"Are you serious about learning *Deitsch*, Guy?" Judith asked.

"Of course I am." He poured steaming milk into the hopper. "At least, I am if you're going to teach me."

"I'll be happy to do it, if you really want to learn. You'll need to speak and read it well if you're going to join the church."

"I don't need to join to fit in around here, do I?"

Glancing at Judith's face, her pink cheeks told him that he had been too blunt.

"You don't have to," she said, clearing her throat. "But understanding what folks are saying will make living in the community easier. We can begin tonight, but it will take weeks for you to pick up the basics."

That brought a grin Guy couldn't hide. Weeks spent in Judith's company? Time he could spend learning to know her, getting close to her. Becoming a friend.

"Okay, I'm game."

Judith smiled then, her joy catching him by surprise. She truly wanted to do this, which meant only one thing. She liked him. Guy felt his own smile spreading across his face…

Jan Drexler enjoys living in the Black Hills of South Dakota with her husband of more than thirty years and their four adult children. Intrigued by history and stories from an early age, she loves delving into the world of "what if?" with her characters. If she isn't at her computer giving life to imaginary people, she's probably hiking in the Hills or the Badlands, enjoying the spectacular scenery.

Books by Jan Drexler

Love Inspired Historical

Amish Country Brides

An Amish Courtship
The Amish Nanny's Sweetheart

The Prodigal Son Returns
A Mother for His Children
A Home for His Family

JAN DREXLER

The Amish Nanny's Sweetheart

HARLEQUIN® LOVE INSPIRED® HISTORICAL

Recycling programs
for this product may
not exist in your area.

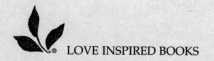 LOVE INSPIRED BOOKS

ISBN-13: 978-1-335-36959-8

The Amish Nanny's Sweetheart

Copyright © 2018 by Jan Drexler

Printed in U.S.A.

Therefore whosoever heareth these sayings of mine, and doeth them, I will liken him unto a wise man, which built his house upon a rock: And the rain descended, and the floods came, and the winds blew, and beat upon that house; and it fell not: for it was founded upon a rock. And every one that heareth these sayings of mine, and doeth them not, shall be likened unto a foolish man, which built his house upon the sand: And the rain descended, and the floods came, and the winds blew, and beat upon that house; and it fell: and great was the fall of it.
—*Matthew* 7:24–27

To my dear aunt, Waneta Bundy,
who sowed sunshine wherever she went.

Soli Deo Gloria

Chapter One

"You're sure you want to do this?"

Judith Lapp grinned at her brother-in-law, Matthew Beachey, as she climbed into the buggy. "I've been looking forward to going to a Youth Singing for years. Why would I refuse this chance now?"

Matthew's grin echoed hers as he turned the buggy onto the road leading to the Stoltzfus family's farm. "That's just what your sister would say."

As the horse trotted down the snowy road, the cold February air pressed close inside the buggy. Judith pulled her shawl more tightly around herself and tucked the heavy lap robe under her legs. A shiver made her teeth chatter, but she didn't care. All those years growing up on the farm near Shipshewana, she had never gone to a Singing. Of course, she hadn't been old enough to go until the last few years. Even so, she and Esther would never have gone if their older brother,

Samuel, had had his way. Living at the edge of the Amish community, just like she had when their father had been alive, Judith had never felt welcome among the young people her own age.

But then, last fall, their lives had changed. Samuel had met Mary. The couple had wed in September, and Esther had moved next door to live with Mary's sister and their aunt. Judith had joined them until she moved to Matthew and Annie's home last week to help care for their growing family. Not only was she delighted to become reacquainted with Annie after their years of separation, her oldest brother, Bram, lived in the same community, and she was learning to know him again, also.

A tingling started in Judith's toes and she tapped them on the buggy floor to warm them. Matthew's shoulders were hunched, and he had pulled his chin into the collar of his coat like a turtle.

Dear Matthew. It had been his idea for her to live with him and Annie after the twins were born. Such wiggly, red, crying babies! Judith's job was to fix meals and care for Eli, her eighteen-month-old nephew. She shivered again, but whether it was from the cold or happiness, she couldn't tell. She had to pinch herself every morning to convince herself that her new life wasn't just a dream.

Matthew turned the horse into the Stoltzfus farm lane and Judith leaned forward as they approached the large white farmhouse. A dozen or more buggies were lined up along the edge of the lane in front of the barn, the buggy shafts resting on the ground. Lights from the house shone onto the snow, and through the windows

Judith could see a crowd of young people milling around inside the Stoltzfuses' big front room.

Her grin grew wider. These girls would be her new friends. And, perhaps, some evening a young man would ask to drive her home from the Singing. A fine, upstanding Amish man who was looking for a bride to share his life with. Finally, the night she had longed for was here.

The barn door opened and closed in a beam of light as one of the young men led their horse into the warm shelter. Ahead of them, silhouetted against the lantern light from the barn, someone walked up the lane toward the house with his hat perched on the back of his head the way an *Englischer* would wear it.

"Is that Guy Hoover?" She nudged Matthew's elbow. "I know I've seen him before."

"It looks like it might be. He lives with the Masts on the farm across the road from us."

"That's right. He brought some milk over on Friday." His smile had been enough to make her like him right away. "I don't remember seeing him at meeting this morning, though."

"He was there, but the Masts left before dinner. David said one of their cows wasn't doing well this morning, and he wanted to get back to her."

Judith smiled at the young man as the buggy passed him. He might have returned her greeting, but she couldn't tell with his face wrapped to the eyes in a wool scarf.

"I'll be back to pick you up at ten thirty," Matthew said as he pulled his horse to a stop at the end of the walk leading to the house.

"What if some fellow asks to take me home?" Judith couldn't resist teasing Matthew.

"Tell him he'll have to wait. It's my privilege tonight." He helped her take the robe off her lap as she slid the buggy door open. "Have fun."

"I will," she said, but her attention was on the icy walk leading to the kitchen door.

Guy reached the back step the same time she did.

"It's sure cold tonight, isn't it?" His words were muffled by his scarf.

"*Ja.* Very cold." She shivered, anxious to get into the warm house.

He pulled the scarf down, revealing a pleasant face and ready smile. "Do you remember me? Friday I saw you when I brought milk to the Beacheys." He spoke in a mixture of *Englisch* and *Deitsch* words, turning his sentence into a jumble.

"For sure, I remember." She remembered how his brown eyes had widened and then crinkled into a grin when she answered the door.

"In a hurry, you were…" He stumbled on the *Deitsch* words and switched to *Englisch.* "You were in a hurry on Friday."

Judith changed to *Englisch*, too, as she reached the door. "You didn't stay long, either."

Guy opened the wooden storm door and followed her into the washing porch. "You surprised me. I didn't know anyone but Annie would be there."

"And then Eli was crying…"

"Those babies were, too."

Judith unwound her scarf from her neck. "They always cry, but I don't mind. There is nothing sweeter than a new baby, and the twins make things twice as much fun." She glanced through the glass window of the kitchen door. The room beyond was crowded, and even though she longed for its warmth, she wished she had an excuse to stay here and continue visiting with Guy. She wondered why he didn't seem comfortable speaking *Deitsch*, but how could she ask that question?

Suppressing a shiver, Judith settled for a smile. "It was nice seeing you again."

Guy unwrapped his own scarf with one hand as he held the door open for her, then she was swept into the crowded kitchen.

Two girls stood between the door and the big kitchen stove, talking with each other, but turned to greet her.

"I'm so glad you came," one of them said. "We met at church this morning. I'm Waneta Zook."

"*Ja*, Waneta, I remember. It's so good to see you again."

"This is my friend Hannah Kaufman."

"I saw you at meeting," Hannah said. Her smile was friendly and welcoming. "You came with Matthew Beachey, didn't you?"

"He's my sister's husband. I came to live with them last week." Judith started to say how thankful she was that Matthew and Annie had opened their home to her, but Hannah's face lit up.

"You've come to help Annie with the twins? What fun!"

Judith smiled as she untied her bonnet. "They are so sweet, but all they do is eat, cry and sleep. Annie keeps busy with them while I watch Eli and take care of the house."

Waneta led the way to a back bedroom where Judith laid her shawl on top of a pile of other shawls and coats on the bed and set her bonnet on a table. She felt to make sure the hairpins were still holding her *Kapp* secure and ran her hand down her skirt to smooth out any wrinkles, then she followed Waneta and Hannah into the big main room. She found a spot against the wall with the other girls and watched the group of boys lounging along the opposite side.

Hannah leaned close to speak into her ear. "After the singing, I'll have to introduce you to my brother. He's that handsome one over there."

Judith looked in the direction Hannah indicated. The young man was tall, and as good-looking as Hannah said. He glanced in her direction as he talked with some other boys who gathered around him, but Guy caught her attention as he stood off to the side, staring at her. He wore the same plain clothes that the other boys wore, but somehow, he looked out of place.

Before she could ask Hannah if she knew Guy, one of the older boys announced that it was time for the Singing to begin. As the girls took their places on one side of the long table in the middle of the room, the boys scrambled to sit across from the girl of their choice. Judith watched to see who would sit across from Waneta. The spot remained empty until a tall young man came in late.

"That's Reuben Stoltzfus, Waneta's beau," Hannah said, whispering into Judith's ear. She giggled as a young man sat across from her.

"Who is that?" Judith whispered back.

"Reuben's brother, Ben."

Hannah looked everywhere except in Ben's direction. Judith didn't dare look to see who had taken the seat across from her. She had never had much to do with boys, since she and her sister Esther hadn't attended the Singings in their home district of Shipshewana. She didn't know if she should say hello, or if she should acknowledge his presence at all. She watched Hannah, who finally looked across the table at Ben, blushing as she gave him a smile.

Judith dared to look at her partner. She drew a breath of relief when she saw it was Guy. His dark brown eyes crinkled as he grinned at her. She could only give him a brief smile before she looked down at her lap. The boys chose to sit across from a girl they were interested in, according to what Annie had told her about the Singings. But was Guy interested, or had he sat there because no one else did?

She took a songbook from the stack that was passed along the table and dared to meet his gaze again just as a voice called out the first song number. She fumbled with her book until she found the right page, knowing he was watching her all the time. The group started singing and she struggled to join in the unfamiliar tune. She glanced up again and was relieved to see that he was concentrating on the songbook.

Holding her book in front of her face, Judith squeezed her mouth shut tight to keep from giggling. She was at a Singing, and a boy was sitting across from her. So, this was what it was like to be grown up. She dared to peek at Guy again, but he was still concentrating on the book in front of him. She suppressed a little quiver that went from her middle all through her, then turned her eyes back to the words of the song. It was a hymn, but not one from the hymnal they used on Sunday mornings, the *Ausbund*.

The tune became more familiar as they started the second verse and she joined in. As she did, she could hear a clear tenor humming the tune without singing the words. It was Guy. He frowned at the book in his hands. If he didn't speak *Deitsch* well, perhaps he couldn't read it, either. Judith lost her place in the song as she let her imagination fill in the empty pieces of Guy's story without success. She would just have to get to know him better if she wanted her questions answered.

Guy Hoover couldn't believe that the seat across from the new girl had remained open long enough for him to claim it. But now, he told himself, he had to quit staring at her. It didn't matter if she was the prettiest girl he had ever seen. She would think he was some kind of fool if he didn't get hold of himself.

Running a finger inside the too-tight neckband of his shirt, he stared at the songbook in his hands. He hadn't wanted to come to the Singing tonight. He hadn't been to one since Hannah Kaufman had laughed at his attempt to talk to her in Pennsylvania Dutch. Three months had passed since then, but the sting of her rejection had kept him away from any gathering of the community's young people. Tonight, though, Verna Mast had pushed him out the door.

"Go have some fun," she had said. "David has you working so hard all through the week that you deserve to spend some time with folks your own age on a Sunday evening."

Folks his own age, yes, but the fellows treated him like the outsider he was. They knew his past, that his pa had abandoned him at the orphanage. That he was an unwanted mongrel, not worth their bother. That he was only a hired hand.

David and Verna had never made him feel that way, though. They were good people.

He sneaked a glance over the top of his songbook. Judith's soft blue gaze, as soft as her voice had been as they talked outside, met his, then dropped to her book.

Looking down at his own music, Guy gave up trying to sing. He could speak a little bit of the Pennsylvania German, but not enough to follow the words on the pages. He knew the tune, though, and hummed along with the singers while his mind wandered.

He let his thoughts drift to the first time he had seen Judith. David had sent him to the Beachey home with a pail of milk and he had knocked on the kitchen door the same as every other time. But when Annie's sister had opened the door...

Guy felt a foolish grin slide over his face and glanced across the table just in time to see Judith's red face before she lifted her songbook to hide it. His grin took over. With some planning, he might be able to talk to her some more before the end of the evening. Perhaps he would even be able to walk her home.

At that thought, his stomach churned like a windmill. Judith sat next to Hannah, and he could imagine what Hannah was saying about him. Why couldn't folks let the new girl get to know him on her own, without gossiping?

After the group had sung several songs, Elizabeth

Stoltzfus announced that refreshments were ready. Guy noticed that several of the fellows were coming out of the kitchen with cups of punch for the girls. This would be his opportunity to talk to Judith, but he saw that Luke Kaufman was already at her side with a cup. As he offered it to Judith, she smiled up at him.

Luke Kaufman.

Guy pushed away from the table and made his way to the kitchen. If she was interested in Luke, then she would never even look at him.

As he reached the table filled with sandwiches, John Stoltzfus thrust a plate toward him. "Glad to see you here tonight, Guy."

Guy nodded at the older man, the father of Benjamin and Reuben. John had always welcomed him whenever he was in the Amish community.

"Denki." Guy switched to English. "Thank you for hosting the Singing."

"Of course." John spoke in English, too. "You know that whoever hosts the morning church services also hosts the Youth Singing in the evening."

"All the same, thanks." Guy took a thick sandwich spread with ground ham and then one with egg salad.

"Don't miss the pie," John said. "Elizabeth makes the best pumpkin pies."

"I know." Guy slid a piece of pie onto his plate, then moved around the table to stand next to John, out of the way. John's wife, Elizabeth, was the best cook he knew of, other than Verna. "I'll probably have seconds if there are any pieces left."

John grinned and clapped him on the shoulder. "I'll

keep one back for you, if you'd like. Although you look like the Masts' table has been agreeing with you."

Guy nodded as he took a bite of the ham sandwich. He had worked for David Mast every summer since he was nine, and those summers had filled his winter dreams with memories of Verna's delicious cooking. When he turned eighteen last year and could no longer live at the Orphan's Home, David had offered him a regular job, including room and board. He had jumped at the offer.

"Verna's cooking is a sight better than—" Guy stopped. He didn't need to remind John or the others in the kitchen of where he had lived most of his life. "Her cooking is delicious."

The short refreshment break was nearly over, and while Guy finished his first piece of pie, the kitchen emptied as the others drifted back into the front room. John cut a second helping of pie for him, and Guy couldn't refuse.

"How are things going? David speaks highly of your help on the farm."

Guy raised his eyebrows as he swallowed a bite of pie. "You wouldn't know it to hear him some days. It seems I can't do anything right."

Especially yesterday. He had driven the wagon too close to the corner of the shed and had spent the rest of the afternoon whitewashing the scraped siding.

John grinned. "I'm sure my boys think that about me, sometimes." He shrugged. "But how else will you learn to be a good farmer?"

Guy stared at the plate in his hand. Is that what David was doing? Teaching him to be a farmer?

"I'm not sure that's what I want."

John scraped the last crumbs of his pie into a pile with the back of his fork. "Don't be too quick to decide. Ask for God's direction."

Guy nodded. "Sure." Ask God. That's what Verna would tell him.

"Meanwhile, soak up all you can from David's teaching. You never know when those skills will come in handy, whether you stay on the farm or not."

"Yeah, you're right." Guy took his plate to the sink. He didn't know how long he'd be living with the Masts. David had never said anything about him staying on past this year. But then, he never had the other years, either.

"David loves you like a son. You know that, don't you?"

Guy glanced at John as he went back into the front room to join the Singing again. He had gone over this time and again in his head, ever since the first summer he had stayed with the Masts. David and Verna seemed to like him, but after all these years, they had never adopted him, and he knew why. He wasn't Amish. He wasn't good enough for them.

Judith leaned away from Luke until her back touched the wall. His hand rested next to her head as he loomed over her. She had to look up at an uncomfortable angle to see his face, but it was worth it. Luke Kaufman was one of the cutest boys she had ever seen and popular with the other fellows.

"How long will you be staying with Matthew's family?" Luke's blue eyes held hers in a steady gaze as he took a sip of punch.

"Quite a while. At least until the twins are a few years old, I think."

He glanced away as a girl's laughter rose above the conversations in the room, then focused back on her.

"Did you leave a lot of friends behind in Shipshewana?"

Judith shook her head. She and Esther hadn't done much socializing before their brother Samuel got married.

Luke leaned even closer. "Not even a boyfriend?"

"*Ne,* no boyfriend." Judith felt her cheeks flush hot. Were all boys this bold?

"Then you'll have to let me be your first beau." He smiled, but his eyes smoldered. "I'll take you home from the Singing tonight."

Judith pressed her lips together to keep from giggling. Luke leaned even closer to her, making her even more nervous, but she couldn't move away with the wall right behind her. "You must already have a girl you're interested in." She turned her punch glass in her hands, not daring to take a drink. She was shaking so much inside that she would spill the punch down the front of her dress, for sure.

He shrugged. Even his shrugs were smooth and self-assured.

"No girl to speak of." He lifted one of her *Kapp* strings with his finger. "Not now."

She couldn't stop the nervous giggle from escaping again. "Then, there was a girl?"

"No one special." Luke breathed the words as he leaned even closer. He smelled of soap and something else that Judith couldn't identify. Something smoky and bitter. His gaze slid from her eyes to her mouth and her stomach flipped over.

Someone clapped their hands to get everyone's attention. "It's time to take your seats." Reuben Stoltzfus's voice carried over the rest of the sounds in the room, but Luke didn't move.

"Let me take you home tonight. Meet me at the end of the lane."

Judith found herself nodding, but then remembered her promise to Matthew and turned the nod to a shake.

"I can't. Matthew said he was coming for me."

"When he sees that you've already gone, he'll understand."

Judith shook her head again and ducked under Luke's arm to head back to her seat. "*Ne.* Matthew said that he wanted to take me home this time."

"I'll get my way." He tugged on the *Kapp* string again and gave her a heart-stopping smile. "Count on it."

As Judith slid into her seat next to Hannah, the other girl grabbed her hand.

"I saw you talking to Luke. Did you like him?"

Judith glanced down the table toward Luke. He was laughing with the fellows sitting on either side of him. Their conversation during the break had been unsettling, but she wasn't sure why. She hadn't had much experience talking to boys.

"He is nice, I guess."

Hannah squeezed her hand. "I knew you'd think so."

Reuben called out the number for the first song, and the group had nearly finished it before Guy took his seat again. He looked in her direction, then at his songbook. Judith kept watching him. He stared at the book, but didn't join in the singing.

The next song was a fun one. Each verse was about two people who had a hole in their bucket, and at the end it repeated the lines from all the previous verses. By the time they reached the twelfth verse, everyone was laughing so hard they couldn't keep singing. Everyone except the young man across the table from her.

After the rollicking fun, someone suggested a quick break. Judith stayed in her seat this time, not wanting to be cornered by Luke again.

A few minutes later, a cup of punch appeared on the table in front of her. She looked up to see Guy smiling at her.

"Denki," she said.

He made his way around the end of the table to his seat and took a drink of his punch. Judith leaned toward him, keeping her voice low so the others wouldn't hear their conversation.

"Why didn't you sing with us?"

Guy rubbed the side of his nose. "I don't talk *Deitsch* well, and I can't read it."

"So why did you come to the Singing?"

"I don't know." He looked miserable.

"You have a nice voice. I heard you humming along with us earlier."

A shadow of a smile flashed at her. "Do you mind if we speak English?"

She switched languages, just as he had. "No." She gave him a mock frown. "But you won't improve your *Deitsch* if you don't use it." She laid her hands on the table and leaned closer to him. "Why don't you know how to speak like us?"

"I wasn't raised here—"

Before he could finish his sentence, the next song was announced. This one was a round, and it took concentration for Judith to keep up with her part. Half of her thoughts were on Guy, though. How could he not know *Deitsch*?

At ten o'clock, the singing was over. Luke and some of the other boys rushed out the door, but the girls stood in groups to chat. With a half hour to wait for Matthew, Judith started helping a few of the young people who were collecting the songbooks.

She had picked up a small stack when she met Guy coming around the other side of the table with his own hands full of books.

"I'll take those for you," he said.

Judith handed him the books she had gathered. "You're speaking English again."

Guy shrugged. "The Penn Dutch is too hard. Everyone here understands English, so why should I learn it?"

"You'd fit in with the other fellows better. Don't you want that?"

"I'm not sure they want me around."

"You should give it a try." Judith stepped closer to him. "All you need is someone to teach you."

He glanced around, then ducked his head toward her. "Could you teach me?"

He was serious, his eyes locked on hers, waiting for her answer.

"I'm not sure I'd be a very good teacher, but I could try."

"Maybe we could get together this coming week?" He grinned. "If you can ever get away from those babies."

Judith frowned. Did he dislike children that much? "Those babies are the reason I'm here, and I don't want to get away from them."

"C'mon, I was only teasing." His cheeks turned red.

Judith grinned back at him. "I'm glad you were, because I love Annie's children. All three of them."

"So, when can we start the lessons?"

"I'll have to check with Annie, first."

He nodded and thumbed at the corners of the songbooks in his hand. "I saw you talking with Luke Kaufman earlier. Is he taking you home?"

If any boy was taking a girl home, it was supposed to be a secret, except for the girls who had steady beaus, like Waneta. Even Judith knew Reuben would be taking her home. But Guy looked at her with such intensity when he asked the question that she had to give him an answer.

"No." She shook her head. "He asked, but Matthew is coming for me."

"Whew," Guy said. "I'm glad."

He picked up a few more songbooks that someone had left on a chair and Judith followed him. If he was asking to take her home, he had a strange way of doing it.

"Why are you glad?"

"No reason." He gave the books to Benjamin Stoltzfus, then turned back to Judith. "Except that maybe I can get a ride with you and Matthew?"

He wiggled his dark eyebrows up and down as he asked, and Judith found herself laughing at him.

"For sure, you can. Matthew will be here at ten

thirty." She glanced at the clock. "I had better get my bonnet and shawl. Meet you by the back door?"

"Yeah. I'll wait for you there."

As Judith went toward the kitchen, she glanced back. Guy had picked up the end of one of the benches, ready to help Benjamin carry it out to the church wagon. After talking with Luke at the break, she had been breathless and feeling a little bit like she was dabbling in deep, unknown waters. But that exchange with Guy…it had been more like talking to a friend she had known for a long time.

Hannah was in the bedroom, putting on her bonnet. Her black shawl was already wrapped around her shoulders.

"You're ready to go home?" Judith asked, reaching for her own bonnet.

"Ja." Hannah peered into a small, round shaving mirror fastened to the edge of the towel rack on the washstand, pinching her cheeks to bring some color into them. "Luke asked me to remind you that he'll be waiting for you at the end of the lane." She turned to Judith with a smile. "He has a brand-new courting buggy and can't wait to try it out."

"But I told him that Matthew was coming for me. I don't need a ride."

Hannah laughed. "No girl ever needs a ride!" She grasped Judith's hand. "My brother is looking for a wife, and I have a feeling you're just the girl he's been waiting for. If you step carefully, you and I could be sisters before you know it."

Judith withdrew her hand. "I'm not ready to be married. This is my first Singing, and I want to get to know other people before I settle down to one fellow."

Hannah picked up a pair of mittens from the bed and pulled them on. "If Luke is set on you, there will be no changing his mind."

"I'm still not going to let him take me home. Matthew asked to be the one to do it on my first night out, and I want to go home with him." Judith found her own mittens tucked in the folds of her shawl. "Besides, Guy Hoover is going to ride with us."

Hannah faced her. "Guy Hoover? You don't want to get involved with him."

"Why not?"

Hannah shook her head, her face set in a frown. "He isn't one of us. Never has been, and he never will be. He's an outsider." She turned toward the door, then gave one last shot. "He doesn't belong here."

Judith's fingers chilled as if she had plunged them into a snowdrift. Hannah's animosity toward Guy was shocking, and not what she had expected from her new friend.

If Guy was an outsider, that explained why he didn't know *Deitsch*. Judith tugged her mitten on. New friend or not, Hannah was wrong. She would do everything she could to help him feel welcome in the community.

Chapter Two

Spring was in the air on Tuesday morning as the weekend's cold spell gave way to warmer breezes and fitful sunshine. Guy turned the team at the end of the field, then threw the lever to start the manure spreader's gears as they made another pass. When David had given him this early-spring job of fertilizing the fields, Guy had chosen to do these acres first. Why? He grinned to himself as he drove the horses toward the fence on the other end. Because from here he could watch the Beacheys' farmyard across the road.

He had only seen Judith once since the Singing two days ago. Just a glimpse, but he knew she was there. Ever since he had said goodbye to her when Matthew let him off at the end of the Mast lane that night, the only thing on his mind was to see her again.

Judith. Even her name sang in his mind.

He shook his head at himself, frowning. Why would he think he had a chance with her? The prettiest girl around, and new in the community, to boot. The boys were going to buzz around her like bees in a flower garden.

Guy turned the horses at the other end of the field and started back across. There, finally, he was rewarded with the sight of a figure in a blue dress and black shawl. She carried a basket and headed toward the chicken house. And disappeared. He hadn't even seen her face, so he knew she hadn't seen him.

After two more trips along the length of the field he saw her again. This time, she had let the shawl slip back from covering her head and held it loosely around her shoulders. She carried a basket full of eggs in her other hand as she picked her way along the wet path to the house. With her white *Kapp* gleaming in the bit of sunshine that had made its way through the cloud cover, she was a lovely sight. Blue eyes, he remembered. Dark blue and thoughtful. She dodged a mud puddle with a graceful step, hurried the rest of the way to the house and disappeared behind the closed door.

He stared at the door. Hannah Kaufman had brown eyes, full of laughter and beautiful. At least, he had thought so until he found out the laughter was at his expense. He had no business getting mixed up with an Amish girl, even though Judith seemed kinder and friendlier than Hannah. He didn't belong here, and he wasn't planning to stay. If Pa showed up—

"Guy! What in the world are you doing?"

Startled by David's shout, Guy slammed back to reality. The horses had pulled the spreader off the straight track he thought they were on and were headed toward the barn.

"Sorry!" he called, and waved in David's direction

as he guided the horses back to the middle of the field.
At least no one would notice his distraction, the way
they would if he had been plowing. He shook his head
as he thought about the ribbing he would have gotten
if the crops had grown in crooked rows.

He finished the field and headed toward the barn to
pick up another load of manure. Without a word, David
met him at the manure pile and started shoveling. Guy
joined him, eyeing his expression to gauge his mood.

David was a good boss, and had always been more
than kind to him, but even David could get riled. He
expected the best work from Guy, just as he expected
it from himself. Mistakes were always fixed, sloth was
never tolerated and attention to the task at hand was de-
manded. Guy had broken that last rule too often, and
he waited for David's reprimand.

It came when the spreader was filled and ready for
the next field.

"You weren't driving the team back there, they were
driving you." David leaned on his shovel, his gaze on
the front acres. "What were you thinking about?"

Guy shot a glance toward the Beachey house. The
first thing he had learned that summer when he was
nine, his first summer with the Masts, was that David
could always tell when he tried to skirt the truth.

"I saw that new girl come out of the house."

David let the shadow of a grin show. "I guess a girl
is a fair distraction for a fellow your age, but don't let it
happen again. When you're driving a team, they need
your full attention."

Guy climbed onto the seat of the spreader and clicked
his tongue as a signal to the horses. He didn't have a view

of the neighbor's house from the back field, but his mind went off on its own thoughts, anyway. Keeping the team on track, he focused on the fence post at the far side.

David had taught him that if he picked a point and kept his eye on it, his path would always be straight and true. Almost everything David taught him had more than one meaning. He had made it clear that Guy needed to have a goal for his life and to keep his eyes on that. He was an eddy in a stream, David had complained. Always doing, but never going anywhere. But Guy just couldn't find that centering point.

When the horses reached the fence post, he turned them around and lined up the next goal, the crooked tree by the farm pond, just beyond the fence.

At nineteen years old, he still had no idea what he wanted out of life.

No, that was wrong. He knew.

He had known ever since Pa had taken him to the Orphan's Home on his fifth birthday. He still remembered the green suit Mama had made and how the wool had made his neck itch. He remembered the smell of the Home. The putrid odor that lingered in the dormitory rooms and drifted down the stairs. The crying that echoed in the hallways.

"I'll come get you when I find work," Pa had said as he crouched in front of him, smoothing the collar of the green suit. "It may be a while, but they'll take good care of you here." And then Pa had patted his shoulder and left, trotting down the sidewalk back to the old dusty black automobile.

Guy had waited for his return, and the years of aching emptiness had about killed him.

He knew what he wanted out of life. He wanted a father who never left his boy behind. He wanted a mother who didn't die. He wanted his family.

But that was a dead-end dream.

The next time Pa had come back, on an early-spring day three years later, he had smelled of alcohol. A woman had been with him.

"Dressed in floozy clothes," Mrs. Bender, the matron at the Home, had said with a sniff.

The fancy woman had taken one look at him and poked Pa in the shoulder. "That ain't your kid. He looks nothing like you."

Then she had leaned close to Guy, grabbing his chin and turning it one way and then the other. "Nothing like you."

She had released his chin from her icy stick fingers and lit a cigarette, walking toward the shiny burgundy-colored car waiting by the road. "It's him or me, Sugar Daddy," she had called over her shoulder as she climbed into the front seat.

Pa had shrugged his shoulders, his eye on the woman and the car. "She won't be around long, and then I'll be back for you." He had straightened his striped jacket and settled his hat more firmly on his head. "You see how it is, don't you, Sport?"

Pa had come by to visit a few times after that, showing up every couple of years. Twice he'd had different fancy women with him. Another time he had shown up on foot, dressed in torn clothes and dusty shoes that were cracked and showing Pa's bare feet through the peeling leather. Every time, he had left with the same promise of coming back to get him. Guy only needed to be patient until Pa's ship came in.

But Guy had learned that Pa's promise was nothing but straw. Easily made, easily broken.

The horses had stopped with their noses at the fence, and Brownie turned his head to look back at Guy.

"All right, all right. Hold your horses." Guy shook off the memories and grinned as he turned the team around to start the next pass down the field. Horses holding their horses. If he'd still been at the Home, he'd have told that joke to the other boys as they shivered on their cots waiting for the lights-out call to drift up the long stairway. But he no longer belonged there. Too old for the Home, he was on his own.

He looked at the big white house at the edge of the barnyard. David and Verna's place wasn't home, either, no matter how welcome they tried to make him feel. He wasn't theirs and never would be. He didn't really belong anywhere.

The memory of Judith's quiet glance sent a cool stream of peace through him. Maybe, just maybe, she could help him belong. The Penn Dutch lessons should help him become more comfortable in the community. Maybe he could put down roots here. Buy a farm. Raise a family. He let his thoughts flow to a home and family like Matthew Beachey's, with a girl like Judith as his wife and children growing along with their love for each other. Guy shook his head with a laugh. That dream was far beyond the reach of an outcast like him.

Judith turned the ham frying in the cast-iron skillet then checked the potatoes with a fork. Dinner was nearly ready, and just in time. She could see Matthew heading toward the house for his noon meal.

"*Ach*, Judith, you're a blessing!"

Annie stood in the kitchen doorway, rocking and bouncing as she held a fussy Viola in her arms. Or was it Rose? Judith couldn't tell the two babies apart yet. They both looked like Annie, with wisps of red curls growing on their soft, pink heads. Meanwhile, Eli squirmed, trying to get down from his perch on her left hip.

As she set him on the floor, she waited until he had his balance before letting him go on a headlong dash toward his mother.

"You never told me what a job it is to try to cook with a toddler underfoot." Judith opened the oven door to check on the green bean casserole. She had quickly learned that this dish was one of Matthew's favorites.

Annie knelt to put her free arm around her son. "And soon enough there will be three of them running around the kitchen, all wanting to help." She smiled as she pulled her son close and kissed his cheek.

Judith took four plates from the cupboard and set them on the table, watching Annie. Even though her sister hadn't slept much last night, with the babies awake and crying at all hours, Annie still kept her good humor. Her face looked tired, though, and Judith was afraid she might fall asleep at the dinner table.

"When I put Eli down for his nap, I'll take care of the girls so you can get some sleep this afternoon."

Annie's eyes widened. "Would you? I don't remember when I last slept for more than a few minutes at a time."

Matthew's feet stamped in the porch outside the kitchen door, Judith's signal to finish setting the table.

She smiled at Annie as she laid the silverware next to the plates. "I'd love to take care of them for a while. Tiny babies are so sweet."

Annie cooed at Viola, who was still fussing. "They are sweet, but exhausting." She kissed Eli's brown curls as Judith lifted him into his tall stool at the table. "I don't know what I would do without you here."

Judith pulled out a chair so Annie could sit down next to her son. "If I wasn't here, someone else would help you. There are plenty of girls in the church who would have been glad to come."

"Did you get to know any of them at the Singing on Sunday evening? I didn't have a chance to ask you about it yesterday."

Judith drained the potatoes. She was serving them boiled, since she hadn't had time to mash them. She added a lump of butter to the pot and shook salt and pepper over them.

"I had met Waneta Zook at the morning service, and she introduced me to Hannah Kaufman. There were others there, but I don't remember all of their names."

She set the green bean casserole on the table and put the ham on a serving plate. Just as Matthew came in, still damp from washing up on the porch, she dumped the potatoes into a dish and set it on the table. She sliced a loaf of bread while Matthew greeted his family, then she put it on the table and stepped back to evaluate her work.

"*Ach*, the peaches. I forgot to get them from the cellar."

"It's all right," Matthew said, pointing to her chair. "I'm too hungry to wait for them."

After the prayer, and when Judith had gotten the peaches and put them on the table, she sat down next to Eli. Annie had cut up some potatoes and a few green beans and put them on his plate, but they were already nearly gone, so Judith cut some ham into bites for him.

"What were you girls talking about when I came in?" Matthew asked, taking a second helping of the casserole.

"Judith's first Singing. I was asking if she had made any new friends."

Matthew grinned across the table at her. "I thought I saw a couple boys buzzing around her when I picked her up."

Judith felt her face heat. "I had a great time, and I hope I can go to the next one. Waneta Zook is such a nice girl."

"Guy Hoover seemed to think you were pretty nice, yourself." Matthew teased her as much as he did his wife.

"Guy is nice," Judith said. "He was easy to talk to." Not like Luke Kaufman. She spooned a few peach halves into her sauce dish.

"What did you think of our young people?" Annie asked. Matthew had finished eating, and Annie handed the baby to him.

"I'm looking forward to getting to know more of them. Reuben Stoltzfus kept everything going, and we sang some hymns, and some new songs I had never heard before." Judith buttered a slice of bread and cut

it into pieces for Eli. "I didn't know it would be so much fun."

When they had all finished eating, Matthew read from the *Christenflicht*, the book of prayers that sat with his Bible on the edge of the table, then went back out to work. By that time, Rose was fussing in the other room and Annie went to care for both babies. Judith washed the dishes while Eli played with a spoon and pot on the floor. After a few minutes, Annie came back to sit at the table while she ate another dish of peaches.

"The girls are both asleep," she said, licking her spoon. "I put them in their cots in the front room."

"That will be fine." Judith finished the dishes and sat with her sister for a bit of a rest. "I'll put Eli down in a few minutes, and you'll all have a nice long nap."

Annie scraped the last of the peach juice from the bottom of her dish and Judith put it in the dishwater she had saved.

"I don't suppose we have any cookies?"

Judith cringed as she got them from the top of the icebox. "I should have remembered to get them out earlier so Matthew could have some." Eli climbed on her lap to eat his, leaning against her and watching his mother.

"He can have his when he comes in before the afternoon chores," Annie said, brushing a crumb off her skirt. "And now that it's just us, tell me about the boys."

"Boys?"

"I'm sure you met more boys than Guy Hoover. Which did you like best?"

Judith thought about Luke's blazing blue eyes, squirming a little as she remembered how small she had felt as he had loomed over her. "What do you think about Luke Kaufman?"

Annie leaned her chin in her hand. "He's very popular with both the fellows and the girls, but I'm not sure that's a good thing."

"Why not?"

"I've seen young men like that put too much store in what others think of them. Pride can be a real danger."

Judith nodded, taking the remains of Eli's cookie out of his hands before he dropped it. He was sound asleep.

Humility was a sign of a true Amish person, but falling into the sin of pride was too easy.

"What about Guy?" Annie said, munching on the last half of her son's cookie. "He seems like a nice young man."

"He asked if I would teach him *Deitsch*. Do you know why he doesn't know the language already?"

"He didn't grow up Amish. He's been working for the Masts since before I married Matthew and moved here. It wasn't until last year that he moved onto the farm, though."

"Why? Did he live with his parents before?"

Annie shook her head. "He's from the Orphan's Home. He doesn't have any parents, except for the father who took him to the home when he was a little boy."

"He's part of the community, though, isn't he?" Judith pushed away the memory of Hannah's face when she claimed that Guy would never be more than an outsider.

"Verna hopes he will choose to be baptized and join the church. If they had been able to adopt him, it would have been much easier for him, and them, too. They have no children of their own, but they love Guy and treat him as a son."

"Does he want to join church?"

"I don't know. It isn't something that happens often, you know, an outsider joining the church. That's why it would have been easier if David and Verna had been able to adopt him when he first started spending his summers with them as a young boy."

"Why didn't they adopt him then?"

Annie stifled a yawn. "I think Verna said his father never signed the papers to release him. But if you teach him *Deitsch*, it will make it easier for him to fit in. When do you think you'll start the lessons?"

"I was thinking about some evening this week."

"That sounds fine. After supper, the twins go down for the night, and so do I. Once Eli is in bed, your time is your own." Annie pushed back from the table. "I'm going to lie down. Are you sure about taking care of all three children this afternoon?"

Judith tipped her chin toward the sleeping Eli in her lap. "Of course I am. I'll wake you if I have any problems."

Annie made her way to her room as Judith carried Eli upstairs to his bedroom across the hall from her own. She laid him on the bed and removed his shoes before she covered him with a warm quilt. She looked out the window as Eli shifted in his sleep, settling into what she hoped would be a long nap. This window faced the road and the Mast farm on the other side.

She wasn't lonely, but Annie was busy with the babies, and Judith missed the hours she and Esther, her other sister, had spent talking when she was still at home. She needed a friend, and Guy promised to be a good one. At least, she thought he would be from the little time they had spent together.

Guy was right. He needed to learn *Deitsch* and she could teach him. She had a picture book she had brought to read to Eli, and she could use that to teach him a few words. A warm feeling spread when she thought of the hours they would need to spend together as he learned her language. Their friendship would deepen, and perhaps turn to… Judith felt her cheeks heat in the chilly room.

She frowned, keeping her thoughts stern. There would be no romance during her lessons with Guy. He wanted to learn, that was all. She shouldn't jump to conclusions. Besides, he wasn't Amish. It didn't matter how attractive or friendly he was, she could never let him get any ideas about wooing her.

Unless he was planning to join the church.

Judith gave her upper arms a brisk rub to chase the chill away, then checked to make sure Eli was covered and warm in his bed. As soon as she found a moment, she would walk over to the Mast farm and see when Guy wanted to start his lessons.

Guy had just finished the afternoon milking and was carrying the warm pails to the dairy in the corner of the barn when Judith opened the door.

"Verna told me you were here, but she thought you'd still be milking."

"I just finished, even though the ladies aren't done eating yet." Guy pointed an elbow toward the two cows still munching on their supper of timothy hay. "It's a surprise to see you here."

"I came over to ask you something."

Judith followed him into the dairy and watched in silence as he set the milk on the bench, then shrugged off his barn coat and hung it from the hook on the wall. He watched Judith from under the shock of hair that always fell over his eyebrows as he started assembling the cream separator. He tried to catch her eye, but she seemed distracted. She stepped forward to help him sort the dozens of rings and filters, chewing on her bottom lip.

"Well?" Guy set the filters in their place and attached the big onion-shaped hopper on the top of the cream separator.

"Are you serious about learning *Deitsch*?" She handed him the clean steel buckets that would hold the separated milk and cream. Guy started the slow, heavy crank, getting the separator up to speed before he poured the milk into it.

"Of course I am." He lifted the first pail and poured steaming milk into the hopper. "At least, I am if you're going to teach me."

Judith leaned on the table, watching until the twin streams of milk and cream came out of the spouts and into the waiting buckets.

"I'll be happy to do it, if you really want to learn. You'll need to speak and read *Deitsch* well if you're going to join the church."

Guy poured the second pail of milk into the top of the separator, then continued cranking at the slow, steady speed the machine required. The look in Han-

nah Kaufman's eyes as she laughed at him last fall still
stung. The only reasons to learn Penn Dutch were so
he wouldn't be laughed at and so he could fit in better
with the crowd. He hadn't thought about joining church.
Becoming one of them.

"I don't need to join the church to fit in around here,
do I? The other guys my age haven't joined."

"Some of them have."

Glancing at her face, her pink cheeks told him that
he had been too blunt. She was disappointed in him.

"It just isn't for me." He tried to make his voice sound
casual. The pink had spread to the end of her nose.

"You don't have to join church," she said, clearing
her throat. "But being able to understand what folks are
saying will make living in the community easier. Like
when you go to the Singings or to the church meetings."

He cranked the separator in silence. She wasn't
laughing at him. It seemed like she really wanted to
help him. The bonus was that getting Judith to teach
him Pennsylvania Dutch meant they would spend time
together. Time he could spend learning to know her,
getting close to her. Becoming a friend.

"When would we do this?"

Her face brightened. "I thought we could get together
after supper, unless you still have chores to do then."

"Naw, David gives me the evenings off." He let the
separator slow as the last of the milk emptied out of
the hopper. "Were you thinking of starting tonight?"

"We can begin tonight, but it's going to take more
than one evening. It will take weeks for you to pick up
the basics."

That brought a grin he couldn't hide. Weeks spent

in Judith's company? He set the pails of skim milk and cream aside and put the empty milk buckets under the separator's spouts. He dumped a bucket of hot water into the hopper and let it pour through all those disks and filters, rinsing out any milk that lingered.

"Okay, I'm game."

"Wonderful-gut!" She started for the door. "I have a children's book we can use to begin with. Come over after supper, when Eli is in bed for the night. Around seven o'clock."

Judith smiled then, her joy catching him by surprise. She truly wanted to do this, which meant only one thing. She liked him. He felt his own smile spreading across his face.

"I'll be over after supper, then." He grinned. "It's a date."

As Judith let the door close behind her, Guy went back to his work, but the grin slid off his face. He was looking forward to spending time with Judith, but what was he expecting to get out of learning that Penn Dutch stuff? It was one thing to live with the Masts and work for them. It was something completely different to become one of them.

He pushed away the warm feeling that started whenever he thought of belonging here. Truly belonging here. That would never happen. He had learned long ago not to get his hopes up. The Masts, as much as they seemed to like him, had never really made him part of their family. It seemed if you weren't born Amish, you'd always be an outsider.

Besides, when Pa came for him...

Guy shook his head, chasing the stale hope away.

Once the room was clean and tidy, ready for the morning's milking, Guy picked up the small pail of cream, leaving the skim milk to feed to the hogs the next day.

If David and Verna had adopted him when he was younger, it would be different. He would have learned the language, grown up with the other boys like Luke Kaufman and been a true part of the community. But that hadn't happened, and it wouldn't. Judith was wrong. He would never be Amish.

Chapter Three

That evening, Guy showed up at the back door right at seven o'clock. He was grinning when Judith opened it, but the smile disappeared when he saw Eli hanging onto her skirt.

"Am I too early?"

She shook her head. "You're right on time. I've just had one of those days." She picked up her nephew and led the way into the kitchen. "Eli didn't sleep well last night, and then had a short nap this afternoon. Annie says he is getting some new teeth."

Guy took a seat at the table where she had set a plate of cookies and a glass of milk for each of them.

"I didn't know you were going to feed me," he said, glancing at the book she had also laid on the table.

"My brother was always hungry for a snack, no matter how soon it was after a meal. I thought you might be the same way."

Eli laid his head on her shoulder, watching the strange man in their home.

"I'll never turn down a cookie." Guy reached for

one, then stopped with his hand hovering over the plate. "Why is he staring at me?"

Judith shifted Eli on her lap. "Probably because we're speaking English. He doesn't understand what we're saying." She held a cookie in front of the little boy. *"Gleischt du Cookie?"*

Guy laughed as Eli put the cookie in his mouth. "I guess I don't need Dutch lessons, after all. I know you just asked him if he wanted that cookie."

Eli held the bitten cookie toward Guy. *"Cookie?"*

"I'll get my own, thank you." Guy held a cookie up and looked at Eli. "Cookie."

Judith frowned at Guy. "You should only speak *Deitsch* during your lessons."

He winked at her. "Then how will Eli ever learn how to speak English?"

She had to smile back at his brown eyes twinkling in the lamplight. She pushed the book toward him.

"I thought we could use this to learn some of the names of common objects…"

He halted her speech with a raised hand. "I'm not going to do this if you're going to talk like a schoolteacher."

"All right. No schoolteacher talk." She opened the book in front of her and Guy scooted his chair closer to her. So close that she could feel the warmth of his forearm resting on the table between them. She tightened her left arm around Eli.

The first page had a drawing of a boy holding an apple. "I know what that says," Guy said. "Apple. The word sounds the same in both Dutch and English."

"You're right, *Appel* sounds the same. But what does the whole sentence say?"

Guy stared at the words with a frown. "I don't know."

Judith read the words. *"Der Buh gleicht der Appel. Er esst der Appel."*

"Wait. You're going too fast."

"I thought you said you could read it." Judith grinned as his face grew red, then she regretted it. She squeezed his arm as she leaned toward him. "I'm sorry. I don't mean to laugh at you."

He regarded her with those brown eyes. "I don't like to be teased, but I know you didn't mean any harm." He looked down at her hand, still resting on his shirtsleeve. "I do like the way you apologize, though."

The twinkle was back.

"Cookie?" Eli asked, looking up at her.

"Ne. No more cookies."

Eli pointed at the book. *"Appel?"*

"He's got it right," Guy said. "He's a smart kid."

"Er ist schmaert."

"That's what I said."

"So say it in *Deitsch. Er ist schmaert."*

Guy repeated after her, then pointed at the book again. "Read this again, slowly, and I'll try to catch it this time."

Judith read the sentences again, one word at a time, and Guy repeated each word after her.

"Now, what does it mean?" he asked.

"It means, 'The boy likes the apple. He eats the apple.'" Eli relaxed against her, his eyes heavy. "I'm going to take him up to bed. You practice those sentences while I'm gone."

By the time Judith returned, Guy had turned to the next page, where the picture showed the same boy petting a cat.

"Don't get too far ahead, now."

"But I'm smart, just like Eli. I can read this one, too."

Judith sat in her chair, leaning back with her arms folded, doubting that he could read any of it. "Go ahead. Let me hear you."

Guy recited a few words, but the only one she recognized was "cat." She shook her head, trying to keep a stern look on her face.

"Sorry, that wasn't right. Let's go back to the first page."

They worked together until Guy could read the sentences with the correct pronunciation, and then she had him recite the different verb forms until the cookies and milk were gone.

Guy ran his fingers through his hair. "Can we stop now? I feel like I'm back in school."

"In a way, you are. It isn't easy learning a new language. I remember my first days at school when we could only speak English. I had older sisters and brothers who spoke it a little at home, but I was still lost." Judith closed the book. "That's enough for tonight, though." She looked at him. "Do you think you learned anything?"

He rolled his eyes. "I'll be saying 'I like apples, you like apples, he likes apples' in my dreams." Then he caught her gaze with his. "But yes, I learned something."

Judith shifted in her seat. He was staring into her eyes. "What did you learn?"

"Amish girls can be awfully pretty."

Her face burned, remembering that Matthew was

in the next room, reading a magazine, and could hear every word. "I'm sure you noticed that before. There are a lot of pretty girls around here."

"Not as pretty as you."

"You're flirting with me."

Guy leaned his chin in his hand, elbow propped on the table. "Of course."

"But you came over for your *Deitsch* lesson, not to flirt."

"The lesson is over now, isn't it?"

Judith couldn't keep a giggle from erupting, even though she covered her mouth. He leaned back in his chair, grinning. When he lifted his eyebrows in an exaggerated way, she giggled even more.

"You're going to get us in trouble," she said between gasps for air.

"I'm not doing anything. You're the one making all the noise." He raised his eyes and pretended to whistle.

"Stop it."

He wiggled his eyebrows at her and she nearly fell off her chair, she was laughing so hard. She grabbed his arm. Unable to speak, all she could do was shake her head.

Guy took her hand and leaned toward her. "I'll only stop if you do one thing."

She hiccupped as the giggles subsided. "What?"

"Let me kiss you."

All silliness disappeared at his words. "You can't be serious," she whispered, hoping Matthew hadn't heard what he said.

The twinkle had left his eyes as his gaze focused on hers with their faces inches away from each other.

The only sound was the clock in the front room ticking away the seconds.

Guy drew back and smiled. "Naw, not really." His rough fingers caressed the hand he still held. "But someday? Maybe?"

She couldn't look away from his warm brown eyes, soft and hopeful in the lamplight.

"Maybe," she said. "Someday."

Just then the clock struck eight and Matthew's feet hit the front-room floor with a thud. He cleared his throat to make sure they had heard him.

"That's my signal to head home." Guy rose and took his coat and hat from the hook by the back door. "Thanks for the lesson. When do we get together again?"

"Is tomorrow night too soon?" Judith opened the back door for him. "We could meet together most evenings, and that will help you learn quicker."

"I'll be looking forward to it." Then he gave her one last wink as he put his hat on and let himself out the door.

Judith's knees shook as she leaned against the door, but she couldn't keep from smiling. In spite of the awkward moment when he had asked to kiss her, it had been a fun evening. The hours until tomorrow night stretched in front of her.

Matthew looked in from the front room. "Guy went home?"

"*Ja*, for sure." Judith picked up the plates and glasses and took them to the sink. "He understood your signal that it was time for him to go."

Matthew grinned. "I have to practice pushing suitors out. I can't imagine what it will be like when Rose and Viola grow to courting age. Thanks for letting me practice on you."

He left as Judith washed and dried the few dishes. Courting? Is that what Matthew thought she and Guy were doing? Is that what Guy thought they were doing?

She hung the dish towel on the rack over the stove. There would be no courting from Guy until he said he wanted to join the church, and that wouldn't happen until he knew *Deitsch* a lot better than he did now.

Guy shoved his hands in the waistband of his trousers as he trudged down the Beacheys' farm lane toward the road and the Masts' farm. He shouldn't have done that. Shouldn't have asked for a kiss. Judith wasn't that kind of girl.

Pa would have done it, though. At least, he figured Pa would have gone ahead and kissed her. The girls Pa had brought around would expect him to act like that. Girls like the one in the floozy dress with a bright smile that looked like brittle painted porcelain. Girls that had hung on Pa's arm and ignored the boy Pa had come to see. The girls that had kept Pa from taking Guy away with him.

Pausing at the end of the lane, Guy looked back at the quiet house he had just left. There was nothing brittle about Judith. When she'd held Eli on her lap and smiled at the little boy, something had tugged at his heart. A long-forgotten memory of his own mother? All he remembered were soft kisses and gentle hugs. Had she held him with the same joy he had seen in Judith's face when she held Eli?

He bent his head against a northeast wind promising snow in the morning. It looked like the brief warm spell they had enjoyed was over.

When he reached the house, he let himself into the kitchen quietly, but David and Verna were still up, sitting at the table. They both turned as he entered.

"Did you enjoy your time with Judith?" Verna held out her arms to him for the quick hug she gave him every time he came into the house.

He gave her a kiss on the cheek and sat in his chair. Verna passed a plate of cookies toward him.

"We had a good time." He grinned at the memory of Judith's laughing fit. "I'm going over again tomorrow night."

Verna gave David a look and folded her hands in her lap. Guy knew what that meant as well as David did, and waited for the talk Verna wanted them to have.

David cleared his throat. "Are you, um, interested in Judith?"

Guy looked at Verna's worried face and back at David. "She's a nice girl, but we're not dating."

The older couple exchanged looks again.

"Then why are you spending so much time together?" Verna's voice was laced with worry.

"She's teaching me Pennsylvania Dutch."

David leaned over the table. "You've never wanted to learn it before. What makes the difference now?"

Guy shrugged. "I feel left out of the other fellows' conversations. They speak Dutch when I'm around, even though they know I don't understand it well. I guess I just want—" His voice faltered. What did he want?

Verna took his hand. "You want to be part of the community? You want to join us?"

"It's a little late for that, isn't it?" A pounding started in his ears. "It would have been different if you…" Should he say it? He had never asked why the Masts had chosen not to adopt him.

David's fist clenched, his head bowed. "It would have been different if we had been able to call you our own son." His eyes were moist as he looked at Guy. "If we had been able to adopt you when you first came to us, then you would have grown up speaking *Deitsch* and knowing our ways. But we only had you a few months a year, and then you went back to the world."

Verna squeezed his hand, her voice a whisper. "That was so hard, every fall, sending you back to the orphanage."

"But why didn't you adopt me? Other kids from the Home were adopted."

David swallowed and exchanged glances with Verna again. "Your father never relinquished his family rights. He never released you to be adopted."

Guy frowned, bitterness rising up in his throat. "So he just left me at the Home."

"Don't think too harshly of him," Verna said.

"Forget it." Guy pushed back from the table. "All he's done is ruin my life."

"Guy, don't let this fester." David folded his hands in front of him. "You need to forgive him and go on with your life. The fact that you're learning *Deitsch* shows that you're ready to become part of our church, doesn't it?"

"I don't know what it means." Guy sighed. "I hate not belonging anywhere."

"You belong here." David took Verna's hand. "You belong with us. We love you as if you were our son. You'll always have a home here."

"But I'm not really your son. I'm just a farm hand. I'm not Amish, and I never will be."

Verna sniffed as the three of them sat in silence. David's head was bowed, his eyes closed. A different kind of bitterness filled Guy. Not the anger at Pa, but regret that he had caused the old couple pain.

"If you feel that way," David finally said, "there isn't anything we can do about it." He looked up and met Guy's eyes. "The decision is up to you. You can be our son, or you can be our hired hand. We'll still think of you as nothing less than one of the family."

Guy glanced at Verna's bowed head and the couple's clasped hands, then headed upstairs to his bedroom.

His bedroom.

He padded over to the dormer window in his stocking feet. That first year, when he was nine, this had become his favorite spot. David had built a small chest for him and set it under the window, and Guy had spent hours sitting here, gazing out at the house across the road, watching the birds, looking for foxes in the moonlight… At the Home he had nothing, but here, everything he looked at was his own. He sank down on the chest and drew his feet up, crossing his legs as he looked around the room as if seeing it for the first time.

His bed. His dresser. His chest that had held all the treasures he couldn't take back to the Home. This was his refuge.

On the bad nights at the Home, he would lie in his narrow cot and dream of this room. Summer and freedom couldn't come soon enough. Every year, David and Verna had welcomed him…home…as if they had missed him as much as he had missed them.

Had he ever thanked them? He had spent so much time waiting for Pa to keep his promise that he had neglected what he had here with David and Verna.

The Masts had never made any promises other than to love him, and even tonight they reaffirmed that promise.

But Pa had never kept his promises, and it was time Guy faced that fact. Pa's promises had broken as easily as spring ice on a mud puddle. Why hadn't he seen the truth sooner? He had wasted time and energy waiting for…

A sigh escaped, ending in a sob. He bent his head on his knees and closed the door on that place in his mind that had held fast to a straw promise all these years.

On Wednesday morning, during the twins' nap, Annie made bread while Judith ground ham for Matthew's favorite sandwiches. Judith had brought Eli's blocks into the kitchen, and he sat under the table, playing with them.

"I didn't stay awake long enough to say hello to Guy last night." Annie turned the dough out onto the bread board and started kneading it. "Did you two have a good time?"

"We did," Judith said, smiling at the memory of how silly they had been. She paused the grinder to cut some more of the ham into the smaller chunks that would fit into the hopper. "But Guy didn't seem to want to learn anything. He kept saying it was too much like school."

"I thought you said he wanted to learn *Deitsch*. It seems like he would apply himself to the task if he really wanted to."

Judith's face grew warm at the memory of the look in his eyes when he said he wanted her to kiss him. "Maybe learning *Deitsch* isn't what he really wants."

Annie stopped her kneading. "Do you think he's interested in you?"

"He shouldn't be, should he? I mean, he hasn't joined church, and I'm not going to keep company with anyone who isn't at least considering it."

"Maybe you can be a good influence on him."

Judith fed more pieces of ham into the grinder and turned the crank. She didn't want to get her hopes up about a future with Guy. Not yet. Not until she knew he wanted more than just a fun time together.

"What do you know about the Kaufman family?" She had turned away from Annie, but heard the small disapproving sound she made.

"I've already told you what I think about Luke."

"But what about the rest of his family? Hannah seems nice." Judith chewed her lower lip. Hannah was very friendly to her, but her comments about Guy made Judith cautious about a true friendship with her.

Annie put the ball of dough into a bowl and covered it with a clean, damp dishtowel. "Let's see." She washed her hands at the sink, staring out the window at the winter-brown fields still covered with snow in the shady places. "Luke's father has a large farm between here and the county line. Their family has lived in the area since the middle of the last century. They were some of the first Amish settlers who came to Indiana from Pennsylvania."

"And they're well liked in the community?"

"Ach, ja." Annie sat on a chair at the kitchen table.

Eli held a block out for his mother to see, then pounded it on the floor. "Block, block, block." Then he looked at Judith and grinned.

She grinned back at him. She was growing to love this little boy more each day.

Annie sighed and stretched her back. "The Kaufmans have been leaders in the church for years, according to what Matthew has told me. Luke's *daed* is one of the deacons. Why are you asking about them?"

Judith leaned her back against the kitchen shelf, facing her sister. "I think Luke is interested in me."

"What makes you think that?"

"The way he acted at the Singing. He singled me out to talk to, and he wanted to take me home. Hannah said his courting buggy was new, so I know he wanted to show it off to me."

"Would you welcome his attentions?"

Judith stared out the window. Luke was handsome, and the family was well established, according to what Annie said. But could she face the future with Luke, knowing how uncomfortable he made her feel? That might change as she got to know him. After all, he had the means to support her and a family, and there was no question about his *daed's* commitment to the Amish faith.

Luke was the kind of suitor she had always dreamed of. A man who could change the course of her life.

Judith sat in the chair facing Annie, wiping her hands on a towel. "I don't want to end up like *Mamm*, working too hard and never having enough."

Annie's face paled. Eli climbed into her lap with a block in each hand, and she made room for him, but her brows puckered. "You mean you don't want to marry someone like our *daed*? You want someone who can provide well for you?"

"I don't want to sound ungrateful or that I'm not honoring *Daed's* memory…but I didn't like him very much."

Annie grasped her hand. "You and Esther had it the worst of all of us, I think. I remember that his drinking became a lot worse after *Mamm* died."

Judith nodded. "I only remember him being angry those last few years, and we could never please him." She pressed her lips together before more complaints about *Daed* slipped out.

"I don't blame you for wanting a different kind of life." Annie squeezed her hand, then released it to help Eli slide off her lap and onto the floor again. "But they were happy once. *Mamm* really did love him."

"Before he started drinking."

"She loved him, even then."

Annie fell silent, and Judith watched Eli stack one block on top of another. Annie was right. Their parents had loved each other at one time. But was love enough to make a happy marriage?

"Still, I don't want to end up poor and living on the edge of the family and community."

"There's nothing wrong with being thankful for what the Good Lord provides," Annie said, her voice quiet.

"But don't you think a marriage has a better chance of being happy if there's enough money to live on?" Judith went back to the meat grinder. She had ground all the ham and she needed to wash the grinder before the gears became crusty and hard to clean. "The Kaufman family is well-to-do, from what you said."

"But Judith, just because Luke's family has a good farm doesn't mean he would be a better husband than anyone else."

"Don't you think it's worth getting to know him better?"

Annie shook her head. "He's broken more than one heart already."

Judith let Annie's comment settle in her mind. She didn't have enough experience to tell what kind of man was the right one to marry, but Annie and Matthew seemed happy together.

She sat down at the table again, next to her sister. "How did you know Matthew was the right man for you to marry?"

Annie smiled. "First of all, he made me laugh."

Judith grinned, remembering nearly falling off her chair the evening before.

"But most important, he showed me how much he loved me."

"You mean he whispered mushy poems in your ear?" Judith wrinkled her nose at the thought of some boy's moist lips next to her ear, breathing words of love.

"*Ne*, nothing like that," Annie said, laughing. She sat back in her chair and looked at the ceiling as she went back in her memories. "He remembered that I like the piece of cake from the very middle of the pan and always made sure I got that one. He let me win when we played games with his brothers and sisters. He always gave me his hand to help me in and out of the buggy."

Annie leaned forward, cupping the top of Eli's head in a loving caress. "Matthew has always put my needs and our family's needs before his own comfort. He works hard to provide for us and never complains."

They sat together for a few minutes while Judith thought about Annie's description of her husband. A swelling rose in her throat…a longing for someone to cherish her in that same way.

A cry from one of the babies drifted from the bedroom. "I think someone is hungry again." Annie started toward the kitchen door, then turned back to Judith. "Don't go chasing Luke. He's not the man I'd want my baby sister to marry."

Judith smiled, hoping to reassure her sister. "Don't worry. I'll be careful."

She let the pieces of the grinder soak in warm, soapy water while she chopped onion, celery and pickles to mix into the ham spread.

"Me?" Eli said, tugging on her skirt.

"For sure." Judith lifted him into his chair at the table and spread some of the ground ham on a bit of cracker. "What do you think?"

Eli opened his mouth and she popped the bite in, then he scrunched up his face into a smile. He nodded and patted his tummy as he swallowed. "More? Eli more?"

Judith prepared another cracker for him, grinning as he opened his mouth like a little bird.

"You love ham spread as much as your *daed* does, don't you?"

"Da?" Eli held his hands up. *"Da* here?"

"He's working now, but he'll be in for dinner."

Eli kicked his feet against the chair. "Go *Da*. Down. Go *Da*."

Judith glanced out the window. The weather was cold and cloudy, but it hadn't started snowing yet.

"After I finish my work, we'll go out and see what *Daed* is doing." She wiped off the little boy's hands and put him back down with his blocks, then started washing the dishes.

As the suds swirled around the parts of the meat grinder, she considered Annie's words. She thought Matthew was the perfect husband. Guy seemed to come close to that ideal, the way he made her laugh. But he was only a hired hand with no prospects, and she wasn't about to live the rest of her life as the destitute wife of a man who wasn't even Amish.

Chapter Four

Guy shifted his feet, waiting just inside the kitchen door for Verna to get ready. She had asked him to carry a basket to the Beacheys' this morning for the quilting, but first she had taken her time putting the donuts in the lined basket and covering them with a towel. Then she had disappeared into the back bedroom. He finished his second donut and reached for a third, careful to replace the towel covering the warm treats.

Leaning against the doorframe, he savored the donut as he thought about Judith. After a week of Penn Dutch lessons, Guy felt a bit overwhelmed. Too many words sounded the same, and even though she tried not to, Judith often giggled at his mistakes. But she was a good teacher, and he was learning little by little.

Even Verna was in on the game. She had stopped talking to him in English as soon as she had learned about the lessons. That was frustrating, but no matter how much he pretended he didn't understand her, he had to admit that he knew more now than he had that first evening. At breakfast, Verna had asked what he wanted on his toast, and he had been able to ask for and get apple butter. A few days ago, he thought he had asked for apple butter, but Verna had given him a dish of applesauce.

Was his Dutch good enough to ask Judith to go with him to the next Singing?

"Are you ready to go?" Verna asked as she came back to the kitchen, setting her bonnet in place. She wore her thick black cape and her heavy winter shoes.

Guy missed some of the words in her question, but caught the meaning. "*Ja*, for sure."

Still munching on his donut, he took the heavy basket in his other hand and followed her out of the house and down the lane toward the road.

"Even with that sharp north wind, you can tell spring is coming," Verna said, lifting her face toward the sunshine.

"It smells…" Guy struggled to come up with the word he wanted. It was one of the new ones on the vocabulary list Judith had given him the night before. He made a guess. *"Frish?"*

"Ja, fresh." Verna took a deep breath. She pulled her cape closer around her and hurried down the lane. "But chilly."

Stuffing the last bite of the donut into his mouth, Guy pulled his chin down into his coat and followed her.

Buggies were coming from both directions on the road, all heading toward the Beacheys' house.

"This is the first quilting at Annie's since the twins were born," Verna said as he caught up with her. "Everyone is coming to see the babies, so there will be a crowd." She lifted her hand and waved to a buggy full of women coming from the north. "There is Annie's sister Esther with the ladies from Shipshewana. Judith will be glad to see them."

Guy walked behind Verna as she headed toward the door and followed her in, holding his hat in his hand. As he set the basket on the kitchen table, he searched for Judith in the crowd of women. When he finally found her, she gave him a quick wave and headed in his direction.

She said something, but he couldn't catch the words. He shook his head and pointed to his ears, feeling more uncomfortable by the minute as he realized he was the only man in the entire house.

Judith grabbed his sleeve and led him out to the washing porch. It was sheltered from the breeze but not heated.

She shivered. "You can't stay here."

"*Ja*, I know." He licked his lips. "I wanted to ask you if—" Now that it came to it, he found his knees shaking. "If I could take you to the Singing on Sunday night. I don't have a courting buggy, but we could walk. It's only at Deacon Beachey's, in the next mile." He cringed as his sentence drifted from Dutch to English.

Judith's face took on a slight frown. "I will walk there with you, but this doesn't mean we're going together."

Guy gave up on the Dutch. "You mean, it isn't a date."

"That's right. I'm not ready to keep company with anyone, but I'll be glad to walk with you. As a friend." She put her hand on the doorknob, ready to join the others in the kitchen. "Matthew is out in the barn. I'm sure he'd like some manly company today."

"Yeah." Guy put his hat back on.

Judith opened the door, disappearing into the sea of *Kapps*, and anything he might have said was lost in the noise.

He stood back to let another group of women into the house, then he headed toward the barn. He thought he had been clear, that he wanted to take Judith to the Singing, but had he said it wrong? Or maybe he had misunderstood their evenings together when he thought she liked him. Maybe Matthew could solve the puzzle.

Guy found Matthew in the barn loft, forking clean straw down into the horses' stalls. He cupped his hands around his mouth and called up to him. "Hello!"

Matthew peered over the edge of the loft. "Guy. Good to see you. I'll be down in a minute."

Three more clumps of straw drifted down into the stalls, then Matthew came down the ladder and shook Guy's hand.

"What brings you here today?"

Guy grimaced, trying to catch Matthew's words. It seemed that everyone was bent on making sure he learned the Penn Dutch.

"I carried a basket over for Verna." He grinned as a phrase came to him. "The house is packed with chickens."

Matthew rubbed his chin. "Chickens?"

"Chickens. *Ja.* A house of chickens. Talking."

"I see. You mean it's a hen party in the house."

Guy shook his head, giving up. He switched to English. "Yeah, that's what I mean. A hen party."

"You're right about that." Matthew sat on a bench and motioned for Guy to join him. "How are the *Deitsch* lessons coming?"

"I don't know if I'm ever going to learn this." Guy

rubbed at a stain on his trousers with his thumb. "It's too hard, and I don't think I'm smart enough."

"Du bischt schmaert." Matthew grinned at him. "You are smart. Judith says you're picking it up quickly."

"But the words keep getting mixed up in my head. Like the chicken-house thing. Why couldn't I remember to say it right?"

Matthew shrugged. "Learning a new language is hard."

"But all of you speak two languages. Three, if you count the German the ministers use for Sunday preaching."

"We learned to speak *Deitsch* from birth. *Hoch Deutsch*, High German, isn't much different, and we've heard that from when we were babies, too. And we learn *Englisch* when we go to school, when we're still young. If I was trying to learn, say, French or something, I'd have a hard time, too."

"Maybe." But Guy doubted that Matthew would have trouble learning anything if he put his mind to it. "I have another question for you, though."

Matthew took off his hat, running his fingers through his hair. "Sure. What is it?"

"Why doesn't Judith want me to take her to the Singing next week?"

"Did she say she wouldn't go with you?"

"She said she'd walk with me, but not like if we were going together."

"You mean, she doesn't want to be more than friends."

Guy nodded. "I'm not sure she even wants to be friends."

"She does, but she's still young. She doesn't want to be tied down, yet."

"Going to the Singing with me won't tie her down."

Matthew stood, clapping Guy on the shoulder. "You might not think so, but Judith is different. Until last year, her world didn't go much farther than her back door. She wants a chance to be a girl and have some fun with the other young people." He picked up a broom and started sweeping up loose bits of straw. "Be patient with her, and let her take her time."

"Sure." Guy frowned. He could understand that Judith didn't want the others to think they were dating.

"I wouldn't worry about another fellow horning in," Matthew said as he swept the straw into a pile. "You have the advantage of seeing her almost every day. When the other boys start buzzing around, she'll remember who her friends are."

Guy waved a goodbye to Matthew as he started back toward the Mast farm and the chores waiting for him there. Matthew was right, as long as one of those friends didn't end up being Luke Kaufman.

Judith was at the door to greet Esther as soon as Guy went out to the barn. Even though it had only been two weeks since they had seen each other, Judith felt like it had been forever. Esther must have felt the same way, from the strength of her hug. But they couldn't linger, because Mary, Ida Mae and Aunt Sadie were right behind her.

"How does it feel, taking care of those babies all day?" Esther asked as she untied her bonnet.

"Annie has charge of the babies." Judith took Mary's cloak from her and put her hand out for Ida Mae's.

Ida Mae handed her shawl to Judith, then helped Sadie with her wraps. "I'm sure you get your turn at holding them and changing diapers, though."

Esther laughed. "I can just see Judith changing diapers."

"Then get ready to be surprised," Judith said. "Eli still wears diapers, too. And all of those diapers need to be washed every day."

Sadie moved past the girls, leaning on her cane as she went. She patted Judith's arm. "I know you're a *wonderful-gut* help to Annie."

Judith and Esther carried the cloaks and bonnets into the bedroom while the others went into the front room where the quilting frame was set up.

"Now that there's just us," Esther said, "you can tell me. How are you doing?"

Esther's eyes were fixed on Judith's face, concerned.

"You were right. It is a lot of work taking care of a house full of people and babies up to our ears." Judith smiled to relieve Esther's worries. "But Annie and I work together well, and we have a lot of fun in the midst of the work. I had forgotten how cheerful she is."

Esther smiled. "She's much happier since she married Matthew."

"And the babies make her even happier, if that could be possible."

"So, who was that boy you were talking to?"

Judith felt the blood rush to her cheeks. "What boy?"

"That handsome young man who headed for the barn as soon as we walked toward the house."

It was just like Esther to jump to conclusions. "He's the neighbor's hired hand. He carried a basket over for Verna."

"I know I saw him talking to you." Esther grinned. "I'd say you're sweet on him, the way you're blushing."

"He's a friend."

"Is that all?"

Judith looked straight into Esther's eyes, dark blue, just like her own. "*Ja*, that's all. I'm teaching him *Deitsch*, and so we've spent some time together. But I'm not ready to settle down to one boy. The Singing next week is only my second one, and I plan to have fun with the other girls."

Esther tapped a forefinger on her pursed lips as Judith's face turned even warmer.

"I think there's more to him than you're saying. Did he ask to take you to the Singing?"

Judith sighed, giving up. "How can you always guess my secrets?"

"Everything shows on your face." Esther pushed the pile of cloaks aside and perched on the edge of the bed. "Tell me all about him. What is his name? Where is he from?" She covered her mouth as an idea struck her. "He isn't one of those bachelors from Illinois or Ohio who has come to look for a wife, is he?"

Sitting next to Esther, Judith was determined to answer her sister's questions as quickly and simply as possible. "He's not from anywhere. He lives right here in LaGrange County. His name is Guy Hoover, and he works for the Masts."

"He has family around here, then?"

Judith shook her head. "He's from the Orphan's Home."

"What Amish family would allow a child to go to an—" Esther broke off, then whispered. "He isn't Amish, is he? I didn't think Hoover sounded like an Amish name."

Judith shook her head. "That's why he wanted me to teach him how to speak *Deitsch*, so he would fit in better around here."

"Then he must be wanting to join church?"

"Not from what he says, but who knows what will happen?"

"Are you going to the Singing with him? He asked you, didn't he?"

Judith picked a bit of lint off the quilt they were sitting on. "He asked, and I told him we could walk together, but we're not courting."

"Why not?"

"Two reasons." Judith ticked them off on her fingers. "One, he isn't Amish."

"But he could be, right?"

"I'm not going to keep company with anyone who isn't Amish."

"I would, if he was part of the community. It isn't much different than seeing an Amish boy who isn't baptized yet, is it?"

Judith shifted on the bed. She hadn't thought of that.

"Two, I'm not going to pay attention to only one boy. Not yet."

Esther nodded. "All right. I can understand that, because I feel the same way. I don't want to tie myself down just yet. There will be plenty of time for that later."

Judith laced her fingers around one knee. "Unless the right boy comes along. How is Thomas Weaver?"

"He still only has eyes for Ida Mae."

Ever since Ida Mae had moved from Ohio with Mary to live with Aunt Sadie, the most popular boy in the Shipshewana church had ignored all the girls except her.

"Have you gone to any of the Singings in Shipshewana, yet?"

Esther nodded. "We've had two since you moved, and both of them were a lot of fun."

"Does anyone special take you?"

Esther grinned. "You know how protective our brother is. Samuel made me promise to only ride with him for the first few times."

"Matthew insisted on driving me to the first one." Judith shifted on the bed so she could see Esther's face better. "But have you met anyone at the Singing? Anyone new?"

Esther shook her head, but her cheeks turned pink. "It's the same crowd of boys that we always saw at church." She stood, heading for the bedroom door. "We had better get in to the quilting before we miss everything."

Judith hopped up and grabbed Esther's arm. "Not until you tell me his name."

"I didn't say there was anyone."

"Esther..."

"All right, but you have to keep it a secret." Esther chewed on her lower lip until Judith nodded. "It's Forest Miller."

"Forest?" The gangly fourteen-year-old had been the bane of Esther's existence when the two of them were in eighth grade.

"He's nicer than I thought he was a few years ago."

"Didn't you hate him when you were in school to-gether?"

Esther shrugged. "He has changed and grown up." She smiled in a way Judith had never seen before. "And maybe I have, too."

Judith dropped her sister's arm and watched her walk away. Esther with a beau? Her eyes prickled as she thought of Forest, an earnest young man who worked on the family farm with his *daed*. As the only son, he would take over the farm when his parents retired, and he would do well. If Esther ended up marrying Forest, her future looked bright and secure.

Perhaps she should reconsider her vow to stay free from romantic entanglements. When Esther married, Judith would be the last one of the family without a husband, and that sounded like a lonely prospect.

A figure waited for Guy at the end of the lane on Sunday evening. He had tried to be early, but Judith had arrived at the meeting place before him. The air was cool, but not bitter, and Judith stamped her feet in the dusky light just after sunset.

"You're late," she called when he got close.

"I'm not. I checked the kitchen clock. I'm right on time, so you're early."

When he got close enough, he could see she was grinning at him, her eyes luminous.

"I don't want to be late to the Singing." She started down the road, leaving him to catch up. "I met some more of the girls at the Sunday meeting this morning, and I'm looking forward to seeing them again."

Guy lengthened his stride, pushing away the familiar gnawing ache of being left behind. "Wait up. We planned to walk together, remember?"

"Then hurry up." She turned midstep and walked backwards. "And you're supposed to be speaking *Deitsch*, remember?"

Jogging the last few steps, he fell in beside her as she faced forward again. "*Ja, ja, ja.* I know. But it's hard."

"It will only get easier if you practice."

Guy caught her arm. "If I promise to stick to *Deitsch*, will you slow down and walk with me?"

"I don't want to be late. Everyone will notice if we come in late together, and we don't want them pairing us off."

"Why not?" A warm feeling filled Guy's chest as he thought of the jealous looks he would get from the other boys if that happened.

"Because we're not together."

As she hurried ahead, he took her arm again and made her walk at a slower pace. By his side. Her arm yielded to the pressure and she matched her steps with his. "We could be."

She looked at him, tilting her head to see past the edge of her bonnet. "But we're friends."

"Yeah. We're friends. What's wrong with that?"

Judith looked to the crossroads they were approaching. The clip-clop of a horse sounded from ahead, coming toward them, the buggy silhouetted against the dusky gray sky as the horse turned onto the road toward Deacon Beachey's.

"Nothing. Except…"

Guy stopped in the road and turned her toward him, forgetting all about speaking Penn Dutch.

"Except what?"

She chewed on her lower lip, not meeting his eyes. "Except that, well, I don't want people to think we're more than friends."

That gnawing ache started again and his stomach clenched. "I'm not good enough for you? I'm not Amish?"

Judith hesitated just long enough for his clenched stomach to spiral toward his feet.

"No, no, of course not." She glanced at him, then away again. "It's just that this is all so new for me, and I want to make friends with both the boys and the girls. If they thought we were a couple, then everyone would leave us to ourselves."

Guy couldn't answer. He didn't know her well enough to figure out if she was telling the truth or just trying to make him feel better.

"Come on," she said, tugging at his arm. "Let's keep walking."

He fell into step beside her. "So which girls have you met?"

"I like Waneta Zook. She's so friendly and kind."

Guy nodded. "Her brother Elias always makes me feel welcome, too. But he doesn't come to the Singings here. He has a girl in Clinton Township he likes, so he goes over there."

"And then there are Mandy and Rebecca Stoltzfus. I found out this morning that my sister-in-law Ellie is their older sister. So that makes us sisters, too, doesn't it?"

A twinge of jealousy surprised Guy. Jealous of Judith? He looked at the side of her bonnet, wondering how she made friends so quickly. They crossed the road as they turned at the corner. Elam Beachey's house was just ahead on the left.

"Anyone else?"

"There's Hannah Kaufman. She's been very friendly. And this morning I met her sister Susan."

"And you already met her brother Luke."

"*Ja*, I've met Luke…" Her voice trailed off.

"What do you think about him?" Guy heard a hard edge to his question. He knew his own opinion of Luke. They had never been friends.

"He's nice."

Such a safe answer.

"I saw you talking with him at the last Singing."

"He brought me some punch, and he wanted to take me home."

"He isn't the kind of fellow you want to spend a lot of time with."

She looked at him. "Why not?"

Guy had a slew of reasons, starting with the rakish smile Luke's face always held when he talked about girls and ending with the disdain in his voice whenever Guy was around. But that was his opinion, and he didn't want to gossip.

"He just isn't the type for a girl like you."

They had reached the Beacheys' lane, and buggies crowded the narrow space, making it impossible to walk side by side.

He slowed to let Judith walk in front of him, but first, she looked straight at him. "You have no idea what kind of boy is right for me, Guy Hoover. I'll make my own decisions about that."

She hurried on, meeting some other girls who had stepped out of buggies and were walking up to the house. Guy stood in the crusty leftover snowbank beside the lane, watching them. Judith was wrong. He knew her well enough to know that Luke was not the right boy for her.

He waited until Judith and the other girls had gone into the house, then followed a group of boys in. The kitchen was crowded and hot, but the front room was spacious. Someone had already cracked a window open to keep the air fresh, and the walls that had been moved out of the way for the morning's service were still off to the side. The young men were lined up along the far wall, waiting for the girls to come in and take their seats, and Luke Kaufman was with them, surrounded by a few friends.

As soon as Guy stepped into the room, Luke spotted him and beckoned him over.

"Look fellows," Luke said. "It's the *Englischer*, trying to be Amish again."

Guy didn't answer. He never answered Luke. In the past, he had a hard time understanding him, but his Dutch must be getting better. He not only understood the words Luke used, but the mocking tone behind them.

"Leave him alone," Benjamin Stoltzfus said. "Guy can come to the Singings. He comes to church, doesn't he?"

"Only because old man Mast makes him."

The back of Guy's neck was on fire. It was one thing for Luke to ridicule him, but to speak of David Mast in that tone was unfair.

"He doesn't make me come."

Luke's eyebrows shot up. "The *Englischer* speaks." He looked around the circle of onlookers. "Be careful what you say, boys. It seems he understands *Deitsch*, after all."

Benjamin pushed out of the group, clasping Guy's shoulder and propelling him toward the table.

"Let's find our seats. The girls are beginning to sit down."

"Did you hear what he said about David?" Guy shrugged Benjamin's hand off. "He needs to know he can't talk about folks like that."

Benjamin stopped, facing Guy. "He's just trying to rile you up, don't you see? He'll keep prodding you until he gets you sent home. Is that what you want?"

Unfamiliar words skipped over Guy's understanding. "Say it in English. What is he doing?"

"Trying to get you to start a fight, and you don't want that."

Guy glanced at Luke's mocking face, still holding court with the group of boys.

"*Ne*, I don't want that." He slipped back into *Deitsch*. "*Denki*. I'm glad you stepped in."

"No problem. That's what friends do, isn't it? Look out for each other?"

Benjamin's words sent an unfamiliar warmth through Guy's middle. He watched as Benjamin slipped into the chair across from Susie Gingerich. He had never thought he'd have friends among the Amish. Too often he only saw the laughing faces and Luke's mocking grin, but maybe he spent too much time worrying about Luke's opinion instead of noticing fellows who were being friendly. Judith had reminded him about Elias Zook earlier, and now Benjamin Stoltzfus. Maybe he could fit in with this crowd.

Guy scanned the girls taking their seats, watching for Judith, but just as he saw her take a chair, Luke pushed past him and sat across from her. Guy finally found an empty seat across from a girl he didn't know. She blushed and giggled, whispering to the girl next to her, but he ignored her, glancing down the length of the table toward Judith.

Her face flushed as she glanced toward Luke, then looked down at her lap. She bit her lower lip, then stole a glance at Luke again before looking in Guy's direction. Judith smiled at him, then opened her book as the first song was announced. The smile was friendly, in spite of Luke's presence. Maybe she still considered him a friend, after all.

Chapter Five

Judith sipped a cup of punch during the break, standing on the edge of the group of girls. Listening to Hannah's story of their pig, which had escaped from its pen yesterday, only took half of her attention while she watched the group of boys across the room. It seemed that Luke was telling the same tale as his sister from the laughs he was getting from his audience.

"*Mamm* was furious by the end of it," Hannah said. "The old sow ran right through the clean wash on the line. The rope broke and she dragged all the sheets through the mud. *Mamm* had to do all that laundry over instead of getting the garden plowed like she wanted."

"How did the pig get out?" asked Waneta.

"My sisters and their families were visiting while the men were at the mud sale over in Granger, and one of the kids opened the gate."

Hannah laughed, but the rest of the girls looked at each other. Judith knew what they were all thinking. If one of their nephews or nieces had done such a thing, there would have been trouble. And what had Hannah been doing while all this was going on? She hadn't said a word about helping her *mamm*.

"If I had been your *mamm*," Waneta said, "I would have made the kids wash the dirty clothes."

"Not them. They won't do anything unless their *daeds* are around." Hannah shrugged. "That's the way it is with kids, isn't it?"

Judith was glad when Waneta changed the subject.

"Are any of you coming to the quilting at our house this week? *Mamm* and I are putting my quilt top in the frame, and I can't wait for all of you to see it."

"Is it a special quilt?" Mandy Stoltzfus grinned at Waneta. "I heard Reuben talking to *Daed* about buying the farm next to ours sometime this year."

Waneta's face turned bright pink, but couldn't hide her smile. "Of course, it's a special quilt."

Mandy nodded knowingly at the rest of the girls. "It's the pattern Reuben picked out."

"Maybe," said Waneta, laughing along with the rest of them. "You never know."

The group of boys had broken up, some of them heading outside and some heading to the kitchen for more refreshments. Luke walked straight over to Judith and her friends.

"What are you girls talking about?" He winked at several of them, but his gaze finally rested on Judith.

"Quilting," said Waneta.

Susie Gingerich stepped closer to Luke's side. "Hannah was telling us about the pig that escaped at your place yesterday. What were you boys laughing about?"

Luke grinned. "What do boys ever talk about?"

"Hmm…" Susie tapped her chin with one finger. "Either horses or girls."

"This time it was both."

"And here I thought you were laughing at the same story we were," Judith said.

Luke caught her eye, his grin changing to a soft smile just for her. Had she been wrong about Luke? He didn't seem as intimidating tonight as he had before.

As Deacon Beachey called the young people back for the next round of songs, the girls scattered to their seats, but Luke moved closer to Judith.

"I hope you'll let me take you home tonight."

In spite of Luke's tall form between her and the rest of the room, Judith's gaze was drawn toward Guy, standing off to her left, his brow pulled down into a frown. She turned away from him and looked up at the handsome boy in front of her. Luke's eyes smoldered as he watched her.

Her insides squiggled, but she couldn't let Guy's worries rule her life. "I'll let you give me a ride."

A movement at Judith's right caught her attention. Guy had come a step closer, still watching her with Luke, frowning even harder.

"Meet me at the end of the lane, then. We'll leave during the next break."

"You're not staying until the end of the Singing?"

Luke lifted her *Kapp* string and rolled it between his fingers. "Not if I get to take you home."

She nodded, then slipped around him to take her seat just as the first song was announced.

The songs followed one after another, Judith singing along with the others automatically. All she could think about was the coming ride home. What would she talk about with Luke? She hardly knew him. Her stomach turned with an uneasy wrench. Maybe she shouldn't have accepted his invitation, but what could it hurt? Perhaps after this ride home, he would stop asking her.

Judith glanced across the table at Luke, catching his grin. Her gaze drifted down to Guy. He wasn't frowning anymore, but he stared at her, his songbook lying on the table. Irritation rose as she looked away from him and turned the pages to the next song as it was announced. Was Guy so jealous of Luke that he couldn't even have fun at the Singing? He was assuming a lot about this friendship between them if he thought he could tell her who she could spend time with.

As the next verse started, Judith risked a glance down the table again. Guy had his book in his hands, singing with the rest of the group.

When the song ended, Luke nudged her under the table with his foot. She looked up to see him mouthing the words, "Don't forget." She nodded as he left the table.

During this second break, instead of dividing into groups of boys and girls, some of the young people paired off, just like they had at the first Singing she attended. Judith started toward the back bedroom where she had left her cloak and bonnet, but when she reached the narrow hallway, Guy was at her side.

"You're leaving already?" He didn't bother to attempt speaking in *Deitsch*.

Judith backed against the wall as another girl slipped past them. "I have a ride home, and he's leaving now."

"Luke is taking you home?" Even though he kept his

voice low so their conversation wouldn't be overheard, Guy's words were harsh.

"That isn't your concern."

"Yes, it is. I heard some of what he was saying to the other fellows about you, and you shouldn't go with him."

Judith stared at him. "What do you mean? Luke was talking about me?"

Guy looked around, but the rest of the crowd was leaving them alone. No one was close enough to listen. "He said he was going to steal a kiss from you tonight, and one of the other boys even dared him that he couldn't."

Judith's cheeks exploded with heat. "Now I know you're lying to me, Guy. No Amish boy would do that."

His brown eyes widened at her words. "I would never make something like this up. I told you before, Luke isn't the kind of boy you want to spend time with."

"And you aren't the one to tell me who I can see and who I can't. I don't belong to you, Guy Hoover."

Judith turned to go into the back room, but Guy grasped her elbow. "Judith, don't do this."

She wrenched her arm out of his grasp and hurried into the bedroom. She searched among the cloaks on the bed for hers, blinded by the tears that filled her eyes. Guy had been such a good friend, but why was he acting this way tonight?

Hannah Kaufman came into the room, smiling when she saw Judith.

"So, you're leaving early, too?"

Judith grabbed her shawl and threw it around her shoulders, leaning down to wipe her eyes when Hannah wasn't looking.

"*Ja.* I have a chance to ride home instead of walking, and he's leaving now."

Hannah settled her stiff black bonnet over her *Kapp,* her eyes twinkling. "I know who is taking you home. Luke said he would take you or nobody tonight."

Judith smiled, willing the uneasy feeling in her stomach to leave. "Is anything around here a secret?"

"Not when it comes to my brother." Hannah put on her shawl and tugged her mittens over her hands. "But if you want to know who I'm riding with, my lips are sealed."

Hannah slipped out of the room by a rear door Judith hadn't seen before. She followed and found herself in the backyard. Hannah had run ahead, but Judith could see through the darkness well enough to follow her until Hannah climbed into a waiting courting buggy.

Judith made her way toward the road, where another open buggy sat at the side of the lane, the black lacquered sides shining in the moonlight. Luke jumped down as she approached.

"I'm glad you came." He reached for her and helped her into her seat. "I was afraid you changed your mind."

"I told you I'd come, and I keep my word."

Luke settled himself close to her and picked up the reins. "So do I, Judith. So do I."

He clucked to his horse and they started down the road.

Guy paced into the kitchen of Deacon Beachey's house, then back into the main room, hoping he had been mistaken. But no, Luke Kaufman had left. He glanced at the bedroom door again, where Judith had disappeared. How long did it take her to put her wraps on? She had been in there for at least five minutes.

"You're missing out on the pie."

Benjamin Stoltzfus held two plates in his hands, each with a big piece of cherry pie on it.

"Denki," Guy said as he took one of the plates. He took a bite, glancing at the door again.

"What are you doing?" Benjamin took a bite of his own pie. "Did your girl disappear?"

"I don't have a girl." Guy swallowed the last bite of his pie, sorry that he hadn't taken the time to enjoy it. But his mind was on Judith.

"Then who are you sitting with?"

Guy shrugged. "I don't know. I didn't ask her name."

"You aren't jealous because Luke sat with Judith, are you?"

"Not jealous. Just worried. I don't see Luke anywhere around."

Benjamin scraped the last bit of his pie off the plate with the side of his fork. "He often disappears during the second break, especially when he's taking a girl home." He licked the last smear of cherry juice off his fork. "My *daed* would give me a good talking-to if I tried a stunt like that."

A girl came by with a tray for the dirty dishes and Guy added his to it. "I don't think David would know if I left early or not."

"He would find out. Deacon Beachey would tell him."

"But what would David do?" Guy gave up trying to find the *Deitsch* words and switched to English. "It isn't like he's responsible for me or anything."

"That doesn't mean he doesn't care." Benjamin's voice was quiet, and his gaze was thoughtful as he watched Guy. "The problem with Luke is that his *daed* doesn't seem to care what he does with his time. I've heard him say that his *daed* treats him like an adult and lets him run his own life."

Guy shrugged. "What's wrong with that?"

"Luke doesn't have the wisdom to make decisions on his own. It's like he's running his horse toward a river and ignoring the warnings that the bridge is out. Sometime, he's going to make a mistake that will wreck his life or someone else's." He rubbed the back of his neck with one hand. "I'm just thankful I have a *daed* who cares about me enough to keep me from doing stupid things."

"Don't you resent it sometimes?"

"Yeah, sometimes." Benjamin grinned. "But then I see what happens to fellows whose fathers don't keep an eye on them, and I'm glad *Daed* is holding the reins for a few years, yet."

Nathan Zook walked up to Benjamin then and they started talking in *Deitsch*, but Guy didn't try to follow their conversation. He was too busy pushing back the bubble of resentment that always appeared when one of the fellows mentioned his father. What would his life have been like if Pa hadn't left him in the orphanage? Would he have been there to help him grow up? Or would he have been one of those fathers Benjamin mentioned, the type who didn't care what their boys did?

He would have liked to find out, but it was too late now. Frank Hoover wasn't coming back.

Nathan nudged him with an elbow. "Did you hear what I said?"

"Sorry, I was thinking about something else."

Benjamin laughed and Nathan grinned. "You mean Judith Lapp?"

Guy grinned back at them, their friendly teasing dispelling his gloom. "Maybe."

"The break is almost over, and Luke isn't anywhere around," Nathan said. "I'm sure Judith would like you to sit in his seat for the rest of the evening."

"You don't think she left with him?"

"She's smarter than that, isn't she?"

Guy glanced toward the bedroom door again. "I hope so."

Nathan and Benjamin went back to their seats as Deacon Beachey called for the next round of singing. The door to the back room opened, but the only people to emerge were two girls Guy didn't know. Beyond them, the room was empty. He ground his teeth when he spied the other door on the far wall, remembering Luke's words from the beginning of the evening. He must have convinced Judith to leave with him, and she'd slipped out during the break. Guy had no idea how long she had been gone, but he knew the risks she was taking. Luke had bragged that he would do more than steal a kiss from her. His innuendos had made the boys in the group laugh, but the thought of what Luke might have in mind for Judith tonight made Guy's stomach turn.

Slipping out of the room just as the singing began, Guy went through the kitchen to the washing porch where he had left his coat and hat. He shrugged on the coat as he ran down the steps to the patchy snow. The yard was quiet. He trotted down the lane toward the road, but didn't see anyone. Stopping at the end of the lane, he fastened his coat and snugged his hat down. At least in Luke's bragging, he had let his destination slip out. Guy started jogging down the road toward Emma Lake, a favorite place for courting couples.

Judith shivered in the night air, even though Luke's shoulder against hers was warm. Slowing his horse to a walk, he circled her shoulder with one arm.

"Are you cold?"

"A little."

Luke's breath warmed her cheek as he pulled her closer. "We'll have to see what we can do to warm you up."

Judith searched her mind for something to talk about.

"Did…did you go to the sale in Granger yesterday with your *daed* and brothers?"

"Naw. I don't have to worry about stuff like that yet."

She shifted in her seat, trying to put a little distance between them.

"I thought you would want to be part of looking for new horses for your farm."

He shrugged. "*Daed* takes care of that. I won't have to concern myself with the farm until he's gone."

"Don't you want to learn about it? It will be yours one day, won't it?"

"There's time enough for that later." He tightened his arm, pulling her close again. "First I have to find a wife, don't I?"

Judith swallowed. He couldn't think she was interested in marrying him.

"Do you have someone in mind?"

"You, of course."

His arm slipped off her shoulder and settled around her waist. The horse turned south at the intersection instead of north.

"Luke, you turned the wrong way. I live in the other direction, up that road."

"I know that." Luke's hand wormed under her shawl and he shifted even closer. "But I thought we'd go the long way around, past Emma Lake."

"I'd rather go home. It's getting late."

"Not that late. We have plenty of time." He urged the horse into a faster walk. "The lake is beautiful on a night like this. We can take a few minutes to stop and look at the moonlight shining on it."

Judith looked up at the clouds scudding across the sky. The horse turned at the next intersection.

"The moon has gone behind those clouds."

"That doesn't matter. We won't really be watching the lake while we're there, will we?"

"What else would we do?"

Luke's laugh was low. "We'll find something to keep us busy."

He urged the horse to a trot and turned again after a half mile. Ahead of them, Judith saw the dark water of a small lake. Luke slowed the horse down to a walk again and draped the reins over the dashboard. He turned toward her on the seat, still holding her around the waist. With his free hand, he untied the ribbon holding her bonnet on and pushed it back. She rescued it from falling to the floor of the buggy.

"What are you doing? Leave my bonnet alone."

He pinned her arm between them and caught her other hand. "You know what I'm doing. It's what you wanted when you said you'd ride with me tonight."

"I don't know what you're talking abou—"

Her words were cut off when he caught her mouth with his wet, slobbery lips, pushing against her until she was off-balance. With both of her hands caught, Judith used the only other weapon she had. She swung her foot against his leg, catching him in the tender calf muscle with the toe of her shoe. She wrenched her hands free and pushed at him until he fell back and she jumped out of the buggy.

"Don't ever try that again, Luke Kaufman." She held her bonnet close to her chest, trying to catch her breath. "I'll… I'll tell everyone what you tried to do."

Luke was bent over, massaging his leg. "And I'll tell everyone that you led me on." He spat on the ground near her feet. "No one turns me down. No one. You'll be sorry."

"I don't think so."

"Fine. Have fun walking home."

Luke slapped the reins on his horse's back harder than he needed to and the horse jumped into a trot, leaving Judith standing by the side of the road.

Judith stamped her foot and turned around to walk home. But as she took the first few steps, her anger at Luke faded. The road stretching before her was unfamiliar, and the night was dark. The wind had picked up, tugging at her shawl.

Ripples covered the black, oily surface of the lake and lapped against the shore along the roadside. From the woods across the water came the hoot of an owl. A night bird trilled in response. Judith backed away and started down the road, hoping she was heading the way Luke had brought her.

They had turned so many corners after they left the Singing that she wasn't sure where Matthew's farm was. Putting her bonnet back on, Judith hugged herself, trying to stay warm. She kept walking. Maybe she would come to a farmhouse, and they would know how to help her get back to Matthew's.

Judith shivered as she walked, the cold air seeping beneath her shawl. She wiped her mouth on the back of her mitten, but the clammy feeling of Luke's lips remained. One thing she knew: she would never accept a ride home from Luke Kaufman again.

She stumbled over a rock and stopped. A lane led off the road to the left, straight as an arrow between two fields and disappearing into a stand of trees. Beyond the trees, a barn roof was silhouetted against the cloudy sky. As the breeze blew the clouds from in front of the moon, she could see the outline of a house in the trees, but there were no lights. No welcoming lantern glow seeping around the window shades.

Indecision planted her feet at the muddy edge of the farm lane. Judith chewed her lower lip as she considered her choices. To go down that lane might help her find someone who could give her directions to Matthew's farm, but the dark house looming in the shadowy trees made her shiver from more than the cold breeze.

On the other hand…she looked around at the empty road, the silent lake she had left a half mile behind her, and the clouds scudding across the sky on the rising wind…there wasn't another house in sight. Not far beyond her was a T-intersection, where she would need to decide to turn right or left.

She glanced down the lane at the house again, and chose the open road. She would take her chances on another house.

At the intersection, Judith turned right. When Luke had headed toward Emma Lake instead of Matthew's, he had taken her south, so she would go north. Her steps faltered. Or was this road leading her west? Or east? In the distance, the lights of an automobile lit up the dark sky, reflecting off the low-hanging clouds. Judith made her decision. She didn't want to be caught alone on a dark road by any *Englischers*, so she reversed her direction, hoping this road would take her somewhere safe.

Chapter Six

As the first cold raindrops pelted his shoulders, Guy hunched into his black wool coat, wishing he was in Verna's warm kitchen. Or back in the room crowded with young people at the Singing. Or in the Masts' barn, milking the cows. Anywhere but jogging down a gravel road in the dark and the rain, chasing after Judith. He was a fool to follow her. She had to have known what she was getting into when she went with Luke. If he found them, he wouldn't be welcome company.

His foot slipped and he slowed to a walk, breathing hard. Emma Lake was ahead, the slow, heavy raindrops plopping onto its dark surface. From here, he couldn't see Luke's rig. Of course, when the rain shower started, Luke wouldn't have wanted to stay out in his open courting buggy. He had probably taken Judith on home and was sitting in the warm, dry kitchen, munching on cookies and flirting up a storm. Guy pulled his collar closer to his neck.

The quick shower let up as the wind pushed the

clouds to the east. The moon came out, giving Guy a better view of the lakeshore. No one was there.

He should just walk home. Judith didn't want him around, and didn't want his advice. He should just forget about her and her beau. Isn't that what a friend would do?

Ne, he thought, snorting when the word came into his mind in *Deitsch*. *Ne*, that's not what a friend would do. He couldn't shake off the feeling that Judith was in trouble. But where was she?

Guy started jogging again, keeping to the center of the slick mud-and-gravel road. Perhaps he should check at Matthew's and see if Luke had taken her home. If Judith wasn't there, he'd keep looking. It was all he could do.

Not all he could do, David would say. He had often said that the solution to a problem, to any problem, was to pray. But what David didn't know was that God didn't listen to Guy's prayers. He had discovered that long ago. But this time he would be praying for Judith. Maybe God would listen to a prayer for her.

Guy slowed to a walk again as he reached the T-intersection west of the lake. He had come from the north a few minutes ago, making his way to the lake. He hadn't run across Luke's buggy on the way, but Luke could have taken a roundabout way to spend more time with Judith. They might not have reached the lake yet. Perhaps he was coming from a different direction.

Leaning on his knees while he let his breathing slow to normal, Guy looked up the road and down. He looked up into the sky with patches of stars showing through the disappearing clouds.

"Left or right, God? Which way should I go?"

Guy waited for an answer. A flashing star. A pillar of fire. Anything.

A cow bellowed from somewhere to his left, but no sign from God. He looked up the road again, toward the north. There was no sound. Nothing moved. He looked south. Something might have disturbed that cow to make it bellow like that. Guy turned south and started jogging again.

Before he reached the end of the mile, he gave up jogging, his side seared with pain. He walked, breathing hard as the discomfort eased. He stopped again, listening for any sound of a buggy. He had never heard such a quiet night.

At the next crossroads, he saw someone walking ahead, just cresting a rise, a shadow against the stars, a couple of hundred yards ahead. The person might have seen something, even if it wasn't Luke's buggy. He started jogging again as the shadow disappeared over the hill. As he came up the rise, the clouds gave way at last, and the moon shone with a clear light. Ahead of him, leaning against a fence post, was the person he had been following. As he came closer, he recognized her.

"Judith?"

She jumped and faced him. "Guy? What are you doing here?"

"I followed you. I didn't think I'd ever find you. What are you doing walking, so far from home?"

He closed the space between them, catching her in his arms.

"I'm so glad you found me." She hiccupped and buried her face in his shoulder. "I don't know where I am.

Luke drove in circles. And it's such a dark night, and the rain was cold…"

Guy wrapped his arms around her as she trembled, trying to control her sobs.

"Shh. It's all right, now. I'm here." He let her cry for a few minutes while his irritation with Luke grew. "Judith, where is Luke? Why are you here alone?"

That stopped her crying. "I don't know, and I don't care." She pulled back from his embrace and wiped her cheeks. "You were right about him. I should have listened to you."

A surge of hot anger went through Guy. "Why? What did he do? Did he hurt you?"

Judith shook her head. "It was so stupid. He thought he could get away with kissing me." She sniffed. "Oh, Guy, it was awful. So wet and slobbery. Like a cow licking my face."

Guy nearly laughed at her description, but choked instead. He was glad his face was shadowed so she couldn't see his reaction. "I hope you told him off for being so fresh."

"I kicked him right in the leg. And then I got out of the buggy and he drove away."

"He left you in the road with rain coming?" If Luke had been here right now, Guy would have done a lot more than kick him in the leg.

Judith sighed, a sob catching her breath. She leaned against the fence post again. "I didn't know which way to go." She rubbed her forehead, her shoulders slumped. "I'm so tired."

"Don't worry. We're near Bram's farm, and I can borrow your brother's rig to take you home."

She hiccupped. "That would be wonderful. All I want to do is get dry and warm."

"Come on, then." Guy tucked her hand in his elbow and started back toward the crossroads. He hoped she was up to the walk, even though Bram's farm was less than a mile away. Judith would be welcome there, that was for sure.

She walked in silence beside him, stumbling once in a while.

"Are you sure you are all right? Do you want to wait here while I walk ahead and get the buggy?"

She clutched at his elbow. "*Ne*, don't leave me. I can walk. Just don't leave me alone."

Guy stopped and turned her toward him, tucking a finger under her chin and tilting it up. The moonlight shone on her bonnet, but her face was in shadow. If he could see her expression, maybe he'd know what to say.

"I would never leave you alone."

She tilted her head, as if she was seeing him for the first time. "You wouldn't, would you? Even if I had kicked you."

Guy grinned at the thought of Luke's sore leg. "I wouldn't give you any reason to kick me."

Judith nodded.

"And I would never leave you alone to find your way home."

"I know."

She didn't move. Their cloudy breaths mingled in the cold, damp air between them, and Guy leaned closer, her dark eyes in the shadowy depths of her bonnet drawing him in.

"If I kissed you," he said, his voice catching, "it would be only because you wanted me to."

"If I let you kiss me," her breath spanned the inches between their lips, "I don't think it would be anything like Luke's kiss."

Guy stroked her soft cheek with one thumb. "I would make you forget all about Luke and his kiss."

She smiled and he could feel a dimple form beneath his thumb. Pa's fancy girl, the last one he had brought to the Home, had had a dimple. The girl had clung to Pa's arm, pulling him back to the car as he had waved at Guy.

I'll be back, Pa had called. *Watch for me. I'll find a job we can work on together.*

One more wave and then Pa's attention had been on the girl with the dimple, the waiting boy forgotten.

Guy stepped back, the mood broken. Judith deserved to be treated better than how Pa treated the fancy girls he hung around with. She deserved someone better than another Luke.

"I need to take you home. Bram's farm is just down this road, the first one past the bridge."

Did he sense disappointment as she turned to walk on? He tucked her hand back in his elbow and started on the last leg of their walk together.

Even though Bram and Ellie's house was dark when Judith and Guy walked up the lane, Bram opened the door quickly at their knock.

From inside the house, Ellie's voice called, "Who is it, Bram?"

A match scratched on the stove top as Ellie lit a lamp.

Bram pulled Judith into the kitchen, her big brother's grasp on her arms as strong and comforting as Guy's. Her knees started shaking. She was finally safe and in a familiar place.

"It's a couple of drowned kittens from the looks of them."

Ellie peered around Bram's shoulder. "Judith! Come in here and get warm."

She set the lamp on the big kitchen table and pulled a chair out. Judith sank into it, every bone weary and sore. And cold. She couldn't stop shivering.

Bram built up the fire in the kitchen stove while Guy pulled off his wet coat and hat.

"You two got caught in the rain?" Bram asked, feeding the growing fire with kindling.

"Something like that." Guy watched Judith in the lamplight as she untied her bonnet, his brow wrinkled with concern. "We were on our way home from the Singing, and your house was the closest after we got caught in the rain. I hoped to borrow your rig to take Judith home."

Judith's teeth chattered.

"Take your shawl off," Ellie said, helping Judith ease the wet wool off her shoulders. "Are you soaked through?"

Judith shook her head. "*Ne*, just my shawl and bonnet." She lifted one foot. "And my shoes."

"Come in the bedroom with me, and I'll loan you a pair of warm socks."

Following Ellie's waddling form through the kitchen and into the bedroom, Judith shivered again. Her shawl had been wet, but at least it had held a little warmth.

Ellie lit the candle on top of the dresser and pulled a knitted throw from the back of a small chair, her movements awkward. The newest addition to their family was due to arrive sometime very soon.

"Here," she said as Judith sat on the chair, "wrap up in this while I find some dry stockings for you."

Judith pulled the warm blanket around her shoulders and relaxed against the chair back.

"And here," Ellie continued, bending down to open a dresser drawer. "These are a pair of Bram's socks. Take off your shoes and stockings, and slip these on."

As Judith removed her stockings, she held her toes for a minute. They were ice cold.

"How did you get caught in the rain, anyway?" Ellie sat on the edge of the bed, facing her. "Our house is pretty far from Deacon Beachey's."

Now that Judith was getting warmer, the memories of her ride with Luke came flooding in. Her nose prickled.

"I made an awful mistake."

Ellie sat on the edge of the bed and waited for her to go on.

"Luke Kaufman wanted to give me a ride home, and I said he could, even though I had gone to the Singing with Guy."

"Luke?" Ellie said. "He's kind of wild, isn't he?"

Judith nodded. "I guess I didn't realize what that really meant."

Ellie took her hand. "Did he do something on the way home?"

"First, he drove all around until I was lost, and then we ended up at the lake."

"Emma Lake? That's at least three miles from here."

A shiver ran through Judith. But she couldn't tell if it was from the cold or remembering the dark lakeshore.

"Then he tried to kiss me."

Ellie nodded. "Some boys think they can get away with anything. Did you let him?"

"It was awful." Judith wiped her lips with her free hand, feeling his wet mouth again. "I don't think I like kisses."

With a laugh, Ellie leaned forward and hugged her. "Someday the right boy will kiss you, and then you'll find out how sweet they can be."

Judith leaned her head on Ellie's shoulder, suddenly sleepy now that she was getting warmer. As she closed her eyes, she saw Guy's face, handsome and ruddy in the moonlight, close to her own, and the way his eyes had flicked to her mouth. She had thought he wanted to kiss her, out there in the dark, but he hadn't. Would his kisses be sweet, the way Ellie said?

Ellie gave her another squeeze, then stood up slowly, leaning backward and pushing herself up with one hand.

"Ach," she said, smoothing her hand over her swollen stomach, "I'll be glad when this wee babe is finally here. Then I'll be able to put it down in its cradle instead of carrying it with me all the time."

Judith glanced at the waiting cradle in the corner of the room. "Is the baby awfully heavy?"

Ellie smiled as she rubbed her back. "It isn't so terrible. But I can hardly wait to see the little one."

"It won't be much longer, will it?"

"It can happen any day now." Ellie kneaded her back with her fist as she led the way back to the kitchen. "Any day."

Ellie made them all some hot tea to drink, and they sat on the chairs Bram and Guy had brought near the stove. Judith hung her wet socks on the line behind the oven so they could dry.

The conversation turned to the Singings that Ellie had attended before she married her first husband.

"Did you ever have a beau other than Daniel?" Judith asked, cupping her hands around her mug of sweetened tea with milk.

Ellie shook her head, her eyes focused somewhere over Judith's head. "Daniel was my only beau. He was handsome and kind. And such a good father." She smiled at Bram. "Almost as good a father as you are." She turned to Guy. "He was an orphan, too."

Guy cleared his throat. "You mean he lived at the orphanage?"

"He came from Ohio to live with his aunt and uncle when his parents died. They are Hezekiah and Miriam Miller, who live in our *Dawdi Haus*, now. He was only fourteen years old, and it was very hard for him. He lived with the Millers until we married. They were a second set of parents for him, and the three of them needed each other."

"Well, he needed a home, I know that." Guy turned the mug in his hand. "But why did they need him? To work on the farm?"

Ellie sipped her tea. "The Millers had never had children. Daniel coming to them was a gift. He gave them a reason to continue building up the farm. A reason to work for the future." She smiled, her eyes focused on her hands as she looked back over the years. "Miriam says that Daniel was the child of her heart, and his coming to them was the greatest blessing God could have given them. And Daniel's children—" she paused to take Bram's hand in hers "—and our new son or daughter, are the light of their old age."

Guy frowned as he drained his mug. "We should get going. It's late, and Matthew will be wondering where Judith is."

"I'll drive you both home," Bram said. He put his mug on the drainboard next to the sink. "You know, I had never thought about it before, but David and Verna are a lot like Hezekiah and Miriam. You're the son they never had, just like Daniel was for his folks."

"Not really," Guy said. His frown deepened.

"Why not?" Judith retrieved her dry stockings and slipped them on.

"I don't belong to them, I just work for them."

"That's not the way David thinks of you," Bram said. "I've heard him tell the other men how glad he is that you're living with them full-time now, rather than going back and forth to the orphanage."

Judith slipped her feet into her damp shoes as Guy and Bram went to the barn to hitch up the horse. Why didn't Guy see how much David and Verna loved him? It was almost as if he pushed away any idea that he belonged here in the community. If it hadn't been for his *Deitsch* lessons and attending church with the Masts, she wouldn't think he had any interest in becoming Amish at all.

Ellie dipped some hot water out of the stove reservoir into a dishpan.

"Let me wash the cups for you."

Ellie shook her head. "I'm not sleepy. I'd rather be up

and doing something until Bram gets back." She rubbed the small of her back with one hand.

"Are you feeling all right?"

"It's only the wee one making himself known. I think he might be making his appearance tomorrow or the next day, the way I'm feeling."

"What if you need help while Bram's gone?"

"Don't worry about me," Ellie said, shooing her toward the door. "If I need someone, I can send Johnny to the *Dawdi Haus* for Miriam."

"If you're sure…"

Ellie laughed. "I'm sure." She settled Judith's damp bonnet over her *Kapp*. "But Judith, are you sure?"

"About what?"

"Luke and Guy. It seems like you're caught in between the two of them."

"Not anymore." Judith tied her bonnet under her chin. "I thought Luke was nice looking, and he is popular, but he isn't the boy for me."

"But is Guy?"

Judith looked toward the barn, where Guy was leading the horse out, hitched to the buggy and ready to go. His only thought through the entire evening had been for her. Making sure she was safe, making sure she was taken care of. Even when she had pushed him away, he didn't abandon her.

"I don't know." Judith gave Ellie a quick hug goodbye. "But he's given me a lot to think about tonight."

Ellie caught Judith's sleeve before she stepped away. "He seems to be a kind and thoughtful man. Someone who will be a good friend for you."

Judith glanced toward Guy, waiting to help her into

the buggy. Ellie was right. Guy had been a good friend tonight. Her words from earlier in the evening echoed in her ears. Had she really told Guy she didn't want folks to see them as a couple?

As she stepped into the buggy, her hand in Guy's for balance, she met his look. Those eyes, so gentle and comforting, lit a warm fire inside her.

She sat next to Bram, and Guy squeezed into the seat on her other side. He laid his arm along the back of the bench, his hand barely touching her shoulder. But at the same time, she felt safe and protected.

Ja, he was a good friend. Someone she could trust.

A light was shining from the kitchen windows when they arrived at Judith's house. The ride had been silent, with Judith sitting next to Guy in the front seat, and he welcomed the pressure of her shoulder against his side as his arm along the back of the seat made room for her to sit close to him. He had hoped that she'd lay her head on his shoulder, but she stared straight ahead.

"Looks like Matthew is up and waiting for you," Bram said as he pulled the horse to a halt by the kitchen door.

Judith stifled a yawn. "Or Annie is up with the twins."

That question was answered as Matthew opened the door wide and trotted down the steps toward them before Guy could help Judith from the buggy.

"Judith? Is that you?"

"You didn't have to wait up for me." Judith stood next to Guy. "We got caught in the rain and ended up at Bram's."

Matthew leaned into the buggy. "I appreciate you bringing Judith home, especially since it's so late."

"Being late is partly our fault," Bram said. "We got to talking while their wraps dried and kept them too long."

"How did they end up at your place? That's out of the way if they were walking between here and my folks' place."

Guy shifted his feet when Bram fixed his gaze on him. He had been responsible for Judith, but she had ended up walking nearly all the way to Topeka.

"It's my fault," he said, blurting the words out. "I should have brought her straight home."

Judith stepped between Guy and the older men. "*Ne.* Guy had nothing to do with me ending up so far from home. If he hadn't come to find me, I would still be out there in the dark and lost. I'm sorry I caused you so much trouble, Bram."

"It is no trouble. Ellie hasn't been sleeping well lately, and I know she enjoyed the company."

"Everything is all right at your place?" Matthew asked.

"She's doing well. She thinks we'll be meeting our little stranger soon, though."

Guy knew that was as close as the men would come to discussing Ellie's condition.

"Then you need to get home. I appreciate you giving these young folks a ride." Matthew shook hands with Bram, then closed the buggy door.

Matthew stepped back as Bram drove away and turned to Judith. "Morning will be here before we know it, and I need to turn in. I know Annie will want to hear all about your adventure tomorrow, but I'm just glad you're home now, and safe."

Judith nodded. "I'll come in a minute."

As Matthew went into the house, Judith wrapped her arms around herself. The night air was brisk as a breeze started blowing.

"You should go in, too," Guy said, turning her toward the door. "It's late, and you're cold."

"Come into the washing porch with me." Judith tugged on his hand. "I'm not ready for sleep, and I want to talk to you. We'll be out of the wind there."

She was right. The washing porch was quiet and snug, even if it wasn't warm. Judith closed the door against the chill and sat on a bench, patting the spot next to her. When he sat, she looked at him, her smile barely visible in the dark.

"All the way home from Bram's, the only thing I could think of was how silly I was to go with Luke." She spoke in English, and Guy was glad he didn't have to work to understand her. "I don't know why I did it, except that it sounded like fun. And Hannah has been encouraging me to get together with her brother, so I thought I'd give him a chance."

"Hannah likes to interfere where she isn't wanted." Guy didn't want to think about Hannah and girls like her.

"She isn't mean about it though, is she? She's always been nice to me."

Guy rubbed at his chin. "She's thoughtless more than mean." He scratched the whiskers growing on his cheek. Hannah's carelessness about his feelings last fall had hurt, no matter what her intentions had been.

"But she's blind where her brother is concerned. All the fellows knew he intended to see how far he could get with you tonight. He wanted to take advantage of your inexperience."

Judith was silent for a moment, and when she spoke, her voice was strained. "Why didn't you warn me?"

"I tried, remember? But you didn't listen to me."

She grasped his hand. "I'm sorry. I thought you were just trying to run my life, but instead you were only protecting me."

Guy closed his fingers over her cold hand and reached for the other one. Clasped in his larger ones, they would warm quickly. "Of course I was trying to protect you. You went to the Singing with me, and Matthew trusted me to watch out for you."

"I was wrong about Luke."

"What do you mean?"

"I assumed that I could trust any of the boys in our church. I should be able to, shouldn't I? I thought he would watch out for me, just like Matthew would or you would. But he didn't."

Guy thought about the fellows he knew from town and the Home. He wouldn't trust any girl with them if they were alone on a dark night. He stroked the back of her hand.

"One of the things I like about you is that you look for the good in everyone, but not everyone is good."

"But Luke's father is a deacon." Judith pulled one hand from his grasp and untied her bonnet.

"That doesn't make Luke so good that he won't succumb to temptation when it comes."

"Like a girl who is trusting enough to accept a ride

home with him." Judith stood and paced the length of the porch. "I actually thought he was going to bring me home. How stupid could I be?"

"Not stupid." Guy leaned against the wall and watched her walk back and forth. "You aren't stupid." He stood and caught her arm as she walked past the bench again. "You are new to this whole thing. The Singings, fellows being interested in you, flirting, all of it." He turned her toward him, wishing he could see the expression on her face in the shadows. "You'll learn, and someday you'll ride home with a boy who actually takes you home instead of trying to take advantage of you."

Judith sighed and leaned against him. "But how will I know which boys I can trust and which ones I can't?"

He tightened his arms and held her close. "Ask me. I know most of the fellows and can give you advice." His stomach turned when he thought of someone else talking with her the way he was now. He couldn't think of boys he trusted, except perhaps Benjamin Stoltzfus or Nathan Zook.

"*Denki*, Guy. You're a good friend."

As she went into the house, Guy lingered on the porch, fastening his coat before walking across the road to his warm bed. Judith was looking toward the future with more confidence than he had. She would go out with those boys and perhaps end up marrying one of them. He could see her standing next to Nathan Zook in a few years, a toddler at her knees and a baby in her arms. Happy and content.

And where would he be? Guy shoved his hat onto his head and let himself out into the night. He tucked his chin into his coat and skirted a puddle. Who knew? Still working for David, most likely, and waiting for something that would never happen.

Chapter Seven

"Why are Mondays always so busy?" Annie, with a baby in each arm, pushed a pile of laundry across the washing porch's floor toward Judith with her foot.

"Well, first of all, it's washday." Judith took a shirt from Eli. He was trying hard to help, but the job would have gone smoother without him handing her the soiled clothes one item at a time.

Annie shifted one of the twins to face front as the baby grew fussy. That one must be Viola. She was always wanting to see what was happening around her, while Rose was more likely to be content watching whoever held her.

"*Ja*, it's washday, but that doesn't explain why things are always in a kerfuffle on Mondays."

Judith grinned at her. "Or it could be because you didn't get much sleep last night. I heard you up with one of the twins soon after I got home."

"Both of them." Annie sighed and jiggled the babies, soothing Viola's fussing. "First Rose woke up, and then before I could get her fed and changed, Viola was crying. Sometimes I feel like I get nothing else done except feeding them and changing their diapers."

Judith watched Annie's expression soften as she leaned down to kiss Viola's red curls and swallowed a sudden longing that had appeared from nowhere. A longing so strong that her throat filled and her eyes grew moist. Such a simple gesture, but one that showed the intimate bond between mother and child. She shook her head and turned back to the next shirt Eli handed her, not wanting to stare.

She smiled at her nephew. "But you wouldn't trade them for anything in the world, would you?"

"*Ja*, that's for sure. Sometimes, when I should be sleeping, I just sit and watch them, amazed at the wonder of babies."

That brought Judith's thoughts to her sister-in-law, and the mysterious labor she might be experiencing at this moment.

"Guy and I stopped at Bram and Ellie's last night. She said she expects their little stranger to arrive any day now."

"I haven't had an opportunity to ask you how the Singing went. Did you have fun?"

Judith's cheeks warmed as she put the rest of the load of clothes into the washtub. Eli had found the handle to the wringer and was busy trying it out. "Most of it was a lot of fun."

"Most of it?"

"Matthew didn't tell you?"

Annie shook her head. "He was out and doing chores by the time I woke up this morning. We haven't had a chance to talk."

Judith had been glad when Matthew didn't mention anything about the previous night at breakfast, but she thought he had already told Annie.

"There was a bit of a problem. I got caught in the rain, and Guy took me to Bram's to dry off and borrow their buggy."

Annie stepped closer as Judith scrubbed a shirt on the washboard. "You went to Bram's? How did you end up all the way down there?"

Judith told her the story of Luke and how she ended up alone on a strange road. "I was so embarrassed. I hope the story doesn't get out to everyone."

"No one will hear it from me. But how did Guy know where to look for you?"

"I'm not sure. He was suddenly there, and I never asked him. I was so glad to see him." Judith stopped her scrubbing and looked at Annie. "But you don't need to worry. I won't be accepting a ride from Luke Kaufman again."

"I hope you'll let Guy bring you home from now on."

"Or someone else. Guy said he would let me know which of the boys I can trust."

Annie didn't answer but chewed her bottom lip as Judith ran a shirt through the wringer and dropped it in the basket with the other clean clothes.

"What is wrong?"

"Guy said that? Why? I thought he would have wanted to bring you home himself, not make way for another fellow."

"We're friends, and that's the way I want it to be. I appreciate his willingness to help me, but he knows that I'm not looking for anything more from him."

Viola squirmed and Annie started rocking from one foot to the other with a bouncing motion, a habit Judith had seen in other young mothers. It worked, though, and Viola's fussiness eased.

"I'm not sure that Guy thinks of you as just a friend."

Judith stared at her, the wringer forgotten in midturn. The memory of how his eyes had darkened when she'd thought he might kiss her last night flashed through her thoughts. "What makes you think that?"

It was Annie's turn to grin at her. "I see the expression on his face when he thinks no one is looking."

Feeding the next shirt into the wringer, Judith started turning it again. "Now you're imagining things. Guy is just the boy across the road."

"That you spend a lot of time with."

Judith put the last shirt through the wringer. "Only because of his language lessons."

"Are you sure that's all it is?"

As she picked up the laundry basket to take it outside to the clothesline, Judith caught Annie's gaze. If she was going to have any peace, she needed to squelch Annie's speculations once and for all.

"Of course that's all it is. Guy and I are friends. Nothing more."

Judith let the wooden door slam, Annie's giggles echoing behind her. Picking up the first shirt, she shook it with a snap, then reached up to pin it to the clothesline. As she did, her gaze wandered across the road to the Mast farm. Looking for Guy? She shook her head and concentrated on jamming the pin down on the shirt's shoulder. Where was her determination to find a boy from a good, Amish family? One who would be able to offer her the security and comfort *Mamm* had never enjoyed?

Guy was a friend. Only a friend.

As she bent down to pick up the next shirt from the basket, her gaze went across the road again. Two figures stood in the barnyard, one a few inches taller than the other. That one must be Guy. David grasped Guy's shoulder as they walked behind the corner of the barn, their heads bent together as if they were deep in conversation.

Annie had been right about Luke, and she might be right about Guy. Security and a good name would be nothing without love. The kind of love Judith saw between Annie and Matthew, and Samuel and Mary. Even last night, she had seen that same love between Bram and Ellie.

Would she and Guy ever share that kind of love? Judith stared at the Mast farm as if the empty barnyard held the answer.

"I didn't ask you how things went at the Singing last night." David held the wagon tongue as Guy fitted the new bolts into place.

"It went fine." Guy finished replacing the bolts and picked up the pieces of the old, worn ones to put in the scrap bucket.

The older man ran a hand over his beard. "You got in later than I thought you might."

"Judith had some trouble getting home, so I stayed to make sure she made it all right."

"Trouble?"

Guy leveled a look at his boss. He didn't want to betray Judith's confidence, but he could use some advice.

He gave David a brief account of what had happened the night before. "I did the only thing I could think of, and took her to her brother's place."

"You did right, son." David gave his shoulder a squeeze as they walked toward the machine shed next to the barn. "Bram is a good man and would make sure she got home safely."

"I tried to tell Judith not to accept a ride home from Luke, but she wouldn't listen to me. How can I convince her I know what I'm talking about?"

"After last night, she might trust your opinion more."

Guy tossed the broken pieces of the bolts in the air a few inches and caught them again. "Sometimes I get the feeling she thinks of me like a younger brother. I don't know if she'll ever listen to me."

"You're her friend, aren't you? You are earning her trust."

Guy couldn't think of how to answer. Every time he thought he might want her to be more than a friend, the sound of Hannah's laughter echoed in his ears.

"Yeah," he said, switching to English. "Yeah, we're friends."

David stopped in the doorway, facing him. "Verna and I started out as friends, sitting across the aisle from each other in school. Some of the best marriages start out that way." He grinned. "Should we look for a courting buggy for you?"

His stomach dipped down and then up again. A courting buggy?

"If I bought a courting buggy, it would be the same as putting a sign on my back saying Bachelor Available. Looking for a Wife."

David laughed, then set to work on the new milking stool he was making. "You're probably right. A courting buggy would declare your intentions to the world." He held up the three legs of the stool he had sanded and finished yesterday, checking them against each other. "It would also tell the world that you're thinking about joining church."

"It would, for sure." Guy tossed the old bolts and washers into the scrap bucket.

"And you're not ready for that?"

Leaning on the workbench, Guy watched David whittle the end of one leg of the stool to match the others. "I never put much thought in it." He flicked at a little pile of sawdust. "I've always assumed that when my pa came back, I'd go off with him."

"Do you still think he will?"

After the years of broken promises? "I don't think he'll ever ask me to go with him. Not after all this time. I'm not sure he'll even show up again."

David fitted one of the legs into the hole he had drilled in the bottom of the stool. "You've put a lot of faith in your father over the years. I've seen you waiting and watching for him. One of your first summers here, you'd perk up every time an automobile drove by the farm, hoping it was your dad coming for you."

Guy glanced at the older man, but David was concentrating on getting the angle of the leg right. "I remember that. Pa had stopped by the Home in April, just before my twelfth birthday." Guy ground his thumb into the little pile of sawdust he had created, pressing it together. "He had promised he'd be back before school was out.

He said he had a job out West somewhere, and I could come with him."

It had been another broken promise.

David dipped an old brush in the glue pot, swirled it in the hole and set the leg in place. "People will always disappoint us. That's why we should be wary of putting our faith in them. Even the best of men will let us down eventually."

Guy snorted. "You've got that right."

"God, on the other hand, will never let you down."

God again. Even when he had prayed last night, God had remained silent.

"What about when things go wrong, or people die, or accidents happen?"

David set the second leg in its place. "We have a knack for expecting something different than what God promises. He never promised our lives would be easy, and He never said we would always be happy. What He does promise is that when troubles come, He will be with us." He looked Guy in the eye. "He has never left you or forsaken you."

Guy couldn't meet David's gaze. He swept the little pile of sawdust away, remembering the silent emptiness after Mama died. "It has sure felt like it sometimes."

David sighed as he set in the third leg. Once it was in place, he gave each of the legs a final thump with the mallet, then set the stool upright on the workbench.

"Life is a lot like this stool." David took a bit of sandpaper and rubbed the seat. "What would happen if I had given it only two legs? Or one leg?"

"I wouldn't want to sit on it."

"I wouldn't, either. But that's what we do when we

try to live without God and a community of believers."
He pointed to the legs, one at a time. "God's Word, the
Bible, is the first leg, and the community, the church,
is our second leg."

"And the third?"

"That's us. All by ourselves we're like a one-legged
stool. We can get by, but it's precarious. So God has
given us the church for support and help."

Guy stared at the stool. He knew what it was like to
only have yourself to depend on.

"Folks don't have to belong to a church, do they?
There are other groups, like the Lion's Club or the Odd
Fellows that have halls in town."

"Run by men, for men. Social or civic clubs aren't
the same as a church, and aren't built on the foundation of God's Word. A man of faith lives by prayer and
the Word of God."

David ran his hand over the stool, then applied the
sandpaper to a rough spot on the edge.

"When I think of all three of the parts of my life, the
church, God's Word and myself, I can see how everything works together. And all three parts are connected
to God Himself." David brushed off the seat and put the
stool on the dirt floor. "Try it out."

Guy sat, feeling the stool's support, even on the un-
even floor. "It will work fine for milking the cows."

David grinned. "It works fine for your life, too. I
urge you to think about joining the church, Guy. Not
for me or for Verna, but for yourself. For your future."

As David turned back to the workbench, putting
away his tools, Guy took the new stool into the milk-

ing parlor. Was David right? That joining the church would give him a future?

Guy grabbed the manure fork and started cleaning out the aisle behind the milking stanchions. Every time he considered his future, he only saw emptiness. If Pa would come, then he'd know what to look forward to. A life like he had before Mama died, with someone he belonged to.

Carrying the loaded fork to the manure pile, he paused to gaze out the open door at the bare tree branches against the blue sky. Ever since Mama died and Pa left him at the Home, he had been waiting. Even knowing that Pa wasn't likely to keep his straw promises, he couldn't give up completely.

Guy turned and shoved the fork under the soiled straw again. Fat chance of that happening.

But until he was sure, until he knew for certain, his feet were stuck in the mire of doubt. There was no moving forward until Pa came back.

Chapter Eight

By Tuesday morning, Judith felt rested after her late night on Sunday. She fixed scrambled eggs for breakfast, with sausage patties and biscuits, hurrying to have the meal on the table by the time Matthew finished with the morning chores. Annie wanted to start clearing out the third upstairs bedroom today, in anticipation of Rose and Viola using it in a few months. The room had been used for storage since Annie and Matthew's marriage, and it promised to be a lengthy project.

Before Judith put breakfast on the table, Bram drove into the yard. He jumped from the buggy and pounded up the porch steps, not taking the time to knock.

"Where's Annie?" He strode into the kitchen, his uncombed hair framing his flushed face.

"She's with the twins." Judith stirred the scrambled eggs then turned to pick up Eli, who had taken refuge behind her skirts at Bram's loud entrance. "What's wrong?"

Bram turned to her, half laughing and half panic-

stricken. "It's Ellie. The baby is coming and she's…
she's…"

Annie appeared in the other door, a twin in each arm.
"The baby is coming? Is anyone with her?"

"Miriam is there, but she wants you and Judith, if
you can come. Ellie wanted her *mamm* to be there, but
Elizabeth has gone to her sister's for the day."

Annie placed a calming hand on their brother's arm.
"It's all right. Ellie has gone through this before, and
she'll be fine. Go out to the barn and tell Matthew that
Judith and I are taking the children to your house for the
day and that his breakfast will be in the oven for him."

She laughed as Bram stumbled out the door. "First-
time fathers! I remember the state Matthew was in when
Eli came." She turned to Judith, her eyes lit with joy. "I
suppose we had better get ready. I'll pack diapers and
extra clothes for the children if you'll finish Matthew's
breakfast. It's going to be a long day!"

As Annie rushed out of the kitchen, Judith jiggled Eli
in her arms. "You get to play with Danny today. That
will be fun, won't it?"

Eli grinned a drooling smile, his fist stuffed partway
into his mouth. "Danna, Danna!"

"That's right." Judith set him back on the floor and
stirred the eggs once more. She took the plate of sau-
sages she had already cooked out of the warming oven
and added some of them to the skillet, then covered the
skillet and put it into the oven. "Danny will be happy
to see you."

"Blocks?" Eli ran toward the front room. "Blocks."

Judith grabbed three biscuits from the covered basket
and split them open, laying a sausage patty inside each

one. She took a fourth biscuit for Eli and cut a sausage patty into bites for him. At least they could eat some breakfast on the way to Ellie and Bram's. In just a few minutes, Annie was back in the kitchen and they were ready to go.

As Bram's horse, Partner, trotted down the road at a faster pace than Judith was used to, she handed the biscuit sandwiches around.

Bram shook his head at the offer. "I can't eat anything."

"You need to," Annie said, leaning forward from the backseat. "You need to keep your strength up."

"All right." Bram's growl sounded like Samuel as he stuffed the biscuit into his mouth, driving one-handed.

"And Bram," Annie added, "don't worry so much. Everything will be fine."

Bram shook his head again and urged the horse to trot even faster. "You didn't hear her. I think she must be dying, the way she was moaning."

Annie patted his shoulder. "That's how it is for women. And after the baby comes, she'll forget the pain because of the delight of seeing her little one."

Judith stared out the window. From what Bram was saying, Ellie must be having a terrible time, but Annie didn't seem worried at all. The woman's part in dealing with babies was a mystery to her, even after growing up on a farm. Judith hugged Eli as he sat on her lap and she jiggled the basket that held little Rose. The baby yawned, her eyelids drooping as the steady movement of the buggy put her to sleep.

When they arrived at the farm, Bram pulled up at the back door, jumping out to help Annie and Judith take the children in. Johnny, Judith's nine-year-old nephew, met them at the door.

"How is your *mamm*?" Bram asked, his eyes on the closed bedroom door at the other end of the big kitchen.

"*Grossmutti* Miriam won't let us in." Johnny swung the door open and stared at the folks Bram had brought with him.

"That's all right," Annie said, taking charge. "You and your *daed* need to go take care of the horse, and maybe you can find another task to keep you busy for a while."

Johnny frowned. "I want to stay here with *Mamm*."

Annie shooed the two of them out the door. "I know you'll find something to do. Don't come back in until we call you."

Johnny planted his feet on the floor. "But I'm hungry. I haven't had breakfast yet."

"I'll make something and bring it out to you," Judith said. As much as she was curious about what was happening in the bedroom, she'd much rather make herself useful fixing meals and taking care of the little children while Annie helped Ellie.

"Coffee cake?" Johnny's hopeful grin made her smile.

"I'll see what I can do."

With Bram and Johnny gone, Annie placed the sleeping twins in their baskets on the table and headed into the bedroom. She paused with her hand on the doorknob.

"Have you ever helped with a birth, Judith?"

Judith shook her head.

"We're going to need boiling water, so keep a kettle on." She hesitated, looking worried for the first time that morning. "Will you be all right with all of the children?"

"Susan will help me, and we'll be fine." Judith loved her sweet niece, and at seven years old, Susan was the perfect little mother with young ones.

Annie disappeared into the bedroom and Judith took Eli into the front room. Susan was there, playing with three-year-old Danny.

"*Hallo*, Susan."

The little girl grinned at her from the floor, where she and Danny were building with blocks. "*Hallo*, Auntie Judith."

"I'm going to make some breakfast. Will you be able to play with both Danny and Eli while I bake some coffee cake?"

"For sure." Susan scooted over to let Eli take her place on the floor, then stood to whisper in Judith's ear. "We're going to have a new baby."

Judith grinned at the excitement in Susan's voice. "I know. Isn't it wonderful?"

"Do you think it will be a boy baby or a girl baby?"

"Either one would be *wonderful-gut*. Which one do you want it to be?"

Susan's face grew serious as she watched her little brother and Eli play. "I think a boy would be nice, because then he can play with Danny." Then she turned to Judith, her face pensive. "But is it all right if I really want a little sister?"

Judith laughed and gave Susan a hug. "I don't blame you for wanting a little sister. I'm Annie's little sister, did you know that?"

Susan's eyes grew big as she considered this. "But you're a grown-up."

"I haven't always been a grown-up. Once I was little, like Rose and Viola."

Susan shook her head. "I don't remember that."

Judith bit her lip to keep from laughing again. "I don't remember it, either. I'm going to be in the kitchen with the babies. Be sure to call me if you need anything, all right?"

Susan nodded and went back to supervising the boys' play. Judith peeked into the twins' baskets when she reached the kitchen, then found a large bowl to use for mixing the cake.

As she put the cake in the oven, a sharp cry came from the bedroom, then the lusty yell of a newborn baby. It seemed that Annie had arrived just in time.

The door opened and Miriam, Ellie's elderly aunt, came out with a basin. "We're ready for some clean water to wash the wee babe." Her face was one big smile, and the midmorning sunlight streamed through the window, making her hair shine in a silvery shimmer.

"Is Ellie all right? Can I tell Bram?"

Miriam nodded as she poured warm water into the basin. "She's a beautiful little girl, with dark hair just like Susan's." The older woman gripped Judith's arm. "Give us a few minutes to tidy things up, then Bram can come in. Ellie's already asking for him."

As Miriam went back into the bedroom, Judith ran out the back door to find Bram, flying as if she had wings. No matter what Ellie had gone through, she was blessed with a baby girl. Maybe this business of becoming a mother wasn't such a scary event, after all.

Later, after the baby had been swaddled in soft cloths, Ellie lay in the bed resting and holding her new daughter. Judith leaned on the doorframe of the cozy bedroom with Eli in her arms, while Miriam and Hezekiah leaned against the wall on the other side of the bed. Bram had brought the other children in to meet their new sister, and at the sight of Susan's glowing face, Judith's eyes grew moist. The love in Bram and Ellie's family was apparent, and so was their joy at the arrival of this new little one.

"What is her name?" The question came from Johnny, and Danny echoed it.

"What's her name, *Memmi*?"

Ellie looked at Bram and he cleared his throat. "We thought a good name for her would be Margaret Ruth, after her grandmother, my mother. We'll call her Maggie for short."

Annie smiled as she stroked the top of the baby's head. "That's a fine name, Bram, and our *mamm* would have loved it. Little Maggie Ruth."

March came in like a lion on Friday, with a storm that left a foot of snow on the ground. But the next day, the sun shone brightly, turning the spring air balmy. Judith sat in the wagon bed with Guy, while David Mast and Matthew rode on the high wagon seat. Matthew had replaced the wagon's wheels with sled runners that morning and had hurried her out the door before she'd even cleared breakfast away.

"So the snowstorm means there's more sap in the trees?" Judith asked Matthew. She still didn't understand why everyone was in such a hurry or why they needed her help.

Matthew spoke over his shoulder. "Cold nights hold the sap back, so the storm we had slowed things down. But this sunshine and warmth means the sap will be shooting up the trees faster than a cottontail running from the hounds. My folks need all the help they can get to collect the sap."

"Their sugar bush must be a large one."

"Last year they made more than three hundred quarts of syrup."

"Annie has a jar in the cellar. I wondered where she had gotten it." Judith could still taste the delicious syrup she had eaten with her fried mush for breakfast. No wonder Matthew was excited. "I've never helped with a syrup harvest before, but it sounds like fun."

"The sap only runs like this for a short time, so we need to bring it in while we can." Matthew turned the horses at the corner, the harnesses jingling. "And we don't harvest syrup. We take the sap from the trees and that's boiled down to make the syrup."

The ride to the Elam Beachey's farm was short. Judith had been to the farm last week for the Singing, but this morning Matthew drove past the farm lane to the wood lot beyond it. As he drove into the woods, following a narrow track, Judith smelled wood smoke. The horses went around a thick clump of trees and a shack appeared, with smoke and steam pouring from the chimney. The yard around the shack was crowded with Matthew's brothers and some older boys, with Elam, Matthew's *daed*, standing on a stump in the middle of the group, assigning chores.

After welcoming them with a wave, Elam went on.

"We have four sleds now, with Matthew's, so we'll have four teams. Four people with each sled, and *Mamm* and I will work here in the sugaring shed, boiling sap."

"Wait here," Matthew said as he jumped off the seat. "I'll get some cans and a barrel for our sap."

As Guy helped Matthew load the big wooden barrel into the back of the sled, Judith watched the other three sleds head into the woods. Matthew rushed to the wagon seat as soon as he could, and drove into the woods, taking a different route than his brothers had.

"Why the hurry?" Guy asked.

Matthew laughed. "It's a competition every year, to see which of us brothers can bring in the most sap. I've won every year so far, but those nephews of mine are getting older. Manassas and his two boys are bound and determined to win this year, but I think we'll beat them."

When he stopped the wagon, the four of them jumped down. A bucket sat at the base of most of the trees, under a little trough that was stuck into the trunk. Clear liquid dripped from each little spout.

Guy pulled on Judith's sleeve. "Come with us. David is going to show us what we need to do."

He grabbed two empty milk pails out of the back of the sled and followed David to the first tree. The bucket was nearly full.

David stepped into the deep snow at the base of the tree. "First, take anything out of the sap that doesn't belong there."

"What kinds of things?" Judith peered into the bucket.

David snatched a brown leaf from the surface of the

sap. "Leaves, like this one. Later in the season, you might find bugs floating in it."

Judith hoped that she wouldn't need to help when the weather grew warmer.

David went on. "Pour the sap into your pail, then replace the bucket under the spout."

Judith crowded close to Guy to watch. "The sap looks like water. Not like syrup at all. Are you sure this is a sugar tree?"

David nodded and moved to the next tree. "It doesn't turn into syrup until it's been cooked down. That's what Elam and Sarai are doing at the sugar shack."

Judith took her pail and went to another tree. The work was simple enough, but her milk pails filled so quickly that she was heading back to the sled after every two trees. Before she had finished a dozen trees, Matthew called to them.

"We've filled our barrel, so I'll head back to the sugar shack."

As Matthew drove off, David pointed out a smaller tree, away from where Judith and Guy had been working. "When I got to that tree, the bucket was empty. Can you see if the hole needs clearing out? I'll go around and see if there are any others that need attention."

Judith watched Guy take the little trough out of the tree. He broke a dead twig off a larger branch and poked it into the hole. He kept poking and wiggling the stick until the sap started flowing, carrying a few wood chips along with it.

"That should do it," Guy said, straightening up. "Listen to the sap ring on the bottom of the bucket."

All around them, drops of sap fell into the buck-

"4 for 4" MINI-SURVEY

We are prepared to **REWARD** you
with 2 FREE books and 2 FREE gifts
for completing our MINI SURVEY!

FREE
Value Over
$20!

You'll get...
TWO FREE BOOKS &
TWO FREE GIFTS

just for participating in our Mini Survey!

Dear Reader,

IT'S A FACT: if you answer 4 quick questions, we'll send you **4 FREE REWARDS!**

I'm not kidding you. As a leading publisher of women's fiction, we value your opinions… and your time. That's why we are prepared to **reward** you handsomely for completing our mini-survey. In fact, we have 4 Free Rewards for you, including 2 free books and 2 free gifts.

As you may have guessed, that's why our mini-survey is called **"4 for 4".** Answer 4 questions and get 4 Free Rewards. It's that simple!

Thank you for participating in our survey,

Pam Powers

To get your 4 FREE REWARDS:
Complete the survey below and return the insert today to receive 2 FREE BOOKS and 2 FREE GIFTS guaranteed!

"4 for 4" MINI-SURVEY

1 Is reading one of your favorite hobbies?

☐ YES ☐ NO

2 Do you prefer to read instead of watch TV?

☐ YES ☐ NO

3 Do you read newspapers and magazines?

☐ YES ☐ NO

4 Do you enjoy trying new book series with FREE BOOKS?

☐ YES ☐ NO

YES! I have completed the above Mini-Survey. Please send me my 4 FREE REWARDS (worth over $20 retail). I understand that I am under no obligation to buy anything, as explained on the back of this card.

❏ I prefer the regular-print edition
105/305 IDL GMYL

❏ I prefer the larger-print edition
122/322 IDL GMYL

FIRST NAME	LAST NAME

ADDRESS

APT.#	CITY

STATE/PROV.   ZIP/POSTAL CODE

LI-218-MS17

ets they had emptied, filling the woods with a ping-
ing noise.

Suddenly, a sharp crack rang through the woods,
followed by a cry. Without a word, Guy ran through
the soggy snow toward the sound. Judith ran after him.
This was the direction David had gone.

Guy stopped at the edge of a small gully, next to a
creek. David lay in the snow below him, his face white.

"Be careful." David held his hand up in warning.
"The edge gave way under me, and that's why I fell."

"There's the problem." Guy pointed to a broken tree
trunk. Snow had been shaken off and the jagged edges
showed where it had broken under David's weight. Guy
tested it by stepping on it, and the log cracked underneath him. "This log has rotted through."

He jumped down to where David was still lying in
the deep snow. The older man's eyes had closed. Guy
knelt next to him, then shot a glance at Judith.

"Go get help. Quick."

Judith turned and ran back through the woods, not
stopping until she reached the sugar shack. Matthew
and Elam were emptying the barrel on the back of Matthew's sled, while one of his brothers waited for his
turn to unload.

"Help!" Judith shouted, trying to catch her breath.
"There's been an accident."

All the men turned toward her, the sap forgotten.

"Who?" Matthew asked, grabbing his team's bri-
dles and turning them to head back the way Judith had
come. "Where?"

"David." Judith couldn't speak, she was breathing so

hard. She pointed with one hand into the woods. "Guy is with him. He said to hurry."

Matthew's brother Manassas jumped onto the sled and pushed the empty sap barrel off the back as Matthew urged the team to go as fast as they could through the wet snow and mud. Elam jumped on, too, and Matthew's nephews followed, running in the packed snow of the trail.

Sarai, Matthew's mother, had come out of the sugar shack at the commotion and grasped Judith's arms before she could strike out after them.

"Don't try to follow them. I'll need your help here."

Judith nodded, and the tears she had held back started falling. Her last glimpse of Guy's face haunted her, full of fear and a deep sorrow. David had been lying still. Too still.

Melting snow seeped through the layers of clothing Verna had made him wear, and Guy was glad he had listened to her. If he was getting wet and cold, sitting here beside David, how cold must the other man be? Since Judith had gone for help, David hadn't moved. Guy had to look closely to make sure he was breathing, but David had lost consciousness and was lying on his back beside the gurgling stream, as still as death.

"Hurry, hurry," Guy muttered. A prayer? Maybe. He swallowed a threatening panic, tasting the bile. He had to remain calm. He had to think clearly to help David.

The older man's face was white above his graying beard, his eyelids partially open. Guy leaned closer. David couldn't die. He couldn't. What would Verna do without her husband?

Guy grabbed the end of his leather glove in his teeth and pulled it off. Touching David's white cheek with the back of his hand, he felt a bit of warmth. The injured man's breathing was shallow, but he was alive. His breath whooshing out in relief, Guy sat back on his heels. What would he do without David's guidance in his life? The old man had to survive this.

Guy bit his lip. David should have reacted to his touch. Before Judith left to get help, he had been awake. He had talked to them, so the fall hadn't knocked him out. Something was terribly wrong.

Grasping David's hand again, Guy leaned close to the still form. "Don't leave me, David." There was no movement.

After too many breaths, too much time, the sound of horses and the jingle of harness echoed through the woods. Then Matthew's head peered over the embankment.

"What happened?"

"That dead log gave way underneath him."

Manassas and Elam joined Matthew, and Elam slid down the slope, landing next to Guy. "Has he been unconscious the whole time?"

Guy thought he understood the question asked in *Deitsch*. "*Ne.* He was awake when Judith and I found him. He warned us to be careful so we wouldn't fall, too."

Elam felt David's face the way Guy had. "David," he said. When David didn't respond, he called again, louder and with more force. "David! Can you hear me?"

David's eyes fluttered, then opened. He took a deep breath and let it out, then closed his eyes again.

"David," Elam called again. "Talk to me. Do you hurt anywhere?"

A groan was the only answer. Guy felt a bubble of panic rise in his chest. Why didn't David wake up?

Elam's expression was determined rather than scared, and Guy took a breath. If Elam could stay calm, so could he.

"David, try to move your arms."

"He moved one earlier," Guy said.

David's hands twitched. "Cold. I'm cold," he said.

Elam frowned. "Move your legs next. First the left one."

David's left knee raised slightly, then fell back to the ground.

"Now try your right leg."

During the pause that followed, Guy's fists clenched and unclenched. No movement. Then David groaned.

"It looks like his right leg might be broken," Matthew said.

"My hip," David whispered. "Hurts."

Guy glanced at Elam's face. The other man frowned as he stroked his beard.

Finally, he stood. "We need to get him to the house, and we need the doctor. His hip might be broken, or his leg. Either way, we need to handle him carefully."

"Just tell us what to do, *Daed*," Matthew said, speaking for all of them.

"All right. You boys go for the doctor. Take my buggy and hitch Storm to it. He's fast and spooks easy, but you can handle him."

The boys ran off before Guy could even gauge their reaction to their grandfather's trust in them.

"Manassas, we need something to use for a stretcher. There's a ladder in the sugaring shed that will work. And tell *Mamm* to send some blankets."

Manassas took off at a run, following his sons, while Matthew turned the sled around, ready for the journey back to the house. Guy didn't move from David's side.

"Will he be all right?"

Elam locked eyes with him for a long minute. "That's in God's hands. We'll do the best we can to keep from hurting him more than he is already, but it's going to be tricky."

When Manassas got back with the ladder, the four of them worked together to move David's inert form from his cold bed in the snow to the makeshift stretcher. Underneath him was the rocky stream bed, covered in stones. Blood had seeped from a cut on David's head and covered a large rock. Guy swallowed at the thought of David falling onto it with no warning.

"Careful now, boys," Elam said. "Keep your movements steady."

By the time they reached the Beacheys' house and laid David on the bed in a downstairs bedroom, the doctor had arrived. Guy pressed against the wall of the little room, giving the doctor as much space as he could, but refused to file into the kitchen with the others. Judith stayed with him, slipping her hand into his.

As Guy watched the doctor examine David, Judith's grip tightened.

"He'll be all right," she said, standing on her toes to whisper into his ear. "Everyone in the kitchen is praying for him, and the doctor knows what he is doing."

Guy squeezed her hand. Her encouraging words flowed through him, easing the tightness and strengthening him. The doctor continued to work in silence while Guy waited. Judith leaned against him and he encircled her shoulders with one arm. He needed her here, with him. As David's white face remained still, fear drummed in his heart. If not for Judith's presence, the earth would be rocking beneath his feet.

After the boys brought the doctor, they had gone again to fetch Verna. Her voice, strong and sure, drifted into the room before her, like waves pushed by a boat in a quiet lake.

"Doctor," she said. "How is he?"

The doctor stood, stuffing his stethoscope into his black bag. He glanced at Guy, then focused on Verna.

"He has had a bad fall, and some bones might be broken. He also suffered a blow to his head, and it concerns me that he remains unconscious. There could be some internal bleeding."

"Can we take him home, doctor?" Verna asked.

"Not for some time, I'm afraid," the doctor said. "We can't risk moving him."

Verna seemed to age several years at the doctor's words, and reached one shaking arm toward Guy. He went to her, willing his strength to support her. She shuddered slightly as he took her in his arms, and she rested her forehead against his shoulder.

"Do whatever needs to be done, doctor," Guy said, feeling Verna nod in agreement as he spoke the words.

The doctor's eyebrows raised. "And you are…?"

Guy felt the pressure of a weight on his shoulders. He took a breath, holding Verna with a tight grip.

"I'm…"

"Our son," Verna said, her hand on his chest, looking up at him. "Guy is our son."

Chapter Nine

Guy woke to the delicious scent of bacon frying, and for a long, comfortable minute he lay still, absorbing the fragrance. Only his nose was out of the covers, and he let his mind drift until the events of the past two days crowded into his consciousness and tugged him into a groggy wakefulness. Kicking the covers off, Guy rolled until he sat on the edge of the bed, his head in his hands.

David. After the morning chores were done, he needed to go to the Beacheys' to see how David was doing and to take Verna the things she had asked him to fetch.

That thought brought him fully awake. He should be alone in the house, but who was frying bacon? That aroma hadn't only been in his dreams.

After he dressed, he tiptoed down the stairs in his stocking feet, trying to talk himself out of his worries. No thief would take the time to fry bacon. Perhaps Verna had come home, after all. Perhaps David was well again, and life could get back to normal.

He reached the bottom of the stairs and peered

around the corner into the kitchen. Judith was there, working at the stove, with Eli sitting at the table eating a slice of bread. As Guy stepped into the room, Eli saw him and grinned. Judith still had her back to him. She had put the bacon on a plate on the stove to keep warm and was cracking eggs one by one and dropping them into the hot pan. The bacon grease sputtered as they hit and Guy's stomach growled.

Guy leaned against the doorframe, watching her. He had taken Verna's work for granted. Her meals were always delicious and on the table right when he and David came in from working around the farm, a methodical efficiency born of long years of practice. Judith worked with as much efficiency, but her movements expressed the grace of a dancer, her skirt swaying, each movement choreographed to perfection as her tasks came together in a meal just for him.

When she turned to set the table, she saw him, but didn't pause in her work.

"I see the sleepyhead has finally appeared. I thought I would have to do the barn work as well as make the breakfast."

The cows. Guy had slept through milking time. Why hadn't their bawling woken him up earlier?

Pushing past Judith, Guy glanced at the frying eggs with regret. "I need to get to the barn. Keep my breakfast warm, if you can."

"Don't worry. Matthew already milked and put the cows out in the pasture. He left the separating for you to do, and the rest of the chores. But you can do those after you finish eating."

"Matthew did that? Why?"

Judith shrugged as she slid the eggs from the frying pan onto a hot serving platter. "That's what neighbors do when there's a need. He knew you returned home late last night and thought you needed the rest." She put the eggs on the table along with the platter of bacon, then reached into the oven for a stack of hotcakes that had been keeping warm.

She pointed to the chair next to Eli. "Go ahead and sit down. I'm not going to eat all this food by myself."

Guy sat, and without a word, they both bowed their heads for the silent prayer. But he couldn't pray, not with Judith sitting across the table from him and Eli staring. His thoughts kept drifting to David and Verna, the responsibilities of the farm. How they were depending on him. He was even beginning to understand why the farm was so important. It was their home and their life.

He squeezed his eyes tight, trying to banish Verna's echoing voice, but the thought still swirled. To the doctor, she had referred to him as their son, but he wasn't a son to anyone but Frank Hoover. He had no home. No life of his own.

Eli stirred, restless at the length of the prayer time, but Guy wasn't done. A fleeting thought, perhaps a prayer, ran through his head. That God would see fit to give him a place where he belonged. A family. A future.

He shook his head, sitting back in his chair as he opened his eyes. That was a pipe dream, like all the others.

As Judith put one of the fried eggs on Eli's plate, Guy let his gaze feast on the breakfast she had prepared for him. He hadn't asked her to do it. He hadn't even considered that she might. But she had thought of him and his needs and had put them before her own.

"Denki," he said, turning his spoon over and back again. He couldn't look at her. "I'm sure you had plenty of your own work to do instead of making breakfast for me." He cleared away a tickle that had appeared in his throat.

"I was hungry, too, and Eli hasn't had his breakfast yet." Judith passed the plate of eggs to him and took hotcakes for herself and Eli. "I knew that Verna was at Deacon Beachey's." She cut Eli's hotcake into bites for him. "And bachelors are notorious for fixing themselves poor meals."

"You can say that again." Guy reached for the hotcakes. "I ate dinner at the Beacheys' yesterday, but only had some bread and cheese for supper last night."

He piled a half dozen hotcakes on his plate, spreading a generous smear of butter on each one. As the golden stream of maple syrup flowed onto the stack, his eyes blurred. Would maple syrup always remind him of David's accident? And what if he wasn't better this morning? What if…?

Half blinded by his watering eyes, Guy set the little glass pitcher down before he spilled the syrup.

"Is everything all right?" Judith paused with a forkful of eggs partway to her mouth.

Guy wiped his forearm across his face. *"Ja,* I'm all right. The maple syrup just reminded me of David."

"How is he doing? We didn't get over there to see him yesterday."

He knew that. He had expected Judith to come, but the long hours by David's bedside had dragged on without her. There were visitors, folks from the church who had heard of the accident and came to offer their support and help, but no Judith. No calm presence to hold him up under the strain.

"The doctor said he's doing as well as we can expect. He woke up and talked to us for a while, but spent most of the time sleeping. The doctor said that was a good sign."

"I'm glad."

Guy looked up to meet her smile.

"I missed you yesterday."

"I spent the day at Bram's. With the new baby, I knew Ellie would need help with the other children."

He ran his fingers through his hair. The irony wasn't lost on him. A new baby's cries filled one home, while at Deacon Beachey's, the day had felt like a deathwatch.

"That's good. Everyone is all right?"

With that simple question, Judith's enthusiasm bubbled up. Guy finished his hotcakes and his eggs, and was down to the last piece of bacon while she talked nonstop about the baby and the other children, and who knew what else.

"And you'll never guess what they named her."

Her words drifted into the swirl of thoughts he had been wading through while she talked. The worry about David, Verna and the farm kept breaking through so that he hadn't kept track of everything she had said.

"What they named who?"

Her face turned bright pink as she glared at him. Without another word, she washed Eli's hands and face and set him on the floor to play. Then she grabbed the empty dishes off the table and dumped them into the dishpan. Seizing the dipper from above the stove, she took the lid off the reservoir and started ladling hot water into the pan.

He watched her stiff shoulders as Eli came over to him, oblivious of his aunt's mood.

"Up?"

Guy absently took the little boy on his knee and let Eli pull on his suspenders.

"Horses." Eli said, pushing on Guy's stomach to get his attention. "See horses?"

"*Ja.* I'll take you to see the horses."

Guy stood up, Eli in his arms. He took a step toward Judith but thought better of getting too close.

"Did I do something wrong?"

Her glare could have peeled paint.

"I'll take Eli out to see the animals, then I'll bring him in before I start the chores." He took a step toward the door as she turned back to shaving soap into the dishpan. "I appreciate the breakfast. More than you know."

He helped Eli put on his jacket and grabbed his hat from the hook. Glancing at Judith's rigid back, he regretted whatever he had done to make her angry. If he knew more about women, he might know what to do to bring back that peaceful feeling that had reigned during breakfast.

"Come on, Eli." He took the little boy's hand. "Let's go see the horses."

Pausing before taking the final step out of the kitchen, he tried one more time.

"I'll be heading over to Deacon Beachey's as soon as the chores are done. Do you want to come with me?"

"*Ja*, I would like to." Her voice was tight with strain. "I'll have to ask Annie if she can spare me, though."

"That's good." In his relief, he slipped back into English. "That's real good. I'd like to have you with me."

Her shoulders relaxed and she glanced over her shoulder. "And I'd like to be there with you." Then she smiled at him.

He whistled as he grabbed Eli's other hand and swung him down the steps to the ground. Giggling, the boy ran ahead toward the barn and Guy ran after him, catching him just as he stumbled on the rough ground and swinging him around.

Clutching Eli close again, Guy covered the rest of their path to the barn like a galloping horse, making the boy laugh with every jolt.

Even if it took David months to recover from his fall, and even if nothing else right ever happened again, Judith's smile would see him through.

Later that morning, Judith peeled potatoes and carrots in Sarai Beachey's kitchen, preparing them to go into the chicken pie Ruthy and Waneta Zook were making. Judith hadn't gotten to know Waneta's stepmother well yet, but as they worked together, Judith appreciated her quick smile and her willingness to work while Sarai took a much-needed rest.

"We are so thankful that David is doing better today," Ruthy said. She boned the stewed chicken faster than Judith had ever seen anyone do that task.

"Do you know if he'll be able to go home soon?" Judith put the diced vegetables into a pot to cook before she added them to the pie filling.

"The doctor said that once he sets the broken leg and puts a splint on the hip, he will be able to be moved." Ruthy strained the broth from the stewed chicken. "It's good that the Mast farm is a short distance. The move will be hard on him, as it is, but they won't try it for a few more days."

Waneta looked up from the piecrust. "He won't be able to work on his farm, though, will he?"

Ruthy shook her head. "Only God knows when he will be recovered enough to work again."

"It's a good thing he has Guy to help him, isn't it?" Waneta eased the crust into the large baking pan. They were expecting to feed more than twelve people for the noon meal with all the neighbors who had come to visit David and help collect the sap and boil it off. "If it was only David and Verna on that farm, they would have a hard time of it."

Judith dumped the potato and carrot peelings into the slop bucket. "But the church will help, won't it? I heard the men talking about a work day to get the crops planted."

Ruthy nodded. "There are still the day-to-day chores that need to be done, though. That responsibility is too much for Verna, so Waneta is right. Having Guy around to help is *wonderful-gut*."

With this talk of Guy, Judith's stomach took a turn. Just when she thought their friendship was growing into something more, he had to prove himself just as infuriating as any man could be. He had let her make a fool of herself this morning as she talked on and on about baby Maggie Ruth and Bram's growing family. Why she had smiled at him as he had taken Eli to see the horses, she had no idea. Just because he'd said he wanted her to come to Elam and Sarai's with him? That one kind offer wasn't enough to make her forgive him for ignoring her, even if he had made Eli happy with the trip to the barnyard.

While Ruthy took the dishpan off the wall and started filling it, Judith decided to start a batch of gingerbread for dessert. The soft cake would be a welcome end to their meal. As she looked through the cupboards to make sure all the ingredients were on hand, Waneta joined her.

"What kind of cake are you planning to make?"

"I thought gingerbread would be good. The molasses will make it sweet, but I can't find any ginger."

Waneta opened another cupboard. "Here are the spices." She picked up one of the small cans and read the label. "Cream of Tartar." She looked at each of the containers, one by one. "Does Guy like gingerbread?"

Judith fetched the can of lard from the cupboard next to the sink. "I'm not sure if I care if he likes it or not."

Waneta found the ginger and set it on the counter next to the mixing bowl. "Why not? I thought you were good friends."

She kept her voice low, and Judith was glad. Guy was in the next room with Verna and David, and she didn't want him to suspect that they were talking about him.

"We are. I mean, we were." Judith broke some eggs into a small bowl and whisked them with a fork. "But this morning I was telling him about spending yesterday at Ellie and Bram's, and he didn't listen to me at all."

"Reuben will do that, too. I think he just doesn't hear me sometimes."

Ruthy shaved soap flakes into the dishwater and swirled them around with her hand, waiting for them to dissolve. "You need to be patient with Guy. David's accident is a shock for everyone, but for him and Verna most of all."

"That's right," Waneta said, scooping the lard into the mixing bowl. "He has a lot on his mind. You'll learn to gauge his moods and know when he's ready to listen and when he isn't."

The whisking fork slowed in Judith's hand. Gauge his moods? That's how *Mamm* had lived with *Daed* all those years, and how she and Esther had treated Samuel after their parents were gone. Every day they had tiptoed around their brother, not knowing what kind of mood he was in or how he would treat them. If that was what living with a man was like, then it wasn't for her.

A soft knock at the back door drew her attention. Levi Zook stood in the doorway, his hat in his hand and a shy smile on his face. "Ruthy, I'm going over to David's with Guy, Bram and Matthew to see what needs to be done on the farm."

As Ruthy dried her hands, Judith happened to see the glance that passed between her and her husband. A private look. A loving look. No tiptoeing around Levi's feelings. It was the same look she had seen pass between Bram and Ellie after Maggie Ruth's birth and the same look she saw often when Matthew and Annie were together. Many words were held within those looks. Private words that only the couple understood.

Perhaps her family's example wasn't the way all couples lived. After all, she had seen those same private looks pass between Samuel and Mary since they got married last year.

Maybe gauging a man's moods had less to do with avoiding his anger and more to do with knowing how to make him happy.

Levi stepped into the doorway of the bedroom where David was and said something to Guy. As the two men headed out the door, Guy glanced at Judith. His face was hopeful, his eyebrows raised. Waiting. Apologizing? She smiled and he broke into a grin before he followed Levi out the door. She turned back to her work. If she remembered right, Guy had said he liked anything sweet—and especially gingerbread.

Guy followed Levi out of Deacon Beachey's house with a light step. David seemed to be recovering, and Judith had smiled at him. Twice. It seemed that whatever he had done to put her off had been forgiven.

Matthew drove the four men to David's. As they rode, Matthew talked about the work that needed to be done.

"Has David started his plowing, yet?"

Guy shook his head. "We were going to start this week."

"That will be the first thing, then." Matthew turned the horse north at the intersection.

"Does he have his seed?" Bram asked. "Do you know what his plans were?"

"He said something about planting sorghum in the lower field and buckwheat in the field next to the pasture. The upper fields, between the house and the road, are being planted to corn this year."

"What about the mint fields?"

Guy whooshed out a sigh. The mint fields along the creek bottom at the back of the farm were a mystery to him. "That's part of the farm I know nothing about. I know we cut the mint last August, but I don't know if he does anything with the crop in the spring."

Last spring, he had still lived at the Home and only worked for David a couple of days a week. It wasn't until after his eighteenth birthday in May that he had left the Home and David had hired him on as a farm hand. In the ten months since then, he had begun to feel the rhythm of farm life, but this was his first spring to work with David full-time. He wasn't ready to step into the older man's shoes, that was for sure and certain.

Matthew let out a thoughtful grunt. "I remember David saying something about checking out the fields after the spring rains. Last year he had to replant some of the areas along the creek bank. We'll have to keep that in mind once May comes."

"You don't think he'll be able to work by then?" Guy looked from one man to another, but none of them met his eyes.

Bram cleared his throat. "David is suffering quite a bit, and the broken bones will keep him laid up for a long time. If he recovers—"

"If?"

"You heard what the doctor said, that his hip is broken."

"But broken bones mend, don't they?"

Bram rubbed his knee with one thumb, not looking at Guy. "*Ja*, for sure they mend, but David is an old man, and he may not be able to work again."

Guy stared at the fields they passed, but didn't see them. David not able to work? The man had always been the first to the barn in the morning, the first to get to work when Guy was lagging behind. When the doctor said David would survive, Guy had never thought that he wouldn't be able to get back to normal.

They rode in silence until Matthew turned into the farm lane. The barn rose ahead of them, on the right, and the house was on the left. Guy's throat closed as he looked at them, strong and steady. Well cared for. And his responsibility. Could he run the farm without David? He was just a kid. At least, he felt that way. He didn't have what it took to run a big farm like this. Especially not to David's standards.

As they got out of the buggy, the other men surveyed the neat barnyard and well-kept grass lawn around the house.

Levi clapped him on the shoulder. "It looks like you're caring for things the way David would want you to."

Guy noticed a loose screw on the door to the milking parlor and the chicken house that David had wanted him to whitewash this week. The others might not have noticed those details, but David would have. "I don't think I would ever keep this place going the way David does."

"You don't have to do it alone," Bram said as he led the way into the barn. "You have the church to help out."

Inside the granary, Guy showed the others where David had stored his seed for the planting season. The lead-lined bins were clean and free from vermin.

"The plow and harrow are all set for the spring." Guy led the way into the machine shed across from the granary where the equipment stood ready, the metal plow-shares glowing in the dim light.

"It looks like all you need is a dry day like today," Levi said, leaning down to test the edge of the plow.

"We should be ready. David and I have been cleaning and sharpening the equipment all winter." Remembering the hours he had spent with a whetstone brought tears to Guy's eyes. David had leaned over him, showing him the right angle to hold the stone, the right pressure to wield to hone the perfect edge.

"I know the harnesses don't need any work," Matthew said, interrupting Guy's thoughts. "David always keeps them in fine shape."

The men wandered out into the barnyard again, and Levi walked over to the empty field between the house and the road, on the north side of the long farm lane. The snow from last week's storm had melted in the warm spring weather they had had since then.

"What is he doing?" Guy asked.

"Checking the soil," Bram said. "That's one thing I've had to learn as I've begun farming on my own. Hezekiah taught me what to look for, but I don't quite have the knack yet. Someone who's been farming for years just knows when the soil is right. It needs to be dry enough to plow, but not so dry that the wind will draw all of the moisture out of the soil when you turn it."

Matthew looked up into the sky. "Doesn't look like we'll be getting any rain the next few days. The high pressure seems to be holding."

Guy gazed up into the clear blue sky. He didn't see anything.

"Now I know you're all pulling my leg. You can't tell

what the weather is going to do any more than Levi can feel when the soil is ready. You make it sound like farming is full of old wives' tales and old timers' signs." He grinned, waiting for them to laugh at the joke.

Bram grinned, but no one laughed. "It might seem that way, but where do you think the signs and tales came from? Experience is what a farmer relies on, and if you're smart, you'll pay attention and learn for yourself."

Guy stepped closer to Matthew. "So, tell me how you know it won't rain tomorrow."

The shorter man leaned back on his heels, his eyes on the trees rising behind his house across the road. "Look over there at the tree tops and tell me which way the wind is blowing."

The breeze was light enough that Guy couldn't feel it on the ground, but the ends of the branches swayed slightly against the sky. "They're hardly moving, but I'd guess the wind is from the northwest?"

Matthew nodded. "And after the snow went through over the weekend, the wind was from the northeast."

"And cold," Guy said.

"Today it's turned to the northwest, which means fair weather ahead. When the wind turns to the south, you can expect a storm, or at least rainfall." He turned to Guy. "A wise farmer keeps track of the weather. Makes notes on the calendar or in a journal. The direction and strength of the wind, the amount of rain. Some even have a barometer and keep track of the air pressure. When the barometer goes down, you know rain is coming."

As Matthew, Levi and Bram discussed the best time to start plowing David's land, Guy hung back. A heavy weight pressed on his shoulders and his stomach soured. Why hadn't he paid more attention when David went on endlessly about soil and manure and seeds and hours of sunlight? With one misstep, David was laid up and now the responsibility of the farm fell on Guy.

He took a step back from the others, but they didn't notice. Panic sent a bitter taste to his mouth. He swallowed. What could he do? He couldn't stay here. He would mess things up, everyone would see that he didn't know what he was doing and…worst of all… David would know how inept he really was.

"Guy!"

He focused on Matthew, who was gesturing to him.

"Come over here. We need to make plans."

What had Bram said? Guy wiped the back of his neck with one hand. He wasn't alone in this. The church would help. That community that David had talked about the day he made the three-legged stool.

The weight lifted a bit as he joined the others.

Chapter Ten

On Wednesday, after her chores were done, Judith took Eli to the Masts' to help Guy ready the house for David's return home on Thursday. The doctor had given Guy and Verna a list of changes that needed to be made for David's comfort, including moving a bed into the front room. And after living as a bachelor for nearly a week, Judith knew Guy would need help with household chores before Verna came home.

Judith let Eli run down the lane to the Masts' house in front of her. He stopped every few feet, bending over to pick another dandelion growing in the fresh, green grass alongside the buggy tracks, then took off again, running in his stiff-legged, toddler way. When he had gathered three or four of the yellow flowers, he came running back to her.

"Die Blumm." Eli opened his sticky fist and held them up to her. *"Blumm."*

"Denki, Eli. The flowers are beautiful."

He grinned and ran off again, stopping to pick another flower every few steps. By the time they reached the Masts' back porch, her hands were full of dandelion blossoms.

Guy must have seen them coming. He opened the door and stepped out just as Judith was laying the mass of yellow flowers on the back step.

"Verna will be glad to see those," he said. Catching Eli in a hug, he sat on the top step with the little boy on his knee. "She loves dandelion tea. I've heard her talking of it often."

"I think Eli has picked enough flowers for a dozen cups of tea." Judith sat on the step next to him. "And I see you've been practicing your *Deitsch*. You only used two *Englisch* words in that sentence."

Guy held up one of the flowers. "What are these called, then? I only know them as dandelions."

"I've heard them called a couple different things, but I've always called them *pusteblumm*. Because when they turn white, you puff on them to scatter the seeds."

"I get it." He twirled the stem, switching to *Englisch*. "Puff flowers. I can just see you as a little girl, picking all the white balls and blowing the seeds everywhere."

"My sister Esther calls them *buddah blummen*." She held one of the flowers under her chin. "Because if you see yellow on your chin when you hold the flower like this, that means you like butter."

"So, butter flowers." Guy grinned. "I can tell you like butter."

Judith snatched the flower away from her face, knowing from the heat in her cheeks that she was blushing. "What do you call them?"

He made a face. "Weeds. The headmaster at the Home wanted the grass in the lawn to be without any weeds, so one of our chores was to dig up the dandelion plants every spring."

"I've never heard of someone wanting to get rid of them. The flowers are good for tea, and the leaves are yummy greens cooked with bacon and vinegar, and the roots are good for medicine."

"I know. But the headmaster made up his mind, and we had to obey."

Something in Guy's tone drew Judith's gaze. He still jiggled Eli on his knee, giving the boy a pony ride, but his eyes were shadowed, as if he was looking into the past.

"What was it like, growing up in the Orphan's Home?"

He shook his head. "You don't want to know."

"In one way, I suppose it could be fun to have so many brothers and sisters. A big family."

"It wasn't like that." His voice was quiet, but with a hard edge. "We weren't children. Not like Eli or the other children you know. We were property." He swallowed, his Adam's apple bouncing down and up. "The headmaster hired us out to whoever was looking for a boy or girl to work for them."

"But the families who hired you, like the Masts. They were good to you, weren't they?"

Guy shook his head. "Not all of them. The summers that I was seven and eight, I was hired out to a farmer who treated me worse than the headmaster." He held Eli tightly and stopped the pony ride. "I remember one time when the rooster fell in the well. The farmer had to get it out before its carcass poisoned the water, so he sent me down there. He tied a rope to my foot and lowered me headfirst."

Judith scooted closer to him as he passed a hand over his eyes, as if he was trying to erase the memory.

"He didn't hear me yell when he had lowered me to the surface of the water, and I nearly drowned before he hauled me up again."

Guy shuddered, then gave Judith a weak smile. "I've been deathly afraid of water ever since. When I came here, I thought the headmaster had made a mistake. This place was too nice."

"The Lord God led you here to a family who loves you." The shadows in Guy's eyes faded as she spoke. "How old were you?"

"I was nine that first summer. David and Verna gave me a room in the house. My own room with a real bed instead of a cot in the lean-to or a pile of straw in the barn. Verna made new clothes for me and fed me the best food I had ever eaten. The best part was that David never whipped me."

Judith's stomach turned. "Were you whipped at the other place?"

"And at the Home." He chuckled, but the sound was more of a sob than laughter. "The headmaster believes that boys need to have evil beaten out of them." He shrugged. "I don't know if he's right or not. But I do know that I was always happiest during the summers when I was here." He looked at the barn and outbuildings. "David and Verna hired me every summer after that, and I'm grateful."

Judith could see that little boy in her mind. A young Guy, about the same age as her nephew Johnny. What would a life like that drive a boy to when he grew up?

"You must be glad that David asked you to work here, then, and be part of their family."

Guy frowned as he flicked at a spot of mud on his knee. Eli leaned against his shoulder, sucking his thumb, his eyes heavy.

"I'm glad they made room for me, but I don't know how long it will last."

"Why wouldn't it last? Why would you go anywhere else?"

He shrugged. "One thing I've learned is that nothing lasts forever. People come and go out of our lives for one reason or another, so I've learned to take life as it comes. Someday David will quit farming and sell out, or he'll hire someone else with more experience than I have, and I'll have to find a new job. That's just the way it is."

Judith stared at him. His words put a cold space between them as if he had reached out and pushed her away with his hand. "You can't think David and Verna would do that to you. I heard Verna talking about you at the quilting a couple weeks ago. They love you and are so grateful you are living with them and helping them. And with David's accident, they need you now, more than ever."

"Yeah. Sure. That's what they all say. That's what Pa said, too, but where is he? Forgotten all about me, I expect." He drew Eli closer in a casual hug. "I'm on my own and always will be."

"You aren't alone."

"Not now. I appreciate the church, Matthew and all them, and their willingness to help on the farm while

David recovers. But it won't last. There will come a time when they don't need me, and then I'll move on."

Judith laid her hand on his forearm, trying to close the gap between them, but his muscles were tense beneath his sleeve. Hard and unyielding.

"Don't you want to stay? To become part of the community? To have a home?"

His arm jerked away and his jaw bulged, but his eyes grew moist. She scooted closer to him.

"Why do you fight against it if you want it so much?"

Guy shifted Eli to her lap and stood. "Who said I wanted anything?" His eyes glittered with unshed tears. "I'm just looking out for myself, that's all. I don't need you to feel sorry for me, and I don't need anyone's help. You got that?"

He stalked toward the barn, not looking back, even when Eli began to cry. Judith felt like joining her nephew. Guy could have slapped her in the face and it would have hurt less. She jiggled Eli to stop his crying and bent close to his ear.

"Should we go in the house and find a nice, quiet place to lie down? Would you like that?"

Eli nodded and wrapped his arms around her neck, his innocent love a healing balm for her sore heart.

Guy took three steps into the barn before he remembered the work he needed to do was inside the house instead of out here. But his only thought had been to get away from Judith. He heard Eli's crying end and turned to watch Judith comforting the boy. Her head bent over his brown curls as she talked to him, then she wrapped him in her arms as he clung to her, safe and secure.

Judith rose and went into the house, but the scene clouded over as tears filled Guy's eyes. He let them fall, leaning his head against the solid wood of the door-frame. He had shut her out and pushed her away just as much as he had shoved Eli off his lap and onto hers. But why?

Because the feelings she brought out stopped his very breath. He dug his fingernails into the oak beam as the pain of those feelings overwhelmed him. If he could be little again…if he could see Mama again…if he could feel safe again…

He tore his thoughts away. He was a grown man, not a child. His life was laid out in front of him. A stark and lonely track with no end.

What was it about Judith that upset his well-ordered life? Before she'd come along, he had been happy.

Well, maybe not happy. But he could work, laugh and enjoy David's company and Verna's cooking. But now that he knew her, it was as if her steady blue eyes looked right into him and saw the scared little boy who needed a friend.

She made him long for things that would never happen. Things like a home. His own family. A…a wife. A partner in life. Someone to love and to love him. Some-one who wouldn't leave him behind.

How could something he wanted so badly hurt so much?

So he had pushed her away when she awakened those longings in him again. But the hurt only grew worse until it felt like someone had sucker-punched him and left him gasping for breath.

"Please, God." The words came out as a whisper,

barely passing over his lips as he breathed out. "Please, God, show me how to make the pain go away."

The pain eased, and in its place came the need to see Judith. To be with her. To patch things up.

But what if she was mad at him? What if she had gone home already?

He stuck his head out the door with that panicked thought, but there she was. She had left Eli in the house and was gathering the discarded dandelion blossoms into one of Verna's mixing bowls. Relief washed over him.

Walking across the barnyard to the porch, he waited for her to lift her head. To notice him. But she had turned away as she retrieved the blossoms that had fallen off the porch. He stopped a few paces behind her and cleared his throat.

Judith turned to him, looking worn out. "Eli was so tired, I put him down to sleep in the bedroom." She took a step closer to him, peering at his face. "Are you all right? You look like you might be ill."

He rubbed at his eyes, wiping away the last remnants of the tears, but he was sure tell-tale redness would remain.

"I'm fine." He took the bowl of dandelions from her. "I was out of line, back there."

"What does that mean, 'out of line'?"

"It means that I acted poorly. I treated you badly."

She didn't speak. If Guy had any doubts that his attitude had hurt her, they were silenced now. He had wounded her sorely.

"I was a real jerk."

She smiled then. "You were a *nah*. A fool."

"Ja. Ich voah der nah." He had been a fool, all right. A fool to think he could ever survive without seeing her smile.

Judith led the way into the kitchen as he followed.

"Why did you act that way, then?" she asked. "We were only talking."

Guy gazed out the kitchen window. Could he open his heart to her? She needed to know what she did to him. She put the bowl of dandelions in the sink under the spout. Guy pumped water for her as she thrust the blossoms below the surface, letting the excess drain off.

"I've haven't had a home for years."

She started to speak, but he stopped her.

"I haven't had a home since my mother died, when I was five." Her eyes fixed on his, and he could feel them boring deep into his soul. "I want…no, I need what you have. A family, friends. A future. But every time I think it's within my grasp, something happens to take it away." Pa's face flashed for an instant, then it was gone. "So I'm afraid that if I join the church, or if I reach out to accept the home David and Verna want me to have, it will melt like a snowflake in my hand."

Judith leaned closer and he stopped pumping, letting the last of the water run into thc basin.

"So you want it, but you're afraid to want it."

His eyes grew damp again. "I want it so badly that it hurts." He turned toward her. "And you. You make me want it even more."

She swirled the blossoms in the water, watching the spiral of yellow.

Guy bent down, catching her gaze. "I like you a lot, Judith."

He didn't just like her. He needed her like a thirsty plant needed rain. He needed her to fill that empty place.

She smiled, not looking at him. "I like you, too."

"Would you…would you be my girl?"

"You mean that I'd only talk to you at the Singings? And only ride home with you?"

When she put it that way, Guy felt her softness sliding away from him. The empty place ached.

"But you want to spend time with other fellows." He backed away. He had spoken too soon.

"Guy, I don't want to see other boys. Not really. I just want…" She bit her lip as her voice trailed off.

"What do you want? I'll do anything."

"I just want to be sure that my future will be secure. That I'll always have a place in the community with my family." She looked at him, her expression serious. "Anyone who courts me has to want the same thing."

The aching feeling flared until his joints burned. Didn't he want that, too?

Or did he? If Pa came by right now and offered Guy a chance at a life together with him, wouldn't he jump at it?

His breath whooshed out. He hadn't been aware that he'd been holding it.

"I don't even know what I want." He swept his hand in the air, taking in the table where he had eaten so many meals, the front room beyond the door where he had spent so many evenings with David and Verna, the staircase leading to his room upstairs. "This and the Home are all I know, but I feel like there's something else out there…"

"Life with your father." Judith's voice was flat as she supplied the answer for him. "The father who may never return."

Guy nodded his head. Even though Pa's promises might be made of straw, they'd been strong enough to hold him captive in the past. Trapped until he knew for sure if Pa would ever come back or not.

Judith woke up early on Saturday, the big work day at the Masts' farm, after what seemed like a sleepless night. So many chores pressed in on her mind that it felt like she'd been making lists in her head all night. Finally, long before dawn, but while the waning moon was still high in the sky, she got up. Lighting the candle she kept on the table by her bed, she found an old envelope and the stub of a pencil and wrote out every item she needed to do before going to David and Verna's in the morning. Finally, she blew out the candle and settled under the covers to get a bit of sleep.

But it didn't work. Even in her sleep, she dreamed of peeling potatoes until the peelings overflowed the dishpan and spilled out through the kitchen door.

Finally, she opened her eyes. The sun was nearly up and there was light enough to see. Now she could start on that list and get plenty done before Eli woke up. Judith sat at the table in the quiet kitchen and started peeling the potatoes she had washed and sorted the previous night.

Matthew had helped to bring David home on Thursday, and the older man was comfortably settled in the front room. David had asked to be there, rather than the bedroom, so he could be in the center of things. Guy had moved the spare bed into the room, and then had gone to town to purchase the special mattress the doctor had recommended. And Guy had altered the bed so that the top half could be raised or lowered and David could recline or lie flat.

Thinking of Guy brought a smile and her peeling slowed. She liked Guy. He was strong and clever and... and he was a friend she could talk to about anything.

But that was all. A special friend. He said he wanted her to be his girl, but she didn't want to go any farther than friendship until he was ready to commit to being part of the community.

Sighing, she reached for another potato. Some days, she felt like he was already part of the church, but then other times it was like he stood on the opposite side of a fence, looking in, but ready to flee like a skittish horse.

Judith put the third peeled potato into the big pot of clean water and eyed the waiting pile. Nearly thirty pounds waited to be peeled, washed, cut and boiled. Then mashed, buttered and seasoned. Then kept warm in the big pans until dinnertime. Meanwhile, she still needed to make the noodles. She tackled the next potato. At least she wouldn't have to make all this food by herself. Perhaps the other ladies would get to Verna's in time to make the noodles. Several had told Verna they were bringing chickens to stew. They would make a half-dozen pans of chicken and noodles, her favorite dish.

As Judith started on the next potato, someone knocked on the door and walked into the kitchen before Judith could dry her hands.

"Judith? Annie? Am I too early?"

Waneta carried a laundry basket covered with a towel.

"*Ach, ne.* I'm the only one up, but I've started on the work already." Judith took the basket and set it on the counter. "Is Ruthy with you?"

Waneta shook her head. "I came along early while the others finish the chores at home. I thought you could use some help with all the folks you're expecting to feed today."

Judith gestured toward the pile of potatoes. "I can, for sure and for certain. All I can think about is how much there is to do, and how little time before noon."

Waneta hung her shawl on an empty hook. "When you see what I brought, you'll stop worrying." She uncovered the basket to reveal a mound of fresh noodles. "*Mamm* and I made them yesterday. She said we might as well make them early and get the chore out of the way."

"She's right." Judith got a dishpan for Waneta's potato peelings. "And I'm so glad you came. We have at least an hour before Eli wakes up, so we can visit while we peel these potatoes."

"I know what we need to talk about first. We haven't had a chance to talk in private since Luke took you home from the Singing." Waneta found a knife in the drawer and sat down at the table. "You need to tell me about you and Luke and Guy." She paused, a narrow peel already hanging from her knife. "Have you chosen one of them?"

"I don't have anything to say about Luke." Judith tackled her own potato, trying to make her peelings as narrow and thin as Waneta's. Her earlier peelings had been thick with the flesh of the potato, which was wasteful, and she worked quickly to hide them under the new batch.

"Why not? I thought he was sweet on you."

"He thought he was, too. But I set him straight."

Waneta leaned forward. "What do you mean? You have to tell me everything."

"I'm not going to gossip." Judith concentrated on the end of her potato and the peeling dropped into the pan in her lap, almost as neat as Waneta's. "But Luke and I found that we don't have a lot in common."

"I thought he would be perfect for you." Waneta sounded disappointed as she resumed her peeling. "He has always said he wanted to marry the prettiest girl around, and when you showed up at church that first Sunday, I saw the way he looked at you."

Judith shook her head. Her? Pretty? "You've got it wrong. Luke was only interested because I was new. Besides, he isn't the type of man I'm looking for."

"What type is that?"

"Someone kind, and willing to work hard, and cute. A good Amishman."

"It sounds like you're describing Reuben, but you can't have him." Waneta sent her a mock frown and Judith laughed.

"I'm not describing Reuben."

"Then it must be Benjamin, Reuben's brother."

Judith shook her head and kept peeling.

"My brother Elias?"

"I've never even met him."

Waneta started in on another potato. "That's right." She sighed. "I suppose you want to keep it a secret for now. But when you're ready to tell someone, you'll tell me first, won't you?"

Judith grinned at this girl who had become a friend so quickly. "I'll tell you right after I tell my sisters."

Waneta laughed. "That's fair enough."

They worked in silence for a few minutes, then Waneta asked another question.

"Are you still teaching *Deitsch* to Guy Hoover? You were pretty upset with him the other day. Are you two friends again?"

Judith studied Waneta's face, but there wasn't any hint of teasing or that she thought Guy might be a special friend.

"He appreciates the community helping out with David's farm work today. He mentioned it several times when Annie and I were visiting David and Verna yesterday."

Waneta pulled some potatoes closer to her from the dwindling pile. "He's always been so standoffish. But since you've been teaching him, he hangs around with the other fellows more."

"I think he feels more comfortable with them now that he can speak our language better." Judith took another potato and changed the subject. "Is there anything new going on in your family?"

"Can you keep a secret?"

Judith laughed at Waneta's eager face. "Is it a secret you can tell?"

"It isn't that kind of secret, and everyone is going to know soon, anyway."

"I think I can guess. There's going to be a new baby at your house."

"How did you know?"

"It was something Ruthy did while we were at Deacon Beachey's the other day. She put her hand on her back, like she felt a twinge there. I've seen my sister-in-law Ellie do that same thing many times." Judith smiled, remembering the soft look on Ruthy's face when she did it, as if she was carrying a treasure only she knew about.

"I need to be careful around you," Waneta said. "You'll discover all my secrets even before I know about them." She grinned. "My brothers want the next baby to be a boy, but I hope Grace can have a sister that's close to her in age."

Waneta's youngest sister, Grace, was the prettiest baby Judith had ever seen, with curly black hair and dark blue eyes. "Grace doesn't look anything like the rest of you, does she?"

"That's because Grace had a different mother and father than we do. Her mother was *Mamm's* best friend, but she passed away when Grace was born. So we adopted her."

"Even though there were already ten children in your family?"

Waneta nodded. "Like *Daed* says, there's always enough love for one more."

Always enough love for one more. That sounded like something Verna would say. How different would Guy's life have been if they had been able to adopt him?

How different would her life be if Guy had grown up in the church, like Benjamin Stoltzfus or Nathan Zook?

No questions. No wondering about the future. She glanced sideways at Waneta reaching for another potato. As sure of Guy as Waneta was of Reuben.

Her life would be perfect. No less than perfect.

Chapter Eleven

"It's a fine day, isn't it?" Verna set a plate piled with hotcakes in front of Guy. "The folks should be showing up soon, so eat your fill. You need your strength."

"How many do you think will be here?" Guy poured maple syrup over the stack of steaming cakes.

"I wouldn't be surprised if the whole church came." Verna poured coffee into a mug she had set on a tray for David. "That's the usual way of things. When someone is in need, the community steps in to help."

As Verna scrambled eggs at the stove, Guy cut into his stack of hotcakes and took the first bite. Light. Fluffy. Sweet. Just the way he liked them.

"Several of the women will be coming, too."

Guy took another bite, enjoying the warm feeling brought by the anticipation of seeing Judith soon.

Verna went on, speaking over the sizzle of bacon frying and the scrape of her spatula in the frying pan. "We'll be working on the noon meal all morning long, so don't think you can come in here to grab a snack anytime you want."

He grunted a response, his mouth full of hotcakes and his mind lingering on Judith. Would she smile at him in front of everyone? Or would she ignore him, insisting that they were no more than friends? Tradition dictated that no one should know he was sweet on her, but Guy wasn't one to stick to tradition.

"We'll be making donuts for a snack for you men, so you won't go hungry."

She brought two plates of eggs and bacon to the table. Setting one in front of Guy, she put the second on the tray. Next came two dishes of stewed prunes: one for the table and a second for the tray.

"When you're finished with your breakfast, will you take David's tray in to him?" Verna patted his shoulder as she took his empty hotcake plate. "He said he wanted to talk to you before the men arrived this morning."

Guy swallowed the last of the sweet prunes and set his plate of eggs on the tray next to David's.

"*Denki*, Verna. Breakfast was good," he said as he carried the tray into the front room.

David was sitting up in bed, leaning against the support Guy had made for him. He was dressed from the waist up, and Verna had helped him with his morning routine of combing his hair and shaving his upper lip, leaving his beard growing long and full as the Amish did. Guy laid the tray on David's lap, then sat in Verna's chair with his plate.

"It smells good," David said, taking a deep breath that ended in a cough.

Guy frowned while David bowed his head in a silent prayer. The doctor had warned them to watch for a cough that could easily turn to pneumonia in a bed-ridden patient.

"Do you need me to prop you up further? Will it help to be more upright?"

The older man shook his head, waving him away. "I'm fine like this." He picked up his fork and took a small bite of the eggs. "Do you have a plan of what work you'll be doing today?"

Guy shrugged. "Matthew and Bram have it pretty well laid out. I thought I'd just do what they tell me."

David picked up his coffee, blowing across the steaming liquid before taking a sip. "This is our farm, Guy. The others will be here to help, not to do the work for you. You need to be the one to organize the men and plan the day."

Setting his fork on his plate, Guy looked at David. "Me? I'm just the hired help. I don't know what needs to be done, or when, or how. All of the others have a lot more experience than I do."

"But they don't know the fields the way you do. And you—" Another cough interrupted David's words. "And you're more than just hired help. You're acting for me today."

Guy ate a slice of bacon in three bites, then finished his eggs. Step into David's shoes? Him? There must be another way.

"Maybe we could move your bed outside so you could supervise. You could be there to answer everyone's questions…" His words trailed off as David shook his head.

"I'm not up to that, and you know it." He shifted

slightly in his bed and grimaced with pain. "I'm tired." He leaned his head back against the pillow. "So tired."

His eyes closed and Guy stood up to leave him alone.

As he lifted the forgotten tray from David's lap, the older man's eyelids fluttered. "I'm counting on you, Guy." He laid a cool, dry hand on Guy's. "I can't be out there, but you can. And you can do this, son. I know you can."

As David drifted off to sleep, Guy carried the tray back to the kitchen. Verna shook her head, clucking her tongue as she scraped David's uneaten breakfast into the slop pail.

"He'll be all right." Guy ducked his head to kiss her on the cheek. "He just needs to rest and recover."

He swallowed as he thought of that cough. David was going to get well. He had to.

Grabbing his hat from the hook, he stepped out into the barnyard and looked up at the sky. The same as David would do first thing every morning.

Guy ran his thumbs along his suspenders. Okay, so he hadn't checked the sky earlier, when he had come out to do the milking. But he'd get in the habit eventually.

He tilted his head up again, this time taking a good look. A gentle breeze blew from the northwest, and the light, wispy clouds didn't seem to move at all. A quiet morning with the sun shining in a blue sky. A dry day ahead, and cool weather. Perfect for getting the work done that they needed to do. He went into the barn, checking the plow and harrow. He ran his hands along the harnesses, feeling for sticky spots that would betray a dirty harness or weak places in the leather. Everything was ready.

Going through one of the big box stalls, Guy opened the back door and whistled for the draft horses. He would hitch up all six of them today to plow the south front field. One of the other fellows could follow him with their team and a harrow. Meanwhile, another pair of men could do the same with the north field. The day's plans ordered themselves in his head as he mentally assigned men and teams to the various fields and different tasks. If all went well, they might even be able to get the buckwheat planted in the back field behind the house. Planting the sorghum and corn would have to wait a few weeks, until the soil was warmer.

The horses came into their stalls, eager for their oats and the work they knew was waiting for them. As they ate, Guy groomed each one, paying special attention to their shoulders and backs, where the weight of the harness would press. He checked their feet for any stones that might have gotten lodged in their hooves while they were out in the pasture, then fastened a lead rope to each halter. After they had eaten, he'd lead them to the trough for some water, then back into the barn to harness them up.

As he fastened the lead rope to Penny's halter, she lifted her nose from her empty feed box and nudged him, looking for another treat. He laughed and gave her a piece of carrot, just as he had the other horses. She munched the carrot slowly, watching him with one eye. Then she winked, as if to say, "We know you can do this work. You're not alone."

Guy laughed at his fanciful thoughts, then smiled as he heard the first team coming toward the barn along the lane. Penny was right. He had the whole community to help him work today. Confidence flowed through him as he headed out to the barnyard to greet the visitors.

By the time Judith and Waneta finished peeling the potatoes, Eli was awake and the day started in earnest.

Breakfast was quick, with fried potatoes, ham and scrambled eggs. Waneta ate with the family, helping Annie care for the babies while Judith dealt with a fussy Eli.

"The children know things are different this morning, with the work day and all." Annie sighed, holding baby Rose to her shoulder and patting her back.

Matthew finished his breakfast and rose from table. "I need to hitch our team, then I'll be heading over to the Masts'."

"Da," shouted Eli, dumping his plate onto the floor with a crash. "I go with *Da*!" He squirmed in his chair, pushing at Judith's hands as she tried to keep him from falling, and Viola joined in the mayhem with a screaming cry.

Waneta's face grew red as she tried to suppress her laughter while comforting Viola. "Now this sounds like home when Grace is out of sorts!"

"Eli, stop that crying right now!" Judith kept her voice firm and the little boy stopped his wiggling. He leaned back in his chair, tears rolling down his cheeks.

"I go with *Da*." He reached his hands out toward Matthew, his voice pitifully sad.

"Not right now, Eli." Matthew picked up his son, holding the sobbing boy in his arms. "You'll come later, with Judith and Waneta. Until then, you help take care of your sisters." Eli cried louder, but Matthew set him on the floor next to Judith. "Do as I say now. I will see you later."

When Matthew shut the door behind him, Eli ran to it. *"Da! Da!"*

Judith went to him, lifting him in her arms. "You need to obey your *daed*, and crying won't change anything." She got a towel and wiped his face. "But you can help me with the potatoes, and we'll go hitch up the buggy in a little while."

"Horse?" Eli's tears stopped at Judith's promise of the work that lay ahead of them.

"Ja, you can help me with the horse." Judith grinned at him until he smiled back, then set him down, satisfied that he was over his tantrum. He loved Summer, the buggy horse, more than any other animal on the farm.

Meanwhile, the twins were quieting down as Annie and Waneta fed them, changed their diapers and put them down for their morning naps. Judith washed the breakfast dishes, then she and Waneta loaded the potatoes and noodles into the buggy. Eli sat on the buggy seat with Waneta while Judith hitched up Summer. While she worked, Eli sang a little song to the horse.

Waneta jiggled him on her lap as Judith climbed into the buggy and picked up the reins.

"I don't know what song he was singing, but he was enjoying himself."

Judith laughed. "Eli sings the same song to Summer whenever he's around her, and she seems to like it. She's always calm and gentle with him."

"They have a special friendship, then." Waneta smiled as Judith drove across the road and up the Masts' lane. "Much like you and…" Her voice trailed off, waiting for Judith to fill in the blank.

"You aren't going to tease me into telling you anything, so you may as well give up trying."

Waneta giggled and leaned down to speak in Eli's ear. "You can tell me, can't you? Who is Judith's special friend?"

Right then, Eli spotted Guy standing in the middle of the Masts' barnyard with Matthew, Bram and a few other men. Judith's stomach flipped at the sight of him, then fell when Eli bounced on Waneta's lap and pointed.

"Guy!" He looked at Waneta, then back at the men. "Guy! *Da!*"

"*Ja*, Eli. There's your *daed*." Judith ignored Waneta's pointed looks as she guided the buggy to the hitching rail by the back door of the house.

Verna's kitchen was fragrant with frying dough as Judith and Waneta brought in the basket of noodles and big pot of potatoes. The kitchen was crowded and noisy, with women talking as quickly as their fingers flew. Three women sat at the table, boning cooked chickens, while two others worked with Verna at the stove, frying donuts. Judith pumped a pail of water at the sink and poured it into her pot, then set the potatoes on the back of the stove to start cooking.

"Here," said Verna, dusting a tray of fresh donuts with cinnamon and sugar. "You girls can take these out to the men." She handed one tray to Judith, another to Waneta and another to Hannah Kaufman. "I'll take care of Eli." She handed the little boy a donut and settled him on a chair.

"Hannah, it's good to see you," Judith said, as she

started out the door with her donuts. "I didn't know you were planning to be here."

"*Daed* said we had to come." Hannah's pretty face was marred by a pouting expression. "I'd rather stay home and sew on my new dress."

"What color is it?" Waneta asked, walking next to Hannah toward the barn.

Judith followed them, not listening to their conversation as she searched the groups of men for another glimpse of Guy. But if Hannah was here, that meant Luke had come, too.

"Just what I was waiting for." Luke's voice came from her right, where he was lounging against some straw bales with a few other boys.

Putting a smile on her face, trying to be friendly, Judith held the tray of donuts toward them. "Would you like some donuts? They're fresh."

The boys didn't hesitate, but took three or four each. Luke waited until they cleared away, then grabbed a few for himself.

"They're fresh, are they?" He grinned at her. "Just like you?"

Judith turned away, meaning to take the rest of the donuts to the barn, where she could see her brother Bram through the open door.

"Wait a minute." Luke grabbed her arm. She spun toward him to keep her balance. "Maybe I want some more of those."

"You have plenty. I'm going to take these to the men in the barn."

"If you stand here, I'll save you that trip."

Judith looked at the half-filled tray in her hands.

"You don't mean you're going to eat all of these, do you?"

In reply, he picked up four more donuts and handed them to one of his friends. "We will, but mostly I want to talk to you."

"We don't have anything to talk about."

"I still have a bruise from where you kicked me."

"I wouldn't have kicked you if you hadn't—" Judith suddenly remembered their audience and lowered her voice to a whisper. "If you hadn't done what you did."

Luke backed away, holding his hand to his chest with a dramatic gesture. "You wound me. I didn't do anything to you."

Judith felt her cheeks burning. "I'm not going to argue with you about it. Take the donuts if you want them so I can go back to the house for more."

"Is anything wrong here?"

At the sound of Guy's voice behind her, Judith's knees went weak. He couldn't think she was talking to Luke because she chose to, could he?

Luke's mouth twisted as he took a step toward Guy. "What's going on here is none of your business, *Englischer.*"

He made the term sound like something you'd find on the barn floor.

Guy's face reddened, but his voice was steady when he turned to her. "Are you all right?"

She nodded, and turned to continue into the barn. "I just gave Luke and his friends some donuts. I'll take the rest to the men inside."

Judith had only taken a few steps when she heard the sickening sound of a fist hitting flesh.

One of Luke's friends yelled, "Fight! There's a fight!" Turning around she saw Luke on the ground with Guy on top of him, pressing his head into the gravel with one hand.

"Have you had enough?" Guy said, holding a handkerchief to his nose.

"Let me up!" Luke's yell was muffled, but his anger gave it a deadly tone.

Guy backed off just as the other men ran up.

"What's going on here?" John Stoltzfus shouldered his way in between Guy and Luke. "This is no time or place for a fight. You should both be ashamed of your actions."

Luke crab-walked away from Guy until a couple of his friends helped him stand up. "He started it," he said, pointing at Guy. "We were talking and he…he punched me."

Everyone looked at Guy. The handkerchief he held against his nose was soaked with blood.

"Is this true? Did you strike Luke?"

"I only pushed him to the ground." Guy's face was stormy, and he avoided looking at anyone.

"He punched me," Luke said, turning to his friends for confirmation. They all nodded.

"The outsider attacked him. I saw it," one of them said. Judith couldn't remember his name.

John looked at Guy with a frown. "This is a serious matter. We don't solve our differences with violence."

When Guy didn't say anything, Judith pushed forward. "This is silly. Look at Luke. He doesn't have a mark on him, and yet Guy's nose is bleeding. It's apparent that Luke is the one who hit Guy."

John looked from one young man to the other, then turned to Judith. "Did you see what happened?"

Judith's breath caught. She shook her head. "I was on my way into the barn." She gestured toward the barn door. Donuts had fallen from her tray when the fight started and were strewn in the dirt.

Turning to Guy, John's frown deepened. "Do you have anything to say?"

Guy's face grew even darker as he took two steps back, then turned and stalked toward the house.

John caught Luke's arm as he turned to go, too. "This isn't over, young man. Your *daed* and I will need to discuss this."

He let him go then, frowning at Luke's jaunty step. Judith stepped back as Luke passed her.

John raised his voice as he addressed the crowd around him. "Let's get back to work. There's still plenty that needs to be done."

Guy disappeared around the corner of the house, away from the kitchen and the group of men in the barnyard. Judith longed to follow him, but she couldn't get the sight of him cruelly pushing Luke's head into the gravel out of her mind. She hugged her elbows, undecided. What had really happened between Luke and Guy?

Guy strode around the corner of the house, heading somewhere. He didn't care where, as long as it was away from Luke Kaufman. At the back of the farmhouse, shielded from the barnyard by a lilac bush, were the old cellar steps. Shaded and cool, this spot had often been his refuge when he was a boy and had done something to make David mad.

He slumped on the third step, where his head was even with the ground, and leaned his head against the cool stone side of the stairway. Cautiously, he pulled the handkerchief away from his face. At least the bleeding had slowed. He pressed the side of his nose, but didn't feel the tell-tale pain of broken bones.

Luke's punch had taken him by surprise. At the Home, he had always been expecting a fistfight from any of the boys there. But here? Among the Amish? He had let down his guard.

Guy dabbed at a trickle of blood. He wouldn't make that mistake again.

But the worst was the expressions on the faces of the people who had gathered around. They had all believed that he had punched Luke, when all he had done was try to keep the bully from hitting him again. It hadn't been hard to throw Luke off balance, but once he had Luke on the ground and helpless, the fool had said it again. He had called Judith the name that had started the fight in the first place, and it had been all Guy could do to control his temper and keep himself from grinding Luke's face into the gravel.

He turned his handkerchief until he found a clean spot, then held it to his nose again, waiting for the bleeding to stop.

Fighting wasn't allowed among the Amish. He knew that. Someone would be in trouble, but it probably wasn't going to be Luke.

Even Judith had to see how useless her defense of him had been. Luke's friends would lie for him, and

Guy would be blamed for the fight. And what would happen then? David and Verna had been good to him, but would they allow him to stay on after this? Not if the whole community was against him.

Sounds filtered into his hiding place from the fields. Someone had organized the men into teams and sent them into the fields to plow and harrow. The day's work was going on without him. He wasn't needed after all. David had been wrong.

Guy dabbed at his nose again. His face felt tight and sore, but the bleeding had stopped. He'd probably have a black eye for days…and have to explain to David how it got there.

He shifted so his back was against the rough, cold stone. His mood was spiraling downward into a black hole, but he didn't care. John Stoltzfus hadn't believed him, and he was a minister. His opinion counted among these people.

And Judith… He had seen the look on her face. His fight with Luke had disgusted her. Maybe she had feelings for the bully after all.

Guy started to shake his head, denying that thought, but the motion sent a shooting pain from his nose to the back of his skull. He leaned against the stone wall again, seeking relief.

He sure had burned some bridges today. No one in the community would want him around. His job was gone, since David and Verna wouldn't want him on the farm. Any friendships he thought he might have…they were gone, too. He closed his eyes, imagining the reception he'd get the next time he showed his face around the other men. The cellar steps were a refuge, but someone would find him here. He had to go someplace until the workday was over and the farm was empty. He couldn't work with any of those men now.

Guy peeked over the edge of the stairwell, across the buckwheat field toward the woods along the river at the back of David's farm. If he could get across the field without being seen… Or if he was seen, he could say he was going to check on the mint or something. He stuffed his handkerchief in the waistband of his trousers and stood up.

"There you are!" Verna came around the lilac bush and stood with her fists at her waist, holding him in her gaze.

Guy's stomach turned as if he had eaten a rock that wouldn't settle. He hated to disappoint David, but the thought of disappointing Verna made him sick.

"I've been looking for you. The men have gone on with their work, and with you no place to be found. What has gotten into you?"

"There was some trouble—"

"We heard." Verna grabbed his suspender and pulled him up the step. She reached up to pull his chin around. "And you have quite the black eye coming on, there." She turned toward the back door. "Come along. David wants to talk to you."

The stone turned on end, but he followed. Looking over his shoulder across the buckwheat field, Guy put his thoughts of leaving on a shelf for now.

David waited for him, lying flat on his bed. The only sign that he was in pain was his pale face and the fixed set to his jaw. When David gestured toward the chair nearby, Guy sat down.

"What is this I hear about a fight?" The older man's tone was hard, but his expression spoke of grief and shame.

Guy swallowed. "I didn't start it."

"Luke says you did."

Guy fixed his gaze on the quilted edge of the blanket covering David's legs. "He said something about Judith, but it wasn't true."

"So you hit him?"

Anger turned the stone to lava. "Is that what you think? That I'm that outsider who can't learn to live like all of you? That the first chance I get I strike out at someone because that's the way I am? Some kind of sinner?"

Tears stood in David's eyes. He reached for Guy's hand and Guy gave it to him. The old man's hands were dry, leathery and tough. Guy's eyes grew moist, too.

"We are all sinners, Guy. There is nothing you can do that can't be forgiven."

For some reason, Pa came to Guy's mind. Any man who would abandon his own son was a sinner, for sure. But Guy hadn't done anything wrong.

"I didn't hit Luke. He hit me, then I tried to keep him from hitting me again."

"I want you to tell me the truth. Luke says you hit him first, and he has witnesses that agree with him."

"You don't believe me, do you?" Guy stood and shoved his hands in his waistband.

"I want to, Guy." David looked tired. "I want to. But the witnesses don't agree with what you've said."

"But I told you what happened. I didn't lie to you."

David coughed, a hollow, racking cough. "Remember, Guy," he said, his voice raspy. "A man of faith lives by prayer and the Word of God."

Then he coughed again. Guy turned toward the kitchen door to call Verna, but she was already coming with a hot compress.

"Lift him up, Guy. Just a bit, so he isn't lying flat."

She opened David's shirt and laid the compress on his chest while Guy made the adjustments to the bed. He slipped up the stairs to his room while Verna was occupied.

He slumped on the chest by the window, drawing his feet up. This was the end. If David believed Luke's lying friends instead of him, there was nothing left for him here.

Finding a clean handkerchief in his drawer, Guy wrapped some socks and another handkerchief in it and gathered it into a bundle. He took the few coins he had and added them.

Looking out the front window, toward the road, he saw the teams of men working in the front fields. Out back, another team would still be working the buckwheat field. But at noon, everyone would be coming to the house for dinner. He walked to the side window and opened the sash. The side porch roof was just below him, and from there he could drop to the ground. He'd just have to wait until everyone was occupied on the other side of the house.

He cracked his door open and listened for sounds of dinner being served. His stomach growled as the tantalizing aroma of chicken and noodles drifted up the stairway. He would miss dinner, but he couldn't risk going downstairs. He'd just have to go hungry.

Judith's voice rose above the other sounds from

downstairs. Somehow, he would get word to her. Let her know where he was.

He ignored the itching eyes that warned him of the tears that were about to fall. He didn't even know which direction to head. Maybe he could try the factories in Goshen or in South Bend. Once he got a job, then he could write to her.

Guy turned his back and leaned against the wall. He was just kidding himself. There were no jobs around. The other fellows his age from the Home had disappeared to the West, riding the rails because they might be able to pick produce in California. But he had seen just as many men riding the rails east. Or south. Chasing the next rumor of a job.

As the dinner bell rang, Guy grasped his bundle and started for the open window. He paused, waiting to hear the sound of Judith's voice one more time, but he couldn't distinguish hers from the others in the crowd. She would probably hate him for not saying goodbye, but it couldn't be helped. He was sure she hated him anyway for the part he'd played in the fight with Luke, whether she thought it was his fault or not.

Guy stuck one foot out the window and let it dangle while he pushed his shoulders and the bundle out. He stretched his foot to reach the porch roof, then climbed the rest of the way out of the window. He glanced back at his room, then across the fields toward the woodlot. The trees in the distance blurred.

It wasn't too late, was it? Could he go back?

The sound of voices and laughter drifting to him from the other side of the house hardened his resolve. He didn't belong here and he never would.

Chapter Twelve

By Monday, Judith still couldn't understand what had happened. Keeping Eli company while he played with his blocks after dinner gave her plenty of time to think. Too much time to remember.

When Guy hadn't shown up to eat with the rest of the men during the work day on Saturday, Verna had told her not to worry. Guy had been upset about the row with Luke, but had had a talk with David and everything seemed to be fine. It wasn't until after the dinner dishes were done and the men were back in the fields, that Verna asked her to take a tray to Guy in his room.

She had knocked on the door, and when there was no answer, she assumed he was asleep. She opened the door to take his tray in to him, but he wasn't there.

Judith blinked back tears and smiled as Eli knocked over his stack of blocks, giggling at the fun.

Absently, she helped Eli stack up the blocks again, but it was like someone else was playing with her nephew while she stood at a distance, watching.

Where could Guy be? The bedroom window had been open, but that was the only sign that he'd left.

"Ran away," Matthew had said Sunday afternoon, after he came home from visiting David. "Verna said he took a few things and was gone."

"But he'll come back, won't he?"

Judith hadn't been able to believe that Guy would disappear without a word to anyone, but he was gone. It had been all anyone talked about during the fellowship dinner yesterday after church. Matthew had volunteered to do Guy's chores, as well as his own, but he wasn't happy about the extra work.

But where was Guy? And when would he come back?

Eli knocked the stack of blocks over again and laughed. He clapped his hands, waiting for her to join in. But Judith doubted if she'd ever feel like laughing again.

When Eli yawned, Judith reached for the wooden box Matthew had made to hold the blocks and started putting them in.

"It's time for your nap."

"Ne." Eli frowned, shaking his head.

When Eli was being stubborn, she found she could easily distract him by inviting him to do something else with her.

"Show me how neatly you can put the blocks in the box," Judith said.

She counted as he stacked them, maneuvering them so they would fit. Once all the blocks were in the box, Eli pushed it toward the toy shelf in the corner of the front room.

"Cookie?" He tugged at her sleeve. "Cookie?"

Judith shook her head as she picked him up. "We just finished dinner, and you had a cookie then."

He rested his head against her shoulder as she walked toward the stairway.

"Cookie?" The word was slurred, and she knew he had his thumb in his mouth.

"After your nap."

As she passed the kitchen, Judith saw a movement at the kitchen door. Guy was on the porch, waving to her through the window. She motioned him in, then took Eli up to his bed. By the time she took his shoes off, he was sound asleep and she flew back downstairs.

"Guy!" She whispered his name as she stopped in the doorway.

She hadn't been imagining it. He was here, sitting at the kitchen table. His face was drawn, with whiskers like bristles on his chin. The left side of his face was bruised, especially under his eye, and his nose was swollen. His clothes were filthy, with mud caking the legs of his trousers. He looked terrible. But he was the best thing she had ever seen.

He didn't move as she slipped into the chair next to his.

"Where are Annie and Matthew? Are we alone?"

Judith nodded. "Annie is taking a nap with the twins, and Matthew is working at his *daed's* today." She rested her hand on his arm and leaned toward him. "Are you all right? We've been worried about you. Where have you been?"

He shrugged. "Here and there."

"Are you hungry?"

Guy gave a raspy *"Ja,"* so she took the loaf of bread

from the counter and brought it to the table with the crock of butter. She sliced the bread and he took it as soon as she spread the butter on it.

"Mmm." He grunted and nodded as he chewed. "This tastes good."

"When is the last time you ate?"

He still hadn't looked at her, but watched the bread in his hand as if it would disappear. "I only had a few coins, and I used that on Saturday to buy some bread and cheese at the store in Emma." He stuffed the remaining part of his slice in his mouth and talked around it. "I almost didn't even go there. I thought I might see someone I knew."

Judith cut another slice of bread and buttered it. While he ate it, she went to the cellar and got the rest of the summer sausage they had eaten for dinner, along with a jar of canned pears. When she came upstairs, Guy was at the sink, pumping water into a glass. As she put the food on the table, he leaned with his back against the sink and took a long drink of water, watching her. He filled his glass again and sat back down at the table.

"You must think I have terrible manners." He took the sausage from her and sliced some for a sandwich.

"I think you're hungry."

"I was."

When Guy caught her gaze with his and smiled, Judith felt a laugh bubble up inside her. She slipped her hand into his as he took a bite of his sandwich.

"I'm glad you're all right. I've missed you."

He squeezed her hand. "I've missed you, too."

She opened the jar of pears.

"Don't bother with a bowl," he said, taking the jar

from her. "I'll just eat them this way." He fished in the jar with his fork until he speared a pear half.

"Have you seen David and Verna? Do they know you're back?"

Guy put the jar down and took her hand again. "I'm not back, Judith. I just had to see you before I leave for good. I didn't want to leave without saying goodbye."

"What do you mean, you're not back?" Judith switched to *Englisch* to make sure he understood her. "You're here. All you have to do is walk across the road and you're home."

His face grew red and he moved his gaze away from her. He picked up the fork again and chased a piece of a pear around in the juice. "I can't go back there."

"Why not? You should see David and Verna. They're worried sick about you."

Rubbing his forehead with one hand, he closed his eyes. "They're only angry because I'm not there to do the work for them."

"That isn't true. Matthew said—"

"I don't care what Matthew said. I don't care what David thinks." Guy pushed his chair back from the table. "I don't care what anyone in this whole Amish community thinks."

"Shh." Judith glanced toward the hallway and the bedroom door beyond. "Don't wake Annie." Her head throbbed. When she saw him at the door, she had assumed that everything would go back to normal, that he would make things right with David and Verna. But it was like he still faced Luke, ready for a fight.

"I don't even care if I wake up Annie." Guy's voice was gruff, but his words were quieter. He leaned his forearms on his knees and caught both of her hands in his. "I only care what you think, Judith. I feel like the whole world is against me right now, but I know you aren't. You have to understand that I have to get away. Start a new life somewhere else."

Leave? Judith drew her hands out of his grasp and leaned back in her chair. He couldn't mean what he was saying.

"You can't leave David and Verna...the church..." She pulled her bottom lip between her teeth as the thought of what he was giving up sunk in. "Guy, this is your home."

"I don't have a home."

The memory of Verna's face on Saturday when Judith had told her Guy was gone told a different story.

"David and Verna love you. You're part of their family. David is so sick—"

Guy's head shot up. "What? Is he worse?"

Judith's eyes blurred. "I thought you knew, but I guess you couldn't. Verna asked Matthew to bring the doctor out on Saturday evening."

"It's his cough, isn't it?"

She nodded. "The doctor says he's getting weaker." She took her handkerchief from the waistband of her apron and blew her nose. "They love you, and they need you. Now more than ever."

Guy didn't speak, but glanced toward the door.

"If you won't go home for yourself, go home for them. They've given you a job when no one else can find one. Verna has fed you and mended your clothes. David has taught you everything he knows. You owe them."

"David was mad about my fight with Luke. How can I work for a man who doesn't trust me?"

"Haven't you listened to what I'm telling you?" Judith rose and paced the length of the kitchen. "David doesn't care about the fight. He cares about you. If you don't think he trusts you, then you have to show him that he can." She came to a stop in front of Guy and leaned over him, her fists at her waist. "All you've done by running away is prove that he can't trust you. You've disappointed him."

Guy's head hung lower. "How can I face him?"

Judith knelt so she was looking into his eyes. "Just tell him you're sorry. Ask for his forgiveness."

"It can't be that easy."

She thought back to when her brother Samuel had changed last summer, after he met Mary. He had apologized to both her and Esther. "Asking for forgiveness is hard, but when you love someone, giving it is the easiest thing in the world."

Rubbing his hand across his face, Guy winced when he pressed too hard on his bruises.

"Go," Judith said. "If you don't talk to David now, you may never do it."

Guy swallowed, then nodded. "The worst he can do is throw me out, right?"

Judith stood when he did, and when he hesitated, she nudged him toward the door. "He won't throw you out. Go over there and see."

Guy stepped onto the porch and looked back at Judith. She gave him a nod and an encouraging smile. He hooked his thumbs in his suspenders and set his face toward the road.

The girl didn't know what she was talking about. She hadn't seen David's face on Saturday. Hadn't seen the disappointment etched in the deep lines around his eyes.

When had David gotten so old?

Stopping at the edge of the road while a blue Studebaker rumbled by, Guy shifted his shoulders. He had everything planned out, but somehow, once Judith started talking, it had all gotten shifted around again.

He couldn't face David and Verna, but he couldn't leave them alone again. Judith was right. He owed them. He had to stay with them until David was well again… or until David decided to sell the farm. They had opened their home to him when he had nothing, and the least he could do was to pay them back by being the farm hand they needed.

The Studebaker had pulled to a stop a few yards down the road, and now the gears ground as the driver shifted it into reverse. The dust rose around Guy as the car slid to a halt in front of him.

"Well, well, well." The man inside took off his hat and swiped his forearm across his dusty face. "You've grown up."

Guy swallowed, recognizing the man he had been longing to see. "Pa?"

Pa opened the door and stepped across the road to him, grasping him by both arms. "You sure are a sight for sore eyes. When the Home told me where you had gone, I never hoped that you were still here." He pulled on one of Guy's suspenders. "Workin' for the Bible thumpers, eh? And dressing just like them, too." He grinned. "But now I've found you."

Pa had come for him? Guy felt his own grin answering his father's. Finally, Pa had kept his promise.

"I haven't seen you for a while, Pa. Where have you been?"

Pa looked up and down the empty road, then thumbed over his shoulder toward the car. "Get in and I'll tell you all about it. We can't stand here in the middle of the road."

Guy trotted around the car to the passenger side and slid into the front seat. The leather seats were worn, but comfortable. Guy ran a hand along the fine woodgrain of the dashboard. The car wasn't new, but she had been taken care of.

"She's a nice-looking car, Pa."

The gears ground as Pa put the car into drive and started down the road, much faster than any horse and buggy ever traveled.

"She's something, isn't she?" Pa patted the steering wheel. "A real looker. But she's hot, and I have to get rid of her."

"Hot?"

Pa glanced at him sideways. "You know. Hot. Stolen."

Guy's insides went cold. "Why did you steal a car?"

Pa shrugged, resting his right wrist on the top of the steering wheel. "Had to get outta town. It'd be unhealthy for me to stick around, ya know?" He looked in the rearview mirror and drummed the fingers of his left hand on the bottom curve of the wheel.

Guy's stomach turned as Pa popped over a bump,

bottoming the chassis on the rough road. "What town was that?"

"You've never heard of it. A little place west of here, just south of Chicago." Pa snickered. "I was a guest of the kind citizens until yesterday morning."

Pa made a quick right into an overgrown lane through a patch of woods and eased the car along until they were out of sight of the road, then he cut the engine. He rolled down the window and leaned out, listening.

"Sure is quiet here." Pa pulled a packet of cigarettes out of his pocket and popped one out with an absent gesture. His face held no expression as he kept listening.

"Pa—"

"Shh!" Pa held out a warning hand, freezing in place. "Do you hear that?"

Guy heard nothing but the sound of a car driving along the gravel road they had just left. "It's just another car."

"It could be the Feds. That's a V-8. I'd recognize the sound of one of their roadsters anywhere." As the car went on north past their hiding place, Pa relaxed and struck a match to light his cigarette. "They've been following me for two days, but it looks like I gave them the slip this time."

Guy shifted in his seat. They were in the woods that belonged to Old Man Ryber, David and Verna's *Englisch* neighbor. Guy had learned early on not to trespass on his land.

"Why are they following you?" Guy waved off the cigarette Pa offered him.

Pa put the packet back in his coat pocket and regarded Guy with narrowed eyes as he blew out a stream of smoke. "You've spent too much time among these hicks, boy, or else you're plain stupid." He flicked some ash off the cigarette out the window. "Do I have to spell it out for you? I'm on the lam. On the run. One step ahead of the coppers. You get it?" He slumped back in his seat and drummed his fingers on the steering wheel again.

Guy looked out his window so Pa wouldn't see the disappointment that had to show on his face. This wasn't what he'd expected of his reunion with Pa. The man hadn't changed at all, with one wild story following the next. He'd tell Guy he was the lost prince of Russia if he thought it would get him something.

Pa finished his cigarette and ground out the burning stub in the ashtray between them. "This is the way it is, boy." His tone softened, and Guy braced himself. "I need your help. I have to ditch this car and find a place to hole up for a while. If you're still working at that Amish farm the Home told me about, it'd be the perfect place. The Feds would never think of looking there."

Drumming his fingers on his knee, Guy looked at Pa. "What do you mean?"

"I figure you've got it pretty good, right? I mean, those Amish are pushovers. You can just tell them your Pa has come to stay for a while and that they need to keep quiet. If they get out of line, I can handle them." Pa thumbed his hat back on his head. "You'll do this for me, won't you boy?"

It wasn't a question. It was an order. Pa had always been the one in charge.

Guy knew what would happen if he took Pa to David and Verna's. He would take over the house, blustering about until he got his way. As frail as David was, this could be the end of him. And what would David and Verna think of the boy they had taken in? After they'd... loved him and taken care of him. He owed them, just like Judith had said. He couldn't let a liar like Pa into the house and into their lives.

He shook his head. "I can't, Pa. It wouldn't work."

Pa's face grew hard. "Make it work."

Guy's pulse raced as he tried to think of a reason not to do what Pa wanted. "They have folks over. All the time. Someone would say they saw you."

"Just tell them not to let anyone into the house. That's easy enough."

Shaking his head, Guy slid his hands between the leather seat and his thighs to keep them from trembling.

"Then folks would know something was wrong. And David is sick. The doctor comes to see him almost every day."

Pa's hand fell on Guy's shoulder. "Then think of somewhere else. Maybe that house you were coming from when I spotted you."

"They're Amish, too. The same thing—" His voice squeaked when Pa's heavy hand closed on his shoulder.

"Then think. There has to be somewhere I can hide."

Guy scanned his memory for something. Anything to solve Pa's problem.

"The mint still." Relief washed over him when the little building along the river flashed into his mind. "It's at the back of the Masts' farm, and it isn't used anymore. No one would know you were there."

"Okay. Let's go."

As they got out of the car, Guy hesitated. The blue

car with the black top gleamed under the trees that were barely leafed out. "You're just going to leave this here?"

Pa ground another cigarette under the toe of his shoes. "You're right. Someone will find it and report it. You'll have to get rid of it."

"Me?"

"Yeah. Just take it somewhere north or east. Anywhere out of the county, or even up into Michigan."

"How would I get back?"

Pa glared at him. "Use your head, boy. Or your thumb. You'll find your way back." He slung his jacket over his shoulder where it dangled from his finger. "Now, show me that still."

"Guy has shown up back at the Masts'," Matthew said as he came in the house for supper that night.

Judith poured the boiled potatoes into the strainer and dropped a dollop of butter into the pot to let it melt. "I know. He was over here this afternoon and talked to me about it."

"I thought I heard voices while the babies were sleeping," Annie said. She was sitting at the table holding Rose and supervising Eli as he put a spoon at each place. Viola was still napping.

"We didn't want to wake you, but I'm afraid we got a little loud."

Annie shook her head. "Don't worry about it. I was just resting, not sleeping." She reached out a hand to guide Eli to the next plate. "How did you find out, Matthew?"

Matthew finished washing his hands at the sink and dried them with the towel Annie kept hanging next to it. "I stopped by to milk the cows on my way home from the folks' and he was in the dairy, running the cream separator."

"Did he say where he had been?" Annie asked.

"Not a word." Matthew glanced at Judith. "Did he tell you anything this afternoon?"

Judith shook her head. "Only that he thought he might leave our area, but I convinced him he needed to stay."

"I'm glad you did," Matthew said. "David and Verna need him now more than they ever have before."

"That's what I told him. I'm glad he has come home." Judith set the potatoes on the table with the rest of the food and sat down. "I think I'll go over to see how Verna is doing after supper and take a pie."

"How Verna is doing?" Annie smiled at her. "Are you sure you aren't going over there to see someone else?"

Judith shrugged, ignoring the heat rising in her cheeks. "If I happen to see Guy, that would be all right, too."

Once supper was over and the dishes washed, Judith left Eli playing happily with his *daed* and walked across to the Masts' farm, carrying one of the dried-apple pies she had made during the afternoon. The quarter moon rode high in the twilight sky and the first star was shining at the horizon. The barn was dark and quiet, but light shone from the kitchen windows and the front room. Verna answered the door as Judith knocked.

"Judith, dear," the older woman said as she ushered her into the kitchen. "What a surprise."

Handing her the pie, Judith hung her shawl on the peg next to the door. "I thought David might like a treat."

"If he'll eat anything, it will be pie." Verna sighed as she put the pie on the cupboard shelf. "The doctor says to give him anything he wants to eat, but he just doesn't have an appetite."

"Did it make him feel better to see Guy again?"

"Guy came home, but he won't talk to David or me. He even ate his supper in the barn. He said he had too many chores to do."

Judith chewed on her lower lip. "When I saw Guy this afternoon, I thought he was on his way over to talk to David and straighten things out."

"I wish he had done that. I don't know what the boy is thinking."

"Where is he now? I can take him a piece of pie."

"He said he was going out to the barn to take care of something." Verna cut a slice and slid it onto a plate as Judith put her shawl back on. Verna covered the plate with a towel and handed it to Judith, then held her back with a hand on her arm. "You'll find out what is bothering him, won't you? We don't want to lose our boy."

Judith tried to smile. "I'll try my hardest. But if he doesn't want to talk, I'm not sure what more I can do."

Verna nudged her toward the door. "If he talks to anyone, it will be you."

The barn was still dark as Judith started across the yard. The sky had gone completely dark while she had been in the house, and there was still no sign that anyone was in the barn. No light shone through the windows or filtered through the spaces around the doors. Judith stopped, unsure. Spring peepers sang their evening song, and in the distance, an owl hooted.

"Guy?" Her voice sounded thin in the evening air.

"*Ja*, I'm here." He came from the river, walking along the lane that skirted the pasture. By the time he reached her, he was out of breath. "What are you doing here?"

"I brought some pie for Verna and David and thought I'd bring a piece out to you. Verna said you were working in the barn."

He took the plate from her and walked with her to the porch where they sat on the steps.

Guy held the plate up and took a deep breath. "Apple pie?"

"*Schnitz* pie. Made from dried apples."

He took a bite. "Didn't you want a piece?"

"I had some with my supper." Judith could see his face clearly in the moonlight and the lamplight from the kitchen window, now that her eyes had adjusted to the dark. "What were you doing down by the river?"

He didn't answer, but took another bite.

"Was one of the cows loose or something?"

Laying the empty plate next to him on the step, he laced his fingers around one knee as he chewed. "*Ne.* I was just down there," he finally said.

"Doing what?"

He glanced at her, then stared into the dark shadow of the barn. "Nothing you need to worry about."

As soon as he said that, worry crept in.

"Verna said you didn't talk to David."

Guy picked up a stone and rolled it between his fingers. "By the time I got here, I had to do the chores."

Judith left that alone, too. He'd had plenty of time after he left her to talk to David before chore time.

"How is David feeling today?"

After another glance her way, he threw the stone

across the barnyard. "Why all these questions? Can't we just talk?"

"But you're not talking." She stood, ready to go home. "Something happened this afternoon, didn't it?"

He didn't answer.

"Why were you afraid to talk to David?"

"I'm not afraid."

"But you didn't talk to him. You didn't ask him to forgive you."

"Forget it. Just forget it."

Judith stared at him. When he had left Matthew's this afternoon, it had seemed like everything was going to be all right. She had thought she'd convinced him to mend the fences he had broken on Saturday and reconcile with David. But now he seemed like a stranger, the outsider he always said he was.

"What are you keeping from me, Guy?"

No answer. He picked up another stone.

She turned her back on him and started down the lane toward home, waiting for him to call after her. Waiting for him to follow her. But there was nothing except the sound of the peeping frogs.

Chapter Thirteen

Guy jerked to wakefulness with the rooster's crow early Saturday morning. He had fallen asleep on a pile of clean straw in the barn after Judith left the night before, not wanting to go into the house until David and Verna were asleep. But he had dozed off while waiting.

As he sat up, a quilt fell from his shoulders. He fingered it, recognizing the black-and-purple pattern of the quilt Verna had made for him years ago. She must have brought it to the barn last night and covered him with it. He could imagine the look on her face when she found him sleeping in the straw.

But he didn't care. Standing, Guy folded the quilt and left it on the straw pile. It didn't matter how Verna cared for him, because Pa was back now, and everything had changed.

Yesterday afternoon he had been exhausted, and Pa had taken him by surprise. He had actually believed that whole story about the car and Pa stealing it. Guy chuckled to himself as he headed down to the dairy to milk the cows. Pa had always been a great one for tall tales, and this had to be one of his biggest.

This morning, he and Pa would make their plans. Real plans, with none of this fooling around and Pa's stories. With the car, they could head west to where there were jobs. He and Pa working together could make a good life for themselves. By the time he finished with the milking and the other barn chores, Verna was calling him for breakfast. He met her at the back porch and handed the quilt to her.

"You can bring my breakfast out here and I'll eat in the barn."

Verna crossed her arms over the quilt, holding the screen door open with her hip.

"You aren't some hobo coming around for a handout, Guy Hoover. You come right on in here and sit at the table." Her face was stern. "If you don't want my company, I'll eat in the front room with David. I want to be in there with him, anyway."

Guilt thrummed, but Guy ignored it. "It isn't that I don't want to eat with you. I just have so much to do and I don't want to take the time to clean up enough to come inside."

It was true, Guy thought, even if it wasn't his real reason for staying in the barn. Going inside meant he wouldn't have any excuse to avoid talking to David, and he wasn't in any mood for a lecture. Besides, Pa was waiting for him.

Verna disappeared inside the house, letting the screen door close with a slam behind her. She appeared a few minutes later with his breakfast on a platter. A mountain of fried potatoes, eggs and biscuits steamed in the cool morning air. Guy's mouth watered.

"Denki." He took the platter from her. "I'll set the plate on the porch when I'm done."

"Go on with you," Verna said, waving him away. "Get done what you need to get done." She handed him a bag. "Here are some more biscuits for your mid-morning. They'll keep you going with whatever you need to do."

As he grasped the bag, she held it for a second, until he met her eyes.

"Don't forget, Guy." Her voice quavered. "We do love you."

He dropped his gaze, his throat swelling. "I know."

She went back into the house and he brought the filled platter up to his nose. The aroma made his stomach growl, but Pa was waiting. With a last glance at the house, still trying to silence his guilt's rising tug, he started down the trail toward the river.

The mint still was in a little shed on a small rise along the low acres next to the river. In the old days, David had said, he'd extracted the mint oil himself and sold it for a cash crop each year. But that had been twenty years ago. These days, the mint was distilled at a big plant near Fort Wayne, and all David had to do was mow the field in the late summer and take his mint to the plant.

But the old still remained in the shed, and it had made a good overnight shelter for Pa. Everything was quiet as Guy approached and knocked.

There was no answer right away, but then the door opened. Pa leaned against the doorframe, yawning.

"What do you want, boy?"

"I brought some breakfast." Guy held up the platter with the rapidly cooling food.

Pa grabbed a potato between his thumb and forefinger and inspected it, then smelled it. "It isn't morning already, is it?" He popped the potato into his mouth and sat on an upturned log along the path in front of the shed.

"The sun's been up for hours." Guy set the platter on another log and squatted next to it. "Here's a fork, and there's enough for two."

Pa took the plate onto his lap and shoveled a forkload of potatoes into his mouth. "You make this?" His words slipped around the potatoes.

"Ne." The *Deitsch* word slipped out before he thought. "Um, no. Verna did."

Pa downed a biscuit in one bite and half turned from Guy, shielding the plate while Guy's stomach growled again. Since it didn't seem Pa was going to share the food, Guy reached into the paper bag Verna had given him. A biscuit would have to tide him over.

"Now that you're here," Guy said, swallowing the buttery bite, "where are we going to go? Do you have an idea for a job?"

"That's why I came for you." Pa tilted the plate up and let the last of the crumbs fall into his open mouth, then handed the empty plate to Guy. "A fellow I met in Chicago has a job in Cleveland for us." He pulled a cigarette pack from his pocket, shook one out and lit it. "It's a two-man-and-a-boy gig, and I told him you'd be perfect." He looked at Guy sideways. "You've grown a bit more than I was expecting though. Not quite a boy anymore, are you?"

Guy cleared his throat. "I'm almost nineteen, Pa. I haven't been a boy for years."

Pa took a drag on his cigarette and looked out over the river that wound gently past the green mint field. Guy stood to stretch his stiff legs then sat on the log next to Pa.

"What kind of job is it? It seems that I can do more work now than I could as a boy."

When Pa didn't answer, Guy scooted closer to him.

"I thought we could go west, out to California. I've heard there's plenty of work there."

"Work? Picking vegetables and fruit? Boy, that isn't work. That's slavery." Pa waved his cigarette vaguely in the air. "I'm talkin' real money. Cash money." He leaned close to Guy, blowing smoke into his face, making Guy's eyes water. "Money is easy to get for a fellow who knows the ropes."

An uncomfortable turning started in Guy's stomach. "What do you mean?"

Pa shrugged, taking another draw on his cigarette before grinding it under the toe of his shoe. "You find a sap and play him. It's a game. No one gets hurt, and we get the dough."

Guy rubbed his sweaty palms on the knees of his trousers. He had heard all about confidence men from one of the fellows at the Home, and what Pa was describing sounded just like what they did. It sounded like Pa's story of being on the run might not be a tall tale, after all.

"I can't do anything illegal, Pa. I won't."

A grin split Pa's face, his teeth showing white against his unshaven cheeks. "Who said anything about it being illegal? We're just taking cash that's…extra. Some poor fools have more money than brains, and all we do is teach them a little lesson in how to be careful." He narrowed his eyes, inspecting Guy. "That job in Cleveland might work. We'll head over to Ohio after the heat is off."

"After the heat is off?"

Pa crossed his legs at the ankle. "The Feds. They'll give up looking for small potatoes like me and go chasing someone else. Once they've given up, we'll head to Cleveland." He punched Guy in the arm. "Just you and me, kid. How does that sound?"

Guy swallowed and stared at the river to keep Pa from seeing what he really felt. He didn't want to go to Cleveland. He wanted his pa back. His boyhood dreams mocked him. This wasn't the father he had longed for as he shivered in his cot at the Home on those long winter nights.

But even though this man wasn't the pa he had been waiting for, he'd stick with him. He wouldn't turn his back on his own. After all, to go with Pa and work with him was what he had been hoping for. It was what Pa had promised. Maybe somehow things would still work out. Maybe they could still be a family.

And he wasn't going to run out on Pa the way Pa had run out on him.

On Sunday morning, Judith ran up the stairs after breakfast. A trip home! That's what Matthew had proposed for this non-church day, and she and Annie had beamed at each other across the table.

"I'm ready to get out to see someone other than you two," Annie had said with a teasing grin.

"The twins are old enough to go visiting now, and I knew you'd enjoy the drive on such a fine spring morning." Matthew had smiled back at his wife, giving Judith the feeling she was intruding on a special moment between them.

As soon as Eli was ready to go, she sent him downstairs to help Matthew with the buggy while she took a few minutes to put on a fresh apron for the visit to see the folks at home. As she tied the apron strings, she went into Eli's room to fetch an extra pair of trousers for him, and the view of the Masts' farm through the window caught her eye. She leaned against the windowsill, scanning the lane and barnyard, but there was no sign of Guy.

She hadn't seen him since Friday evening, even though she had hoped he would walk over. But no. No word. No visit. Not even a trip across the road to talk to Matthew. It was as if he had forgotten she existed. Once again, the idea that something was wrong probed at her mind, but there was nothing she could do about it if he wouldn't talk to her.

The trip to Shipshewana seemed longer than she had ever experienced before. She shifted in her seat again, trying to make herself comfortable with Eli on her lap.

"You must be in a hurry," Annie said, looking over her shoulder at Judith and Eli in the backseat. "I thought Eli would be restless on such a long ride, but you're worse than he is."

Judith set Eli on the seat next to her, letting him

stand to watch the horse through the windshield of the buggy while she held his hand to help him keep his balance. "You're right. I didn't know I'd be so anxious to get there."

"I know you miss Esther." Annie jiggled Viola gently as the baby fussed.

"I do. I've never been away from her this long. Even though we got to see each other at the quilting, it wasn't enough."

"I think you even miss Samuel."

The thought of their older brother brought a smile to Judith's face. "Even Samuel. It's nice to be with you all the time, and close to Bram in Eden Township, but I miss the Shipshewana folks."

Judith concentrated on sitting still for the rest of the trip while Annie and Matthew visited in the front of the buggy. Eli was content watching Summer, the buggy horse, even though he couldn't see more than her back and her two ears pointed forward.

When Matthew turned Summer into Samuel and Mary's farm, Judith could hardly wait until the buggy came to a stop at the new house that rose clean and white next to the lane before she was climbing out of the buggy. Mary came out of the kitchen door to greet them.

"What a wonderful surprise!" She took Viola from Annie and cooed to the baby as Annie jumped down.

Annie took Rose from Matthew's arms, then helped Eli out of the buggy. "I hope you don't mind a visit. I just had to come see you and Samuel today."

"Not at all." Mary stroked Viola's cheek with a finger. "Samuel and I had thought about coming to see you this afternoon, but we weren't sure if you'd be up to it."

"A visit with the family was the only thing I wanted to do today," said Annie. "I have to admit, I'm getting a bit of cabin fever staying at home."

"We'll have a nice long visit, then." Mary made a silly face at Viola. "Samuel is in the barn, Matthew. And Judith, I'm sure you'll want to go visit with Esther for a while. I'll give Annie a hand with Eli and the babies. Tell Ida Mae and Esther to bring Aunt Sadie over for dinner."

Judith didn't need any more encouragement, but started down the path toward Sadie's farm. The way was familiar; she had walked this path since she had been a child. Sadie had been their next-door neighbor all of Judith's life and had tried to help her and Esther with various things after *Mamm* passed away. She hadn't made much headway until Mary and her sister, Ida Mae, moved here from Ohio to help take care of Sadie last year. Not only had the two sisters become her good friends, but Mary even became her sister-in-law. Now Esther was living with Ida Mae and Sadie, helping to provide the care Sadie needed as she grew more forgetful with time.

Sadie's little house appeared through the trees. Judith heard voices as she approached, and when she came around the hedge she found the three women sitting in the spring sunshine.

Esther was the first one to see her coming. "Judith!" She ran to meet her, welcoming her with a hug. "How did you get here? It's so good to see you! Is Annie with you? Did you bring Eli and the twins? How long can you stay?"

Judith tightened her hug, drinking in the familiar feel of her sister's arms around her.

"Don't ask so many questions at once," Ida Mae said, joining them.

Judith gave Ida Mae a quick hug, then went over to kiss Sadie on the cheek.

"It's so good to see you," Sadie said. She put her hands on either side of Judith's face and looked into her eyes. "So good."

"It's good to be here," Judith said. She hadn't seen Sadie for a month, and she could notice the changes. Sadie looked older. Tired. Judith kissed the elderly woman's cheek again, then sat in the chair that Esther brought out from the house and set next to Sadie. "And to answer your questions, Esther, Matthew and Annie are at Samuel's, and I'm supposed to bring you all over there. Mary says we're to have a nice long visit."

"I can't wait to see the twins again," Ida Mae said. "Have they grown much?"

Judith nodded. "I can't believe how quickly they're changing. They are smiling more every day and taking an interest in everything that is going on around them. And Eli is so much fun."

"It sounds like you still enjoy being nanny for Matthew and Annie." Esther sat down next to Judith. "And how is everything else going? How is that boy who asked you to the Singing?"

"Guy?" Judith pressed the seam of her skirt between her fingers, the uneasiness still probing at her mind. "He's doing well." She cleared her throat, wanting to move the conversation away from her relationship with her neighbor.

"Didn't we hear that David Mast had a bad accident? And isn't that who Guy is working for?"

Judith nodded. "David is recovering at home, but isn't able to get out of bed yet." Judith's eyes grew moist at the thought. "We had a work day last week and the men got his fields plowed and harrowed, and planted the buckwheat."

"That's good. Is Guy able to keep up with the rest of the farm work on his own?" Esther leaned forward, interested in Judith's reply.

As she thought of how to answer Esther's question, Judith's throat grew dry. She twisted her fingers together, not knowing what to say.

"He seemed to be doing fine the day of the work frolic."

"What is wrong?"

Ida Mae's quiet voice broke into Judith's thoughts. She looked from one face to another. Sadie reached out to take her hand.

"I'm not sure. Guy had a fight with Luke Kaufman during the frolic, but I thought that was resolved."

"Until?" Esther laid a hand on her arm, prodding gently with her question.

"I don't know what happened, but suddenly he's different. Like a stranger." Judith sniffed. She wouldn't start crying. She wouldn't.

"Men worry about different things than we do," Ida Mae said. "Perhaps taking on the responsibility of the Masts' farm is too much for him."

Shaking her head, Judith thought back to the events of the past few days. "After he came to see me, he was going to talk to David and set things right. But for some reason…" Judith's mind went over the path Guy would have taken from Matthew's to the Masts'. The only thing that would have changed his mind about talking to David was if he had met someone on the road who talked him out of it. Or pulled his attention elsewhere.

"When I talked to him the other night, he seemed distracted by something." Judith wiped her cheek with the heel of her hand, concentrating. "He wasn't in the barn, like Verna thought. He was walking toward the barn from the direction of the river…"

"What are you talking about?" Esther asked. "You're rambling and making no sense."

"Never mind." Judith put a smile on her face, determined to think through this problem later. "Let's go over to Samuel's. I brought some ham salad to have for lunch, and Annie brought some fresh spinach from the garden."

As they gathered up the chairs to put them back inside the house, Judith's mind raced. Somehow, she would find out what Guy had been doing at the river.

By Monday morning, Guy could tell that Pa was in no mood to hide out in the mint shed any longer. He had never heard anyone complain so much about everything. The frogs were too loud, the mosquitoes were a nuisance and Guy never brought him coffee with his meals. Sometimes he wished Pa would just take his car and disappear…

But no. Guy shook his head at his own thoughts. He didn't want to go back to not knowing where Pa was. At least this way he had stopped waiting for Pa to show up. Now he could get his life started. The life he was meant to have with his own father, where he belonged.

After missing out on Saturday morning's breakfast, Guy made sure he ate part of the food Verna made for him before taking the plate to Pa. He was always careful to push the food around though, so Pa wouldn't notice some was missing.

When Guy carried his breakfast plate to the mint still, Pa was waiting for him. He grabbed the plate from Guy, almost causing it to spill.

"Be careful, boy. Watch what you're doing." He sniffed the plate. "Cold again, but I guess that can't be helped." He looked at Guy, his eyebrows raised. "No coffee?"

Guy shook his head.

"I'd give my eye teeth for a good cup of java." He shoveled an entire slice of ham into his mouth. "That's the first thing I'll find when I get back on the road."

Guy waited until Pa was finished eating and took his plate. "How will you know when it's time to go find work?"

"I have to know that the Feds have moved on." Pa wiped his mouth with his sleeve and took the last cigarette from his pack. "Go into town today, will you? Get me some more cigs and ask around. See if anyone has seen any cops." He struck a match and bent his head to shield the flame from the light breeze.

Pushing down his rising irritation with Pa's demanding ways, Guy watched the man beside him. He had looked forward to Pa's return for so long, but now that he was here, it was like Guy was the father and Pa was the wayward son.

"I have work to do this morning, but I'll try to get to town this afternoon."

"I'll get a list ready." Pa pulled on his cigarette as if he couldn't get enough of the stuff into his lungs. "There are some other things I need while you're there." Smoke poured out of his mouth as he spoke.

Guy headed back to the house, carrying the empty plate with him. He could imagine what would be on that list. Things a young Amishman wouldn't be buying, that was for sure. He'd have to avoid the store in Emma, where David and Verna usually shopped.

The path was starting to wear from his coming and going the past few days. If David hadn't been laid up, Pa couldn't have stayed hidden for long. But Verna never ventured this far from the house, especially with David as badly off as he was. The thought of David's gray face the last time Guy had seen him prodded at him. How was he doing now? As he reached the house, Guy hesitated. He could go in. Talk to David. Apologize for taking off the way he did. Apologize for…everything.

Guy set the empty plate on the back porch and went to the barn. He was in a hole, that was for sure. If he talked to David but didn't mention Pa, the old man would be able to tell he was hiding something. David had always known what Guy was thinking. He'd know something was wrong.

Wrong? Guy slumped against Billy's stall and the horse nudged him for the carrot Guy often brought. Yes, wrong. Pa being here was wrong. Hiding him was wrong. Even knowing about the shiny Studebaker hidden in the woods was wrong, especially if it was stolen, like Pa said.

And there was the problem. He couldn't trust anything Pa had told him. Broken promises and lies. That's all Pa had ever given him.

"Guy?"

Judith's voice echoed through the barn. She stood in the doorway, silhouetted against the morning light. Tension drained from his shoulders. He wanted nothing more than to take her in his arms. It had been too long since he had seen her. But the easy camaraderie was gone.

Ever since Pa had shown up.

"What do you want?"

She came closer to him. In the shadows of the barn, with the light streaming in the open doorway behind her, he couldn't see her expression.

"I just want to talk." She leaned against the stall next to him and stroked Billy's nose.

"Don't you have work to do?" Guy frowned at the gruff sound of his own voice.

"Annie took Eli and the twins to visit Matthew's folks today, so once I put the laundry on the clothesline, I have the rest of the morning free."

"And you chose to come over here? Why?"

Judith moved closer to him, pushing Billy's nose out of the way. Now he could see her face, and he had a sudden urge to run his finger along her soft cheek. Before Pa came, he would have. Now this secret stood between them.

"I know something is wrong." She faced him as she spoke. "You haven't been the same since the work day. First, you ran away from David and Verna because of that silly fight with Luke."

He shook his head. "I had forgotten all about that."

"But between then and when I saw you on Friday evening, something happened, didn't it?"

He couldn't answer, even when she leaned closer and the clean, fresh scent of her clothes teased his nose.

"I miss you, Guy."

Judith looked up at him, waiting. He missed her, too. He missed their friendship and the way she had of making him feel like he had a future here with David and Verna.

He gave in to the urge and ran his finger along the soft skin of her jawline. She leaned her cheek into his hand and he stepped closer to her. Close enough to slip his arm around her and pull her close. She turned her face toward him and received his kiss. Longing to lose himself in her, he deepened the kiss, pulling her closer. If he could have, he'd have stayed with her forever and never faced his pa or David again. Ending the kiss, he held her against him, tucking her head into his shoulder. She fit so well that she might have been made for him. Only for him.

After a few minutes, Judith drew back, holding his gaze with her own. "Tell me what's wrong, Guy. Let me help you." She rubbed her thumb over the whiskers on his chin. "Whatever it is, you don't have to face it alone."

Guy felt the truth of her words ring deep in his chest. It was the same thing Matthew had told him before the work day. But this…this was different. This wasn't about the Amish community, and it wasn't about family.

As he stared into Judith's eyes, he saw his reflection. Not a stranger, not an outsider, but part of her.

And Judith was part of him. They belonged together, and knowing that ripped him apart, because he couldn't give up the dream of following Pa. The boy in him held fast to that dream, but the man reached for Judith. He needed to tell her, to convince her to come with him.

"You're right. Something has happened to change things. Pa showed up."

"Your *daed*?"

Guy nodded as she drew back, still watching his face.

"Where is he? What did David and Verna have to say about him?" She clutched his hand. "He isn't going to take you away from us, is he?"

Billy pushed against Guy's shoulder with his nose, impatient with him and waiting for his carrot.

"What if I did go with him?"

Tears stood in Judith's eyes. "And leave me? Leave your home?"

The pain in her voice was like a stab in his heart. He reached out, trying to bridge the chasm. "Come with me."

She turned from him. "You know I can't, and you shouldn't, either."

"But if I leave with Pa, we'll go somewhere. I'll find a job." He pushed the thought of Pa's job in Cleveland out of his head. "We'll make a new home, you and I."

"And your *daed*? The man who left you in the orphanage for all those years? The man who broke his promises to you?"

Guy slumped against Billy's stall, melting under her words.

"I won't go with you, Guy. You need to decide between me and him. Between a life on the road with that man or a home here with us." She spoke through her tears, her voice a hoarse whisper.

She walked toward the door, silhouetted once more against the bright spring sunshine.

"But I have to go." Hope rose when she paused in the doorway, and he pleaded once more. "I have to go with him. He's my pa."

"Then you've decided." She wiped her tears away. "Goodbye."

And she was gone.

Chapter Fourteen

As Judith left the Masts' barn, she caught sight of Verna waving to her from the kitchen window. Judith waved in return, then walked as fast as she could down the lane. Away from Guy. How could he believe that anyone, even his father…especially the father who had abandoned him…was more important than their friendship? More important than the home he said he wanted?

Before she reached the end of the lane, a stitch in her side forced her to slow down. She paused to catch her breath, looking back at the house and barn. Guy wasn't coming after her, but she hadn't thought he would. The kiss he gave her had been a surprise, but it had made her hope that he'd made the right choice, that he was staying here with Verna and David.

But his choice was to leave, no matter how much it hurt her.

Since Annie was at Deacon Beachey's with the children, Judith didn't go straight into the house. The day was fine, but the blue sky grated on her. The weather should be cloudy and damp to match her mood. But even the songbirds ignored her, singing with melodies that would normally make her pause and listen. She went into the barn, banging the door shut behind her.

"Hallo!" came Matthew's call from somewhere above her in the high haymow.

"It's me. Judith."

She climbed up the ladder. Matthew was forking hay through the chute to the horses' mangers.

"You're back earlier than I expected." He leaned the pitchfork against a beam and beckoned to her. "I have something to show you."

On the far side of the stack, he parted the strands of hay, revealing Judith's favorite gray-striped barn cat, Belle, with a litter of newborn kittens.

"Ach, how sweet!" Judith sank to her knees next to the nest. Belle purred and reached her head toward Judith for a scratch. "Look how tiny they are! They must have been born this morning."

Matthew knelt next to her. "Belle thought she had hidden them well, the way mama cats do, but when I started moving the hay, I heard her meowing. We'll leave them here until the kittens are big enough to come out and play." He covered the little family up again and stood.

"How are David and Verna?" he asked, grabbing his pitchfork again.

Judith sat on the floor next to Belle's hiding place and stretched her legs in front of her. "I didn't see them. I went to the barn first to talk to Guy, and then…" She brushed a piece of hay off her skirt. "I guess I just forgot."

Matthew stopped his work and stared at her. "You

forgot to see how David is doing? I thought that was
why you went over there."

She didn't answer but brushed another piece of hay
off her lap. She should have gone to the house and talked
to Verna first, but she had been more concerned about
Guy than David. A hot tear trickled down her cheek and
she dashed it away. She had to stop this crying.

"All right." Matthew waited until she looked at him.
"Tell me what is wrong. If you didn't see David and
Verna, it must be Guy."

Judith nodded. "What is it about boys? Why are they
so…selfish and pigheaded?"

"I should feel insulted." Matthew thrust the pitchfork
into the sweet-smelling pile and sat next to her. He stuck
a piece of hay in his mouth and chewed on it. "But I
think I understand. Guy did something you didn't like?"

How much could she tell Matthew? Judith sucked
in her lower lip and watched him. He could be trusted,
she knew that, but would he give her good advice, or
would he take Guy's side?

"Guy's *daed* came back."

Matthew's brows raised. "When?"

"Friday. Guy has been keeping it a secret."

"He hasn't even told David and Verna?"

Judith shook her head. "And he wants to go away
with his *daed* and live somewhere else."

Matthew threw the piece of hay off to the side and
laced his fingers around one knee. "It's too bad that he
wants to leave us. I know David was hoping Guy would
be able to take over the farm one day."

It was Judith's turn to be surprised. "Does Guy know
that?"

"*Ne*, and don't tell him. That is something David needs to discuss with him at the right time." Once Judith nodded her agreement, he went on. "Where is he thinking of going?"

She shrugged. "He didn't tell me."

"There's more to it, isn't there?"

Judith crumpled a piece of hay between her fingers. "I've always hoped he'd choose to stay here, to join the church."

Matthew sighed. "I know that's what David and Verna have prayed for, but I feel sorry for Guy. He has a tough decision to make."

"What do you mean? Guy is taking the easy way, going off with the father that he's been waiting for all his life. Now he can start living the way he's always wanted to." Her last words disappeared in a hiccupping sob.

"I've seen you and Guy together. That young man has it bad."

Judith blinked away her tears. "What do you mean?"

"He's in love with you."

"That can't be true. He's never said anything…" Except that kiss. That sweet kiss that had taken her by surprise.

"He might not even realize it." Matthew stretched his legs out, leaning back on his hands. "Don't you see the position Guy is in? Men can be fiercely loyal to their families, but sometimes they have to make a decision that is going to hurt the ones they love the most."

"I thought men always did whatever they wanted to and women just had to learn to accept it." Judith sniffed again. That was the way her *daed* had been and the way Samuel had been until he met Mary.

"Not always. A real man sacrifices everything for the ones he loves. That's why this decision must be agonizing for Guy. Do you think he wants to leave David and Verna?" Matthew put one hand on top of Judith's. "Do you think he wants to leave you?"

"You don't think he wants to go?"

Matthew shook his head. "Not the Guy I know. I think he has made this decision out of loyalty to his *daed.*" He laced his hands around his knee again. "Instead of being angry with him, you could look for a way to help him."

"You mean I should help him leave?"

Matthew shook his head. "Give him a reason to stay."

All morning, as Guy went from one chore to another, Judith's final words rang in his ears.

She was right. He had made his decision. But if he didn't go with Pa, wouldn't he be doing the same thing Pa had always done? Putting his family second to what he really wanted?

If only Judith could see that.

When the time drew close to dinner, Guy put the tools away. If he was going to make that trip to town for Pa and get home in time for milking, he had to get going. He knocked on the back door.

"You're early," Verna said as she opened the oven door and slid in a chicken potpie. "I'm just putting dinner in the oven now."

Guy's mouth watered as the thought of Verna's delicious cooking filled his mind. "I'm going into town. Do you need anything?"

"Going to town on a Monday?" Verna went back into the kitchen and picked up a knife and a loaf of bread. The golden crust crackled as she cut thick slices.

Guy stepped closer to the kitchen door, still waiting on the porch. "*Ja.* It can't wait." Pa couldn't wait.

"You'll have your dinner first, won't you?" She turned from her work, watching him with narrowed eyes as if she was trying to figure out something. "Come and sit at the table for once."

He shook his head. "I have to get going. Can you put mine in a lard pail or something?"

"Do I hear Guy?" David called from the front room, his voice raspy and weak. The question ended in a cough.

Verna went to the doorway on the opposite end of the kitchen. "For sure, it is. He's going into town."

Another cough, then David said something that Guy couldn't hear. Verna beckoned to him.

"He wants to see you."

Guy swallowed, the taste of his guilt like bile. But he couldn't take time to talk to David now. Pa was waiting for him.

When Guy didn't move, Verna stalked across the kitchen and out on the porch. She took his arm.

"I don't know why you're acting this way," she said, tears standing in her eyes, "but it's time for you to decide to put someone else ahead of your own feelings. David is very ill, and worrying about you is likely to kill him."

Guy's face grew hot. "I'll see him later. I have to get going."

Verna leaned close to him, peering into his face. "Nothing you have planned is as important as saying hello to David. Just let him see you."

Everything in him wanted to do what Verna said, but Pa—

"Now, Guy. Or no dinner."

He knew the look on her face, and he couldn't go back to Pa without his dinner. He kicked off his work boots and hung his hat on the hook.

"I'll pack some lunch for you while the two of you are talking." Verna stood back to let him pass her, then grabbed his sleeve. "But don't say anything that will upset him, all right?"

Guy leaned down to give her a kiss on the cheek. He did it from habit, but as he caught a whiff of the rose-scented soap she always used, his throat filled. He would miss her when he left with Pa.

David was propped up in his bed with the wedge Guy had made. The old man's eyes were closed, his face tight with pain. As Guy paused in the doorway, David coughed again, a racking, dry cough. When it was over, he fell back against the pillows.

"You wanted to see me?"

Guy asked the question softly, but David's eyes popped open as he tried to turn in his bed to see him. Guy moved to Verna's chair in its place next to the bed, facing David.

"Guy." David reached out his hand and Guy took it. The skin was soft and papery, and the strong grip Guy expected was gone. "Where have you been?"

"Didn't Verna tell you? I've been keeping the farm going."

"*Ja, ja, ja*, I know you've been around the farm, but you haven't come to see me."

"I'm here now." Guy tried to keep his voice light, but David wasn't fooled.

"What has happened, Guy?"

David's grip clung, in spite of his weakness. Guy couldn't turn away, couldn't run. He glanced at David's eyes and was trapped by his gaze. This man was his boss. His teacher. His friend. The best…father he had ever had.

Guy dropped his gaze to the floor. To the toes of the wool socks that Verna had knitted during the winter. They had sat in this very room, the fire in the stove keeping them warm, Verna with her knitting needles and David rocking in his chair while Guy read aloud to them from the *Farm Journal* magazine or the weekly newspaper from LaGrange. This was his home. His family. How could he leave them?

His jaw tightened until it ached. The chasm yawned wide, reminding him that he couldn't stand with a foot on each side. He had to choose one or the other.

He had to stick by Pa, to prove to him that family was the most important thing, whether Pa thought so or not. If only…

His nose prickled and he rubbed it with his free hand. There was no use wishing Pa would be any different than he was.

"Nothing has happened," he said, giving David's hand a squeeze before he pulled free and stood up. "Nothing you need to worry about." He put a smile on his face and leaned over to straighten the blanket around David's waist. "I'm going to town this afternoon. Is there anything you need?"

Exhaustion showed in the tight lines at the corners of David's mouth. "I have a hankering for some licorice, if they have any. Ask Verna for a nickel."

"I'll look for it. If they are out, do you want some of those root beer barrels?"

The older man nodded, resting his head against the pillow. "*Ja*, that would be good."

Guy resisted the urge to kiss the old man's bare forehead. Instead, he squeezed his shoulder. "I'll be back in time for milking."

When he walked through the kitchen, Verna handed him the covered pail.

"I made some ham sandwiches, since you'll miss out on the potpie. And the piece of bread on top is your favorite."

"Buttered, with cinnamon and sugar sprinkled on top?"

"*Ja*, for sure." Verna patted his cheek. "There's a napkin in there, too, and don't you go losing it."

"I won't."

"You'll have to drink water instead of milk." Verna's brow wrinkled as she thought of that.

"I can drink water, don't worry." Guy stepped into the porch and shoved his feet into his boots. "David said he wanted some licorice. Did you think of anything you need?"

"Some baking soda." Verna reached into the cupboard for the pint jar where she kept her coins. "A dime's worth will be fine. Here's a quarter."

"I'll bring you the change." Guy settled his hat on his head.

Verna waved away the idea. "Buy yourself a soda pop. You deserve a treat after working so hard."

Guy let the porch door swing shut behind him as he left before Verna could see his reaction. He didn't deserve a soda pop, or even the dinner pail he was carrying. He deserved to be shot. Or hung. Or at least put in jail for planning to leave them like this.

He went into the barn through the buggy shed, then out the back door and toward the little shed by the river, his stomach churning. Every step felt like he was wading through a mud hole.

The night Judith had gone home with Luke, he had asked God for help. Somehow, he had found Judith and been able to help her. Had that been God's answer to his prayer? Or had it just been chance?

Guy glanced at the sky as he walked. High, white clouds floated overhead. He knew what David would say. He had heard it often enough: "A man of faith lives by prayer and the Word of God."

David was a man of faith, for sure and for certain. But was Guy? He put his hand on his middle, where the churning seemed to be easing.

"God, if You're there, help me feel better about what I'm doing. I don't want to leave, but I have to, don't I?"

The shed came into view as Guy got to the corner of the buckwheat field and descended to the edge of the mint fields. Pa stood next to it, waiting for him.

The churning came back with a vengeance.

Matthew's words echoed in Judith's mind as she cleaned up after the quick dinner she had fixed for the two of them. Matthew had gone back to his work in the barn and the house was empty.

"Give him a reason to stay?" She dried the plates and bowls while the pan she had used for the soup soaked in the dishwater. "How?"

She put the clean dishes away, glad that no one was in the house to hear her talking to herself. After she was done, she started up the stairs to fetch her sewing, but stopped halfway. Verna might know how to help her keep Guy at home, and she could see how David was feeling while she was there.

Verna answered the door as soon as Judith knocked.

"I saw you coming up the lane." Verna welcomed her with a hug and helped her hang up her shawl. "David and I are in the front room, and I could use your help."

"What can I do?" Judith hung her bonnet from the hook on the wall and followed Verna.

"I need to put a new mustard plaster on David's chest, and I also need to change his sheets. Two pairs of hands will make the work go much easier."

Judith's mouth went dry. "But I've never made a mustard plaster before."

"There's no better time to learn. I'll show you what you need to do." Verna went to the table where she had been mixing a yellowish colored dough in a bowl. "This is flour and dried mustard mixed with warm water. It's a very simple remedy for chest congestion." She spread a wide strip of cloth on the table. "I need you to hold the edges of the cloth down while I spread on the paste."

Judith wrinkled her nose at the strong mustard smell but held the cloth until Verna had used all of the paste.

"Now we'll take it in to David." Verna folded the

cloth so the paste was enclosed in a square envelope large enough to cover a man's chest. "We have to work quickly so he doesn't get chilled. I'll need you to take off David's shirt and undershirt, and then I'll put the compress on and we'll dress him again. I just need you to be an extra pair of hands for me."

Judith face grew hot at the thought of what Verna was asking her to do. "I can't undress your husband. It wouldn't be right."

Verna nodded. "Normally, it wouldn't be. But part of being a woman in this world is knowing how to care for the ill and infirm in your family." She lifted the plaster, holding it by the corners. "Someday you'll be a wife and a mother. I hope you'll never need these skills, but you probably will."

Judith's future suddenly looked very frightening as she followed Verna into the front room. "You mean I'll need to know how to do this, even though I may never use it?"

"You never know. But you'd hate to need this knowledge and not have it, wouldn't you?"

David was drowsing as he sat propped up in his bed. Verna caressed his forehead to wake him and he smiled when he saw her.

By the time the compress was applied and the bedding changed, David was exhausted. Verna tucked the blankets around him, then took his soiled clothes and bedding back to the kitchen.

"I'm glad you were here to help Verna," David said, grimacing as he shifted to a more comfortable position.

"How are you feeling?" Judith helped him straighten his pillows.

"The hip is healing, and my fever is staying down, so I hope we've passed the danger of pneumonia." David coughed. "But other than that, I'm feeling wonderful. I saw Guy today, and talking with him brightened up my day."

He coughed again as Verna came back into the room. She gave him a handkerchief and helped him lean over to cough as the mustard plaster started loosening the congestion in his chest.

"You must have seen Guy leave," Verna said. "He was going to town, and left not long before you got here."

"I didn't," Judith said. "I must have just missed him."

Her fingers grew cold. Had he gone to town, like Verna said, or had he already left with his father? When David said he had talked with Guy, a brief hope that Guy had changed his mind had flitted through her mind, but with this news…perhaps Guy had only been saying goodbye.

"He's a fine young man," David said, settling his head back against the pillows. "He thinks a lot of you."

Judith fingered her apron absently. Had Guy taken the buggy? Or had he walked? Was his father with him?

"He certainly does," said Verna. "He's going through a hard spell right now, but we keep praying for him."

"Praying for him?" Judith had heard folks say that, and she had prayed for others before, but she had never thought about what it meant. "You mean, you're asking God to make Guy act the way you want?"

"Ach, ne!" Verna covered her mouth at the idea. "We don't ask God to do what we want. We ask Him to do what He wants. As the Lord's Prayer says, 'Thy will be

done.' And we hope that His will is for Guy to become a member of our church and our community."

"What if he doesn't become part of the church?"

David took Verna's hand in his. "Then that is as God wills it to be, and we submit to Him. But we will never stop praying for our boy." He ended with another fit of coughing.

Verna nodded, her mouth set in a grim smile. "The mustard plaster is working better today than it has the past few days. I think he's getting better."

David's coughing continued, but Verna didn't seem concerned as she supplied a clean handkerchief and rubbed his back.

Judith's thoughts went back to Guy. If Guy left with his father, that would tell her exactly how he felt about her. Even though Matthew was sure Guy loved her, and even with David's encouraging words, the truth would come out in Guy's actions. Any man who loved her had to love the Lord and His people first. He had to be willing to become part of the community.

But Guy had already made his choice. And if he was gone, then how could she convince him to stay?

As David settled back on his bed, he said, "I know I'll never be able to work again, not the way I've always been able to."

He held up a hand as Judith started to protest. "It's the way of the world, Judith. Our lives are just wisps of fog in the moonlight. We get older, then we die and someone else takes our place."

David's face was calm. Relaxed. Secure. It was as if he was talking about planting a field rather than his own death.

He went on. "I've thought Guy would take over the farm when I wasn't able to work any longer, but I always thought we had a few more years left. With this accident, it seems it's time for me to retire and for Guy to have the farm. It will be a good place for him to live with his wife and to raise his family." He let his eyes close. "I just hope I'm here to watch his children grow."

His voice drifted off and Verna beckoned for Judith to follow her to the kitchen.

"Does his talk of dying worry you?" Judith asked as Verna indicated for her to take a seat at the table.

"Ne." The older woman's mouth quivered. "I don't want to lose him, but I don't want him to suffer, either. I keep praying that God will heal him, but some days it seems like he's only getting worse."

"He said that today was a good day."

"Ja." Verna's smile strengthened. "Guy talked to him for quite a while before dinner, and it made David happy to see him. I hope Guy decides to spend more time with him."

Judith followed a line of wood grain in the top of the table with her finger. When Guy left, it would break David's heart. Verna's, too. Couldn't he see that?

"I have been hoping that you would be the one Guy chooses to marry."

"We will have to wait and see what happens."

Verna covered her hand with her own. "I know he is restless. I've seen it even more during the past week. I can't help but think that something has gone terribly wrong for him, but he won't talk to me about it."

Judith shook her head. "Right now he isn't talking

to me, either." Not since he had chosen his father over her and his family.

"Then we must pray for him. Constantly." Verna touched her *Kapp*. "We are always ready to pray as we keep our heads covered, so we can pray for our loved ones all through the day as they come to mind."

Judith turned her hand over so she could give the older woman's hand a squeeze. "I will pray for him. Always."

Chapter Fifteen

As Guy drove the blue Studebaker into Goshen, the county seat of neighboring Elkhart County, he pushed in the clutch and tried to shift gears. A grinding sound growled from somewhere underneath the car and he cringed when folks turned to stare. Hunching down as far as he could behind the steering wheel, he drove past the courthouse and the bulletproof police booth on the corner.

Pa had insisted that he drive the Studebaker. "Take it and ditch it somewhere," he had said.

So Guy had taken it, but where in the world would he ditch it? And why? Guy couldn't believe that Pa would steal a car. It was more likely that he had made up that story, too. Pa was a liar, for sure. And probably a petty thief and con man. But to steal a car was crossing a line. Pa wouldn't go that far.

He parked outside the drugstore on Main Street, a block from the courthouse square, and read through Pa's list again. Cigarettes, chewing gum, sock garters, matches, hair pomade and a cake of bay rum shaving soap.

After purchasing the things on Pa's list, Verna's baking soda and a ten-cent sack of licorice for David, Guy opened the door to leave. Two men inspecting the Studebaker made him pause in the doorway. One walked behind the car, writing on a notepad, while the other man leaned inside the vehicle, his head out of sight. Guy looked up and down the street and caught sight of the police box. At least help was nearby if these men were trying to steal Pa's car.

"Can I help you?" He tightened his grip on the box of items from the drugstore as his voice quivered.

The man with the notebook stepped onto the sidewalk next to him, flipping open the lapel of his jacket to show a shiny badge. "Who are you?"

"Guy Hoover." He took a step backward as the second man joined the first.

"Hoover, eh?"

The second man put his hands on his hips, drawing back his jacket just enough for Guy to get a glimpse of his badge and the shoulder holster he wore.

"We're looking for Frank Hoover." He moved so that he was on one side of Guy while his partner stood on the other side.

Guy backed toward the drugstore. "Frank Hoover?" Pa.

"Same last name as yours." The first man's smile didn't go past his mouth. "I don't suppose you know him, do you?"

The pieces fell into place. These were Feds. G-men. Guy had seen a movie a couple years ago with G-men and James Cagney, and these men looked and acted just like the cops in the movie. Was Pa a wanted man? Had he been telling the truth the whole time, after all? A stone sank in Guy's gut as the thought crossed his mind.

"I know him. He's my father. Has he done something wrong?"

The first man took the box from Guy and sorted through it while the second man stepped forward.

"I think you need to come with us."

"Where?"

The Fed grasped his elbow and started walking him down the street. "To the police station. We can talk there."

Guy tried to stop, but the man propelled him on. "Am I under arrest?"

"We just want to talk to you."

Folks stared as they walked the short distance to the police station, and Guy was glad he wasn't in Emma or Shipshewana where someone might recognize him. The Feds nodded to the police sergeant as they passed the front desk, then climbed a wide, creaking stairway to the second floor. The first man led the way into a room and motioned to a chair on one side of a table. The second man closed the door behind them, and then sat next to his partner across from Guy.

"I'm Murphy," the second man said, and threw a thumb toward his partner. "This is Sanderson."

Sanderson picked the items out of the box from the drugstore one by one. "Licorice. Hoover hates licorice." He glanced at Guy. "This must be for you."

Guy shook his head. "It's for a friend."

"Baking soda." The can rapped against the table. "Cigarettes. Chesterfields. That's Hoover's brand." The package hit the table as he pulled out the can of pomade. "Murray's. He's a man of habit, that's for sure."

Murphy leaned toward him. "Where is he? Here in Goshen?"

Guy shook his head in answer to the question as Pa's lies and stories swirled through his head. He still didn't know which were true. Or were any of them true? The stone in his gut turned to ice. Perhaps all of them were true.

"Can you tell me why you want him? What has he done?"

Sanderson and Murphy exchanged glances.

"He hasn't told you?" Sanderson tapped his finger on the can of pomade.

The room closed in on Guy. What would Pa do if he was sitting here? Lie his way out?

David's voice echoed in Guy's head, "A man of faith lives by prayer and the Word of God." He sent a quick prayer up. Would God hear it?

He took a deep breath. Pa's way would only land him in jail, and he didn't have to ask himself what David would do at a time like this. More than that, he knew what Judith would want him to do. She would want him to be like David, not like Pa.

Guy looked at the two men in front of him. "Pa tells me a lot of things, and I never know if I should believe him or not. But he showed up at the farm where I work a few days ago after being gone for years."

"Did he tell you that car you're driving was stolen?" Murphy was making notes as he spoke.

"He said it was, but I thought he must be lying."

"And his escape from prison. He must have bragged about that."

Guy swallowed. "He said it was some city jail, and I thought sure that was another lie."

"Did he tell you he robbed a bank, along with another man?" Murphy's eyes drilled into Guy.

"Robbed a bank?" Guy shook his head, his feet growing cold. If these men were right, Pa was much worse than a con man, and Guy didn't know him at all. Suddenly the chasm he had been straddling was gone. Learning the truth about Pa made it easy to determine which side was the one where he belonged.

Sanderson slapped the table. "Quit fooling around and tell us what you know."

A firm, strong sensation flowed through Guy. He knew what he had to do.

"I'll tell you everything." Murphy and Sanderson leaned back in their chairs. "But what will happen to Pa?"

"I won't lie to you, kid." Murphy crossed his legs and thrust his hands into his pockets. "When we catch up with your old man, he'll go to prison for a long time."

Guy swallowed. He wouldn't wish prison on anyone, but Pa was a crook. And he was dangerous. The sensation strengthened. He had to do what was right, even if Pa was his only family. He couldn't help Pa escape the punishment for his crimes.

A lifetime of hopes and dreams, the anticipation of reuniting with his father and being a family again fell away like river ice melting on a warm spring day, disappearing into nothing. He bent his head, eyes closed. He never thought doing the right thing would be so hard.

Facing Murphy and Sanderson, he started at the beginning.

* * *

Judith took a shirt off the clothesline, folded it loosely and dropped it into the basket on top of the rest of the clean laundry. From this spot at the edge of the backyard, she could see across the road and up the Masts' lane. As far as she could tell, Guy hadn't come back from town yet, and it was almost milking time.

If she was right and he had left with his *daed*, what could she do? Retrieving a few stray clothespins that had fallen to the ground, she lifted the basket and started back to the house. She would die an old maid, that's what she would do. Guy had made his choice, and it didn't include her or their faith. Ever since his father had shown up, Guy's future had been ruined.

She shook her head, picking her way through the yard to avoid stones with her still spring-tender feet. *Ne*, not ruined, but changed from what she had hoped for and dreamed of for him. He would never have a life here, at home in the community. They would never have a future together, and it was Guy's *daed's* fault.

Ach, here she was, letting hatred and resentment seep into her heart. She paused at the bottom of the porch steps and looked across the road once more. She would have to ask the Good Lord to forgive her wayward heart. The sun was lowering in the sky to the west, making the eastern sky a deep blue over the Masts' house and barn. It was a lovely farm, and the Masts were wonderful people. How could Guy leave them?

The sound of an automobile speeding along the gravel road made her move closer to the house. She opened the door to the back porch but lingered as the vehicle came nearer. The black car slowed to a stop at the end of the lane. Judith looked closer, risking discovery by the strangers as she leaned out to see Guy get out of the back of the car. He spoke to the men in the front seat before giving them a wave and heading up the lane toward the Masts' farm.

Judith set the laundry basket in the porch and waited until the car drove off before she followed Guy. She needed to be home in time to fix sandwiches for supper and to help Annie when she got home from her visit, but she had to find out where Guy had been and why he had come home in an automobile.

An automobile! The thought made her insides quiver.

She hurried along the grassy verge next to the lane, not wanting to run on the gravel. "Guy!" she called.

He waited for her to catch up, and they walked to the barn together.

"I can't stop to talk," he said, shifting the box under his arm. "I need to get the cows in for milking."

"I can help you. I saw you come home in an automobile. What is going on?" She followed him into the milking parlor.

Guy didn't look at her as he opened the gate to let the cows in from the pasture. "I went to town to get a few things, and some guys gave me a ride home. No big deal."

Judith gave each of the cows a measure of grain from the feed box while Guy washed their udders. As he sat on the stool to milk the first cow, she stood near him.

"When Verna told me you had gone to the store, I was afraid you had already left with your *daed*."

"Naw," he said, grunting as he stripped the last of the milk, filling the bucket. He set the full bucket out of reach of the cow's hooves and tail. "That's done with. Plans have changed."

Judith followed him to the next cow in line. "You mean you're not going? That's *wonderful-gut*."

"Maybe." The sounds of milk streaming into the pail stopped. "You can't talk to anyone about it, though." He resumed the milking, still not looking at her.

"Why not?"

"There's more going on than you know, and I don't want you involved in it."

Judith stood back as he finished the second cow. When he said his plans were changed, she'd hoped they would continue the romance that seemed to be blooming. But Guy was being as hard and secretive as ever.

When he picked up the full milk pails to take to the dairy, Judith followed him. In the clean, whitewashed room, Guy lit the lantern hanging on the wall, then started assembling the cream separator. Judith stepped up next to him to help.

"If you're involved in something, I do want to know. This morning, I thought you had chosen your *daed* over me and your family. Now it seems you've changed your mind, but you still won't talk to me about it."

Guy sighed as he faced her. He put the last pieces of the separator together, then took her hands in his.

"Some things became clear to me today. I had been wrong about Pa, and I have to work to make things right."

"What do you mean? How can you make things right?"

"You can't tell anyone else what I'm going to tell you. Not until it's over."

Judith drew her hands back. "What are you talking about?"

"Pa is a bad guy. A crook. I've been talking to a couple agents from the FBI, and I'm going to cooperate with them so they can arrest Pa."

Judith shivered, even though the barn was warm. "You would turn your own father in to the authorities?"

A muscle clenched in Guy's jaw. "David is more of a father to me than that man has ever been. When I found out what Pa has been convicted of, and that he escaped from jail, I knew I would be wrong if I tried to help him." He smiled at her. "I thought about what David would want me to do, and the way was clear."

"Will it be dangerous?"

A shadow passed over his face. "The agents think it might be."

"Then I want to be there, too."

"No."

"What if something happens to you? I want to be there—"

"No. I don't want to risk you getting hurt." He ran his thumb down her cheek. "If something did happen to me, I'd want to know that you were safe." He started the crank on the cream separator. "But nothing is going to happen. The FBI agents and the police will make sure everything goes smoothly, so you don't have to worry."

Judith chewed her lower lip, watching as he poured the milk into the separator. No matter what Guy said, she had to be there. She would stay far enough away to be out of danger.

"When is this going to happen? And where?"

He glanced at her, eyes narrowed with suspicion. "Why do you want to know?"

"So I can pray for you. And for the police." And she would be praying.

"The agents will be here at sunset." Guy leaned into the crank, looking tired and worn as he turned it. "I'll come over to tell you when it's done."

Judith nodded. "I'll be waiting to hear."

After Judith went home, Guy carried the pail of cream into the house, along with the baking soda and licorice he had picked up at the drugstore.

"*Denki*, Guy," Verna said, lifting her cheek for his kiss. "You shouldn't have brought so much licorice for David, though. You'll spoil him."

"Don't you think he needs to be spoiled once in a while?" Guy used a teasing tone that he didn't feel. His stomach churned at the thought of what he had to do after supper.

"Take it in to him. I've heated up leftover potpie for your supper." She laid a hand on his sleeve. "You will eat in the house with us tonight, won't you?"

Guy couldn't look her in the eye. "Not tonight. I have something else to do."

She dropped her hand and went back to the stove without a word. Guy pushed back the urge to tell her everything. She would know soon enough.

When he went into the front room, David was watching the western sky through the window.

"I brought your licorice."

David grinned. "You found some!"

Guy couldn't suppress his own smile at the pink

tinge in the old man's cheeks. His breathing wasn't as raspy, either.

"The store had plenty, so I bought a dime's worth."

"*Denki*, son. This will be a fine treat after supper."

Guy put on a frown. "You'll share with Verna, won't you?"

David's brows lifted in surprise. "Of course. You wouldn't think otherwise, would you?"

"I know how you love this stuff."

David nodded, smiling. "But I love Verna even more."

Putting the bag on the table next to his bed, David said, "Are you going to tell me what is bothering you?"

Guy drew his hand over his face. David always could read his mind.

"I can talk to you about it tomorrow, but not now. Not yet." He stepped toward the door. "I have some things I need to do."

David's face wore a worried frown. "Take care, son."

Guy nodded and left. He picked up the plate Verna had fixed for him as he passed through the kitchen, and ignored her frown. She was just as worried as David, and he didn't blame them. But everything should be cleared up tonight. And once Pa was in FBI custody, then Guy would be free to mend the fences he had broken in the past ten days.

He stopped by the barn to collect the box from the drugstore and started toward the shed by the river. He had just enough time to give Pa his dinner and the things from the store before sunset. Enough time to ease Pa's feelings and to pretend that tonight was just like every other night.

"Been waitin' for you, boy," Pa said when Guy reached the shed. "I've been missing my cigs." He took the box and looked through it, inspecting each item. He tore open the package of cigarettes, shook one out and lit it before he reached for the plate. The warmed-over potpie smelled delicious, and Guy's stomach growled in response.

"How did things go in town?" Pa asked, his mouth full of food.

"Fine." Guy didn't trust his voice enough to say more.

"Got rid of the Studebaker?"

Guy nodded. "It's all taken care of."

Impounded in the police lot.

"See any Feds?"

Guy heard a crack in the undergrowth behind the shed, but Pa didn't react.

"Maybe. I saw a couple guys wearing suits."

Pa laid the plate down on an upturned log, the potpie only half eaten. He ground his cigarette out in the gravy and leaned his elbows on his knees.

"Did they notice you? Follow you?"

Shaking his head, Guy wiped away the sweat beads tickling his upper lip. "No, Pa. They didn't follow me."

Pa turned his head in the growing dusk, looking for all the world like a wolf sniffing out its prey. "You sure, boy?" His eyes bore into Guy. "I've always taken care of you, haven't I?"

Guy's stomach turned. "Pa, you put me in an orphanage."

"I made sure you had people to care for you. Give

you clothes. Give you schooling. I did what I promised your ma."

"Yes, Pa."

"I promised her, even though you weren't my flesh and blood."

Guy's head snapped up. This was the worst lie of all. "That isn't true."

Pa went on. "Your ma had you before we even met. I let her tell you I was your pa, even though taking you on along with her was more than I had planned on." Pa shook another cigarette out of the package and put it between his lips but didn't light it. He spoke around it, his words muffled. "Your ma was one fine woman, though. A real looker."

A soft noise came from the dark underbrush toward the river, and Pa cocked his head, as if he was listening.

He leaned forward, speaking softly, and Guy found himself moving closer to him to hear the lies, drawn like a bird to a snake. "You were always in the way. Useless. Until now."

Pa grabbed Guy's arm and yanked him upward and around, securing him with a choke hold around his neck. He backed toward the shed, using Guy as a shield. Struggling to breathe, Guy clutched at Pa's arm.

"All right, you Feds. I know you're out there."

Through his blurred vision, Guy saw a gun in Pa's free hand.

"Come out where I can see you, or the kid gets it."

Guy got a grip on Pa's forearm, pulling it away from his throat long enough to suck air into his burning lungs. Murphy and Sanderson approached from the direction of the river, both of them holding guns. Pa tightened the grip on Guy's throat.

"Drop it, Frank," Sanderson said, coming forward with cautious steps. "You don't want to have murder on your conscience, too."

Pa—Frank—laughed. "You don't think I've killed before?" He shoved the barrel of the gun against Guy's temple. "What do you think happened to his ma?"

As if a door had opened, a scene from the past roared into Guy's consciousness. Mama screaming, prostrate on the floor, Pa standing over her, and Guy watching from behind the door. He was hiding, waiting for Pa to leave. Waiting to run to Mama so he could help her stop crying. Then Pa kicked with his heavy black boot, and Mama never cried again.

The realization of what Frank had done so many years ago exploded in Guy's brain. With a rasping cry, he threw his arm up, knocking Frank's hand away. The gun fired as he planted his heels in the soft ground and shoved backward, slamming Frank against the shed wall. Guy fell to the ground, his ears ringing. He rolled away from the shed and Frank. Shots from Frank's gun and the agents' guns flashed in the growing darkness, but Guy only heard soft pops muffled by the roaring in his ears. More men ran up, and one wrestled Frank to the ground.

Guy shook his head, trying to clear his ears, but the roaring hum continued. Murphy was in front of him, pulling him upright, his face contorted as his mouth moved. If he was talking, Guy couldn't hear. He grasped Murphy's outstretched arm and stood, but fell again. It was as if someone had tilted the ground under his feet.

As Frank was taken away, Guy closed his eyes, letting his head press into the soft ground, waiting for the throbbing to ease. Tears soaked into the grass, turning the dirt to mud.

Chapter Sixteen

After a quick supper of sandwiches and canned fruit, Judith put Eli to bed. During the meal he'd fussed, refusing to eat anything but bread and butter.

"He didn't take his afternoon nap," Annie had said. "*Grossdawdi* Beachey took him out to the barn and he loved it. He had a lot of fun, but we're paying for it now."

"He'll fall asleep early, for sure." Judith had been glad, because her mind was filled with worry about Guy.

Now, as she left the house with the excuse that she was borrowing a sewing pattern from Verna, she glanced behind her at the western sky. The clouds glowed with orange and pink as the sun set, but the beautiful sight only added urgency to her worry. Guy had said something would happen at sunset.

Along the lane leading to the Masts' house, six police cars were parked. She walked past them, unease growing as she saw that they were empty. Where were the policemen?

Lamplight glowed from the Masts' parlor window,

where Verna and David were probably wondering about the police, but Verna would stay with David, not wanting to leave him alone. Judith went to the barn, pushing the dairy door open. She listened, but there were no sounds other than a hoof stamping on the dirt floor, and all was dark. Guy had gone. But where?

Looking down the path that ran beside the buckwheat field, Judith hesitated. That was the direction Guy had come from when this started. His *daed* must be down by the river. She walked slowly, listening for any sounds, but even the spring peepers were silent. The hair on the back of her neck prickled. The evening was too quiet.

When she reached the corner of the buckwheat field, where the path sloped down toward the river and the mint fields, a movement at the corner of her eye made her duck down, crouching next to a fence post. She saw it again. A policeman was ahead of her, moving slowly toward a shed at the edge of the mint field.

The light from the setting sun was fading, and the scene in front of her became less distinct in the faltering light, but as she watched, she saw more men heading toward the shed with slow, stealthy steps. In the quiet, loud voices rose from the shed, and then a gunshot punctuated the dusky air.

Judith clung to the fence post as the scene in front of her exploded in gunfire and shouts. She couldn't distinguish one policeman from another with their uniforms, and she didn't see Guy anywhere.

Then silence fell again. Two men emerged from the confusion, supporting a handcuffed man between them. Once they'd gone by, Judith ran toward the shed.

When she saw Guy lying on the ground with two

men standing over him, she started toward him, but a policeman caught her, holding her back.

"Let me go." Judith tried to pull out of his grasp. "I have to see him."

One of the men standing near Guy waved her over and the policeman let her go. "Do you live around here? Do you know where we can take him to get some help?"

Judith's hands trembled as she saw Guy lying motionless. She knelt next to him, afraid to touch him. "Was he shot? Is he hurt?"

"Nope. Not shot. He probably broke an eardrum when Hoover fired his weapon." As the man turned Guy over, a policeman shone a flashlight on him. Guy squinted his eyes against the bright beam.

"Judith?" His voice was loud, like he was shouting at her from a long distance. Blood trickled from his right ear.

"Can you hear me?"

"What?" He pointed at his ear.

"We'll take him to the house." Judith stood. "Was anyone else hurt? I heard a lot of gunshots."

The man helped Guy stand. "No injuries. Your boyfriend pulled off his part of the deal perfectly. Frank Hoover is in custody, and he'll be put away for a long time."

When they reached the house, Verna was waiting for them. Her eyes widened when she saw Guy being supported by the two *Englischers*.

"He can't hear anything," Judith said, "but otherwise he isn't hurt."

"What has happened? We saw the policemen come,

but I couldn't leave David to find out why they were here."

"Everything is fine, ma'am. Guy helped us capture a dangerous fugitive, but that man is in custody now and we'll be leaving. Do you want us to call a doctor with our car radio?"

Verna shook her head. "We'll take care of him." She took Guy's arm, and he put it around her, giving her a hug.

"We'll be on our way, in that case." The second man touched the brim of his hat in a kind of salute, then shook Guy's hand. "Thank you for your cooperation."

Guy nodded, still looking a bit dazed.

When the men left, Judith and Verna helped Guy into the front room and the soft chair in the corner. Judith explained to David and Verna what she knew about Frank Hoover and the arrest, but she left the details of Guy's involvement to him. Verna gave Guy a wet towel to clean away the blood that still trickled from his ear.

"You won't be able to hear well for a few days," Verna said in a loud voice, making sure Guy could see her mouth as she over-enunciated the words, "but the hearing should come back in your left ear. We'll have to wait and see."

Guy nodded, leaning back in the chair. He looked at Judith. "I told you not to come. I told you it was going to be dangerous."

"I stayed out of the way until it was over." She spoke loudly, like Verna had, and he nodded to show that he had heard her.

"I'm glad you're here now, though." He took her hand and squeezed it.

David sighed. "That's a good way for the evening to end."

Over the next two days, Guy slowly regained the hearing in his left ear.

When the doctor came to visit David, he examined Guy at Verna's insistence. Sitting at the kitchen table, Guy tilted his head, wincing as the doctor inserted something into the sore right ear.

"Whew." Doctor Bradley gave a low whistle. "You blew out that eardrum. Have you had any bleeding?"

Verna hovered over Guy. "He had some the first night after it happened, but I haven't seen any since then."

After looking in his other ear, the doctor sat in front of Guy and pressed his stethoscope against Guy's chest. "Any other problems? Coughing? Trouble breathing?"

Guy shook his head. "Why?"

"I'm trying to figure out what you did to end up with your ear looking like that."

"Someone fired a gun next to my head." Guy had told Verna and David part of the story, that he was present when the police arrested a fugitive, but he hadn't wanted to tell them everything until both he and David were better.

Doctor Bradley stowed his instruments back in his black bag. "I'm afraid the damage to this ear might be permanent, but the other one should be right as rain soon enough." He snapped his fingers next to Guy's right ear and then his left. "Can you hear all right out of your left ear?"

"It's a lot better today than it was yesterday."

"Take it easy while the right ear heals. And no swimming, either, or ducking your head underwater. Not until it heals completely."

Verna twisted her fingers together. "How is David doing, do you think?"

The doctor smiled at her. "You are one of the best nurses I've seen. The threat of pneumonia has cleared up, and the broken bones are mending. Now the hard part starts."

Guy took Verna's hand as her eyes widened, and he grinned at the doctor. "You mean that the hard part will be keeping him in bed now that he's feeling better, right?"

"That's right." Doctor Bradley shrugged on his worn overcoat. "He shouldn't get chilled, and he needs to remain quiet. He needs fresh air and sunshine, though, so when you can, open up the windows and move his bed so he can catch the afternoon light. In a few weeks, once the bones are mostly healed, we'll see about letting him sit outside."

After the doctor left, Verna wiped her eyes. "I've been so worried, but I didn't want to let David see."

"He's been pretty sick."

She shook her head. "You're the one I've been worried about."

"Now that David's feeling better, and I am, too, I'll tell you both what has been going on."

Facing up to the way he had treated David and Verna was one of the hardest things Guy had ever done. The three of them gathered in the front room as the afternoon waned, and he told them every detail of what had happened since the work day two weeks before.

"I should have realized that you have been my family more than Frank Hoover ever was."

Verna squeezed his hand. "What is done is done and past. You never need to question our forgiveness, and we hope you will forgive us."

Guy looked from Verna to David. "What do I need to forgive you for?"

David cleared his throat. "We should have spent more time looking into your situation. There must have been a way to claim that your father abandoned his rights, even if he never signed them away. We should have pursued any way we could to adopt you."

"Don't call that man my father." Guy forced the words out through clenched teeth. "I hope he never gets out of jail."

"Guy." The one word brought Guy's eyes up to meet David's. "You must forgive him. Don't harbor that hatred. Frank Hoover is a man who has done unspeakable things, but if you can't forgive him the way you have been forgiven, then you will never be able to move toward your future."

The vision of Frank kicking his mother had replayed itself in Guy's mind over and over. The last couple of nights, ever since that distant memory had come back, he had even dreamed that he attacked Frank, saving his mother. How could he ever forgive that man?

"Don't forgive me, then," Guy said, staring at the floor. "Frank Hoover doesn't deserve forgiveness."

"None of us do." David spoke so quietly that Guy had to lean close.

"But you forgave me."

"Of course we did, because we love you. But I've also been forgiven by God for my sins because of our Lord and Savior, Jesus Christ. I couldn't truly forgive you unless I understood how vast my own sin is and how I've been forgiven."

Guy shook his head. "You don't have any sins. Someone like Frank does, but not you."

"We all have sinned and come short of the glory of God."

"That's from the Good Book, isn't it?"

"From Romans. Do you know what it means?"

Guy rubbed the side of his nose as he leaned his elbows on his knees. "I guess it means we're all sinners? But that can't be true."

"There was only one sinless man in all of history."

"Jesus."

"*Ja*, that's right. Every other man and woman is a sinner and needs to be forgiven. We are weak mortals, subject to committing sin knowingly and unknowingly."

"Then where is there hope?" Guy held his head in his hands. "We might as well all live like Frank, taking whatever we want."

Even as he said it, Guy felt a wrench in his heart. That wasn't the answer. That wasn't the way David lived.

"There is hope." Verna's words were soft but fervent.

David nodded. "There is hope in the blood of the Lord Jesus Christ. He died for our sins, so we could be forgiven. We take on His righteousness when He lives in us."

Guy swallowed. "So, if God forgives me…"

"When you belong to God, He looks at you and sees the sacrifice of Jesus. Your sins are forgiven. All of them. You no longer need to fear the penalty for your sins."

The penalty for his sins was much worse than what Frank Hoover was facing here on Earth. The orphanage made sure every child went to Sunday School, and Guy had heard of the destruction waiting for sinners. His knees trembled.

"How do I…" Guy swallowed. "I mean, what do I need to do?"

"Ask God to forgive you. Believe in what He has told you in His Word."

"That's all?"

"That's everything."

"And then what?"

"Then you belong to God. You are His."

Guy couldn't stop the prickling behind his eyes. He could belong to God. As bad as he was, as much as he had shrugged away everything David, Verna and the Sunday School teachers had tried to tell him about God, he could belong.

He felt the sudden urge to be alone. "Do you mind?" He stood, on his way to his room. "I need to…" What? Pray?

"Of course you do," David said. "Spend time talking with God. He will lead you in the way you should go."

"Story." Eli patted his bed, his way of telling Judith to sit with him. "Story."

"Only a short one." Judith sat, catching both of Eli's hands in her own. She leaned down to kiss his soft cheek. Her stories always helped him go to sleep faster. "What should the story be about?"

Eli's eyes lit up. "Horses."

Judith told him a story about Summer running in the meadow, looking for a kitten to play with. By the time Summer went to the barn for her supper, Eli's eyes had closed.

Sitting for a minute to make sure he was asleep, Judith let her mind and her gaze drift to the Mast farm. She had a good view from Eli's window, as the large white barn was lit with the golden beams of the setting sun. The scene was calm and peaceful on this Thursday evening, but Monday's events played through her mind once more. She hadn't seen Guy since that night, but he had sent word through Matthew that he was better today and would be over for his *Deitsch* lesson tonight.

He had been speaking only *Deitsch* in every conversation they had had lately, and rarely made a mistake. What more could she help him with? She grinned at the thought. It didn't really matter, when they could spend a quiet hour together.

A figure appeared at the side of the Masts' house, hurrying toward the lane. Coming to see her.

Judith rose from Eli's side slowly, but the little boy was sound asleep. She descended the stairs as quickly as she could, then let herself out the back door. Guy had just crossed the road and she met him next to the lilac bush at the corner of the house.

"Matthew said you might be coming tonight."

He grinned. "You must have been waiting for me. Are you that anxious to see me?"

"The last time we talked, you couldn't hear me. So, *ja*, I'm that anxious. How are you feeling?"

"Much better. Great, even."

Judith let the quiet of the evening settle in around them as she watched Guy's face. She had never seen him look so calm. So relaxed. As he stared at her, she realized that he was happy. More than happy. A deep peace smoothed over his features and lit his eyes with a glow.

"Do you really think you need more *Deitsch* lessons?"

He held out a copy of the *Ausbund*, the book of hymns they used at Sunday meetings. "I thought we could move to High German, so I could follow along with the singing on Sundays." As she took the book from him, he said, "Let's sit on the front steps as long as the light lasts."

He took her hand and led the way around the lilac bush to the seldom-used front porch. Sitting on the steps, they faced the same scene Judith had enjoyed from Eli's window.

Judith took the book and opened it. "You'll have to learn to read the old German script. It's quite different from the letters you're used to."

"*Ja, ja, ja.* I realize that. But to start with, just read one of your favorite hymns to me. We'll start there."

"Hmm." Judith leafed through the pages of the worn volume until she reached number thirty. "Many of the hymns talk about martyrs and their faithfulness, but I've always liked this one the best."

"Why?" Guy scooted closer to her, looking over her shoulder at the book.

Judith pointed at the page. "It's a hymn of praise in

the midst of persecution. There's an introduction here that explains. 'This hymn was written by George Blaurock at Claussen in Tyrol with Hans from the Reve, who was burned in the year 1528.'"

"Burned?"

"Our ancestors suffered martyrdom in the old country. Many of them were burned at the stake for their beliefs, and the rest were finally driven out of their homes in Switzerland. They lived in Germany for a time but then came to America."

Guy's breath warmed her neck, his head next to hers as she read the first lines of the song, translating it into English as she read.

"Lord God, I will praise Thee from now until my end, that Thou gave me the faith by which I recognized Thee."

Taking the book from her, Guy ran his finger along the line of the text. "It really says that?"

"*Ja*, for sure." They held the book between them as she read the words in German and he repeated them.

Closing the book, Guy laid it on the step. He put his arm around Judith and held her close to him. "I'm glad you chose that hymn to read."

"Why?"

"That line about how God gives us the faith to recognize Him. It's what I've been feeling, but I didn't know how to put it into words."

Judith leaned her head on his shoulder. Across the fields, Verna lit the lamp in the front room, sending a warm glow into the twilight.

Guy went on. "Things have changed since I saw you on Monday. I understand some things a lot better now."

"Things about your *daed*?"

His head nodded, brushing against her *Kapp*. "*Ja*, and things about myself." He took her hand in his, stroking her fingers with his thumb. "I never thought of myself as someone who needed God. I would compare myself to someone else and always think that I wasn't as bad as that other person."

Judith waited for him to continue, pulling her lip between her teeth to keep herself from interrupting him. She knew...or she hoped she knew...what he was going to tell her next.

"But David showed me that it doesn't matter what I've done to sin against God, I'm just as much of a sinner as the next man."

His voice faltered and she turned to look into his face. "*Ja*, I know that I am, too. But God..."

Guy nodded. "*Ja*, but God forgives me, anyway. Like that hymn said, He gave me the faith to see Him, and to know Him."

He drew her close again and she relaxed against his strong shoulder. "I thought you looked different tonight. You're more confident, but not the way Luke is. He tends to talk himself into his confidence, but you've learned to rely on the Lord."

"I just needed a solid foundation under my feet, I guess. And now that I've found it, I don't have to live in the past. I have the future to look forward to."

Judith took a deep breath. "Are you still going to leave? Do you think your future might be somewhere out West?"

Guy kissed her *Kapp*, then leaned his cheek on her head. "*Ne*. I think my future is right here in my arms."

They sat together as the twilight faded softly away. Spring peepers sounded from the direction of the river, and a chill crept over the ground and up the porch steps.

"I could sit here all night with you," Guy said, planting another kiss on her *Kapp*, "but tomorrow is another work day. I'm going to visit the bishop in the morning to ask about baptism."

"Tell him that if he will be teaching a class soon, I'd like to join it."

Guy rose, pulling her up with him. "We could take the instruction together and be baptized on the same day. I'll tell Bishop we want to do that."

Judith nodded as he kissed her. Then he started back across the road, whistling a tune as he went. She watched until he disappeared into the dusk and sighed, hugging herself. A future with Guy Hoover sounded like the best future of all.

Chapter Seventeen

When Guy went to ask about membership the next morning, the old bishop was wary of his intentions. He invited Guy into the *Dawdi Haus* where the elderly man lived alone, and asked him to sit at the table.

As Guy took his seat, Bishop leaned his elbows on the table. "It isn't a usual thing, for someone not born into the Amish church to become a member." The old man's eyes closed as he spoke, just as they did when he preached, as if the world around him was a distraction to his thoughts.

"I might not have been born here, but I belong here," Guy said. He leaned forward on the table, anxious for the bishop to understand. "The Lord God brought me here to be part of David and Verna's family. Now that I belong to God, I want to be part of the church."

Bishop's eyes opened at that, his bushy eyebrows raised. He steepled his fingers and leaned back in his chair. "Tell me how you know you belong to God."

As Guy related his conversation with David, and the conviction he'd felt as he realized the depth of his sin, the old man nodded. A smile passed over his lined features as Guy concluded.

"All is well and good, and I will be happy to help you take the steps toward membership. But one problem remains."

"Whatever it is, I'll take care of it."

"Luke Kaufman."

Guy felt heat rush to his face. As far as he was concerned, his fight with Luke was old news and in the past. Did he really have to face this again?

"When you take your membership vows, you are promising your life to the church. This isn't a social club that you can join one day and leave the next. The church is a body. A community of believers. We are to be holy and without blemish. If there are ill feelings between members of the community, the entire congregation suffers. Before we can admit you into membership, and even before you begin instruction for baptism, you must reconcile with Luke. There must be no division among brothers."

Before Guy left, promising to talk to Luke, Bishop set a week to begin the instruction. The classes would be held before the church services on Sunday mornings, during the first hour.

"There may be several who want to join the class, once I announce its formation."

"I know Judith Lapp would like to be part of it."

Bishop gave him a wink as he nodded. "I thought she would."

Instead of going straight home, Guy drove the buggy to the Kaufman farm. He had been there once before, last summer when the Kaufmans took their turn at holding the church meeting in their home, but he felt a new twinge of…jealousy. Or envy. The Kaufmans had three barns rising from well-tended fields and meadows. Brown-and-white cows grazed on lush grass, while a half-dozen Belgian mares drowsed in the midday sun, their foals lying at their feet with gangly legs sprawling. The house had been placed on a slight rise, surrounded by gardens and orchards. Everywhere he looked, Guy saw wealth. Compared to the Kaufman home, David's farm looked small.

His jaw clenched, and he worked it loose. It didn't matter how well-off the Kaufmans were, he needed to mend this rift between Luke and himself. As he turned into the farm lane, he breathed a prayer that Luke wouldn't take a swing at him again.

Tying Billy to the hitching rail outside the largest barn, Guy walked through the open door into the big bay. The roof soared above him, with high lofts waiting to receive this summer's hay. The walls were lined with stalls and the harnesses on racks in the tack room glowed with polish.

"Hallo!" Guy called. "Is anyone here?"

A noise came from one of the stalls, and Luke's head popped up.

"Guy Hoover?" Luke walked toward him, brushing straw off his clothes. "You're the last person I thought I'd see walking into my barn."

"Ja, well, I never thought I'd do this, either." Guy rubbed his chin. "I came to apologize."

Luke's eyes narrowed. "Why?"

"We shouldn't have had that fight during the work day, and I want to apologize for my part in it."

"What do you get out of it?"

Guy shrugged. "Nothing. It's just that I'm going to be taking baptism instruction, and I want to start with a clean slate." He glanced at Luke's face, but couldn't read his expression. "So, no hard feelings?"

Luke ignored the hand Guy stuck out to seal the deal and only stared at him.

"Baptism instruction? You're joining church?"

Guy nodded.

"Why?"

"Because I want to. I have to."

Luke barked out a laugh. "You want to marry that Judith Lapp, don't you? That's why you want to join church. You can't marry her unless you do."

Marry Judith? Down deep inside him, Guy felt a puzzle piece fall into place with a satisfying ease of pressure. Of course, he wanted to marry Judith. It had been a vague idea in the back of his mind, but now that Luke had put words to it, the idea became reality. He was going to marry Judith.

"*Ne*, that's not the reason." He took a step toward Luke, but halted when the other man backed away. "I've done a lot of thinking lately, and I've come to realize that I belong here."

"I heard about your *daed*. He was arrested by the police, wasn't he?" Luke's swagger was back. "Bishop will never let you join church, not with a *daed* like that. You're just like him, you know that. Bishop knows it, too. He won't risk letting an outcast like you into the church."

Guy's fists clenched, but he released the tension with a sigh. Pray. A man of faith lives by prayer and the Word

of God. He must pray for himself. For Luke. He closed
his eyes, all his thoughts focused on Luke and the de-
structive path he was following.

He opened his eyes. "Let me tell you a story, Luke."
He motioned to a couple of stools near the doorway,
where someone else had sat and talked in the shade of
the barn, enjoying the breeze on a warm day.

Luke sat, but his movements were stiff, as if he expected Guy to strike out at him. But Guy leaned his
arms on his knees and started his story from the beginning. He told Luke about his mother, about Frank
Hoover and about the events of last Monday evening.
He told Luke about his hatred of Frank, and how David
convinced him that he needed to forgive the man he
had once called Pa.

At the end of it, Luke stared at the barn floor. "I
had no idea. I was a fool, riding on you and calling you
names when you were going through all that."

"How could you have known? I didn't tell anyone
about it."

"And here you are, asking me to forgive you, when
it really should be the other way around."

Guy waited as Luke left his seat and paced back and
forth across the open bay.

Luke stopped in front of him, pointing a belliger-
ent finger. "If you think you're going to get me to go
to baptism instruction with you, you're more of a fool
than I am."

"That's not why I came here. I just thought maybe…
well, maybe we could be friends."

Luke paced again, coming to a stop in front of Guy,
his hands on his hips. "You know the other fellows

would tease me, since I've always run you down in front of them."

Guy shrugged and Luke resumed his pacing.

The next time he stopped, his eyes glistened. "And I'm supposed to believe that you're going to forgive me after the way I've treated you?"

Guy shrugged again. "I have to. I've been forgiven, so I must forgive others."

Luke sat on his stool. "Why did you come here today?"

"To reconcile with you. To make things right."

"That's all?"

Guy nodded.

"Then you've got it. Things are right between us. No more fights. No more teasing."

Guy stuck out his hand and Luke shook it, then let go of him just as quickly. "I'm not going to promise I won't ask Judith out again, though."

Guy grinned. "I don't think you're going to have a chance."

Judith followed Eli along the lane leading to the Masts' house. Carrying a hot casserole dish wasn't easy when the little boy stopped every time he saw another dandelion.

"Eli, keep walking. We'll pick dandelions on the way home."

He held up his latest prize to her. "Flower. Pretty flower."

"*Ja*, very pretty." She balanced on one foot, nudging him toward the house with the other one. "But we need to give this casserole to Verna. She's waiting for it."

Eli headed toward the house again, this time at a run, and Judith hurried to keep up with him. Before they reached the side porch, Verna was there with the door open.

"*Ach*, what a pleasure to see you on such a nice spring day!" Verna leaned down to help Eli up the steps. "What brings you here?"

"I made a meal for you, and I thought I'd visit for a few minutes." She followed Verna into the kitchen and set the dish on the stove.

Verna lifted the lid as Judith put the dish towels she had been using to protect her hands on the counter and lifted Eli in her arms before he could do any damage in the clean kitchen.

"Potatoes and ham." Verna took a deep breath, then slid the casserole into the oven. "I haven't fixed anything for dinner yet, so this will be perfect. Come into the front room. David will want to see you and Eli."

David reclined in his bed, not quite in a sitting position. He smiled when he saw her.

"It's so good of you to come." He reached out and patted Eli's knee. "You too, young man. I saw you picking dandelions."

Eli opened his clenched fist and let a crushed dandelion flower fall onto David's lap. "Flower."

Picking up the wad of yellow and green, David inspected it. "*Ja*, for sure. That's what it is."

Judith sat down while David and Eli chatted about the flower. She hadn't seen any sign that Guy was at home, even though she thought he must have returned from his visit to the bishop by now.

"I think David is Eli's favorite person," Judith said. "He is always ready to come over here for a visit."

"He's my favorite boy," David said, smiling as Eli pulled the flower apart and gave him the pieces one by one. "How are folks at your place?"

Judith told about Matthew's farm work and the twins, who were already almost three months old. While she talked, she watched Eli, but also glanced out the window, wondering if Guy would be home soon. She would be able to see the buggy turn from the road into the lane from her vantage point.

"Guy went out early this morning," Verna said. "We expect him back any time."

Judith laughed. "I came over to see you."

Verna and David exchanged glances.

"For sure, you did." David gave Eli a small piece of licorice and grinned as Eli tasted it and made a face. "And we appreciate the company. But I've also seen how you are watching the lane for his return."

Judith's face exploded with heat and she knew she must be beet red.

"Don't let him tease you so," Verna said, patting Judith's hand. "It just shows that he's feeling better."

When Guy's buggy turned into the lane, Judith pretended not to notice. The conversation shifted to the weather, the sprouting buckwheat and when Matthew expected to plant his corn until Judith heard Guy come in the back door.

When he entered the front room, his grin widened when his eyes met Judith's, then he bent to give Verna a kiss on the cheek.

"Well, everything is set." Guy perched on the end

of David's bed. "Bishop said he would announce the baptism class on Sunday, and we will start the next meeting day."

Verna and David looked at each other. Verna folded her hands in her lap and gave a nod in her husband's direction.

"*Ach*, what is it now?" Guy looked from one to the other. "I hoped to take a walk with Judith."

"Before you do," David began, "we want to talk to you about something."

"I should go." Judith stood, taking Eli in her arms.

"Stay, please. I think you'll want to hear this, too." David shifted his position, grimacing as he did. "Guy, I hope you know that we've always considered you to be our son."

Guy nodded. "I know that now, and I appreciate everything you've done for me over the years."

"I'll never be able to work like I did before the accident. That's something I've had to face over the past couple weeks." David reached for Verna's hand. "So, it's time to do something we planned years ago. As I retire, I want you to take over the farm."

Guy looked from David to Verna. "But I thought you would sell it, or give it to one of your nephews."

"Not when we have you to carry on after us."

"Why haven't you said anything before?"

David and Verna exchanged glances again. "We wanted to be sure you were committed to the farm and to our way of life."

Guy nodded. "I had always planned to go with… Frank Hoover, if he ever came for me."

"But now, I think you have a goal for your life. A

future to plan for. The farm will do well for you and give you a living for you and your family."

Judith tightened her hold on Eli to keep him in her lap. Her eyes grew moist as she thought of what this meant for Guy. He would have a home and a family.

Guy cleared his throat, his own eyes glistening. "One more thing. I don't want to carry Frank Hoover's name." He met David's frown. "I've forgiven him, I think. At least, I've begun to forgive him. But I don't respect him, and he'll never be my father. Not the way you have been. If it's all right with you, I want to change my last name to Mast. You might not have been able to adopt me legally, but you did in all the ways that mattered."

Verna hiccuped as tears streamed down her cheeks. As she reached out to take Guy in her arms, Judith slipped out the door with Eli. This was a time for the family to be alone.

During dinner, David and Verna helped Guy make his plans for the farm.

"We'll need to build a *Dawdi Haus*," David said. "Verna is ready to care for a smaller place, and I need to have a house I can get around in. I won't be able to run up and down stairs like I used to."

"But this is your home." Guy looked from one to the other. "And I can't live here alone."

Verna smiled. "I don't think you'll be alone very long." She gathered the empty plates to take back to the kitchen. "Judith will make a *wonderful-gut* wife for you."

As Verna left the room, David's grin made Guy laugh. "Is it that obvious?"

"I think I knew you two would be getting married when you first started going over there to learn *Deitsch*."

Guy glanced out the front window. All was quiet at the Beacheys' farm.

"I might head over to see if Judith can go for that walk, now."

David took a book from the table next to his bed and opened it. "She's probably waiting for you." He winked at Guy.

Guy left the house, whistling. The tune was one of the songs he had learned at the Youth Singings. He and Judith wouldn't be attending many more of those, if he had his way.

She must have seen him coming, because when he walked up the farm lane, she was waiting for him. Standing on the bottom step by the back door, one bare foot swinging through the long grass at the edge, she looked like a young girl. Guy drank in the sight with the sweet knowledge that she was his. His girl.

"Have you come to take that walk with me?" Judith smiled, the dimple in one cheek drawing him close.

"Are you free?"

"Everyone is napping in the house, and Matthew has gone to work the upper field."

Guy took her slim hand in his and led her around the back of the house. Passing the clothesline and the hedge of blueberry bushes, they reached the orchard. Matthew and Annie had a dozen fruit trees, and the spring blossoms filled the air with fragrance.

Stopping by an apple tree, Guy tried to keep his knees from shaking. Judith didn't seem to notice. Holding on to a sturdy branch with one hand, she swung around it, finally facing him with a smile.

"I think I'll always remember this day."

Guy ran his finger along the branch until he reached her hand. "Why this day, in particular?"

"Because of how your life has changed. Did you have any idea that David and Verna were going to give you their farm?"

He turned to look across the road at the white barn and house with the freshly plowed fields surrounding them.

"I never thought I could hope to find my home here."

"But it's true. I'm so glad for you."

Guy's shaking knees stilled. Now was the time. Now or never. He swallowed and stepped closer to Judith.

"You should be glad for yourself, too."

"Why?"

"If you want to, it can be your home."

Her smile disappeared and she ducked under the branch so that nothing was between them.

"What are you trying to say?"

Guy stroked the spot where her dimple had faded. Her expression was serious, waiting, anticipating.

"I don't want to live there unless you'll join me. I love you, and I want to spend the rest of my life with you."

The dimple was back. "I love you, too."

Guy's knees were shaking again, but he grinned. "Say that again. You were on the side of my bad ear."

She leaned close to his left shoulder, laying her hands on his chest. "I love you."

"So, what is your answer?"

"You haven't asked me a question yet."

He took her in his arms, holding her close, breathing in her fragrance. "You know the question," he said into her ear.

"I want you to ask it." Her whisper tickled.

"Will you marry me? Will you be my wife?"

Her hug nearly choked him. "*Ja*, you know I will."

Guy unwrapped her arms from around his neck. "You're sure?"

"You are the only man I want to spend my life with."

He bent his head to kiss her, and nothing else mattered.

Epilogue

Judith fastened the suspenders on two-year-old Eli's trousers as he stood on the bed.

"Church today?" His face wore a puzzled frown.

"*Ja*, even though it is Thursday." She kissed his round cheek. "It's a special day."

"Cake?"

"*Ja*, there will be cake at dinner."

As he slipped off the bed and thumped down the stairway, Judith was drawn to the view from his window. Sunshine had turned the orange and red leaves into glowing flames of fire dancing in the September breeze. Across the road, the corn stood tall with the tassels beginning to turn harvest gold. Next to the white farmhouse stood the little *Dawdi Haus* that Guy had finished with the help of Matthew and Bram. David and Verna had moved into it last week.

The sound of footsteps on the stairway reminded Judith that she had plenty to do yet this morning, and time was flying by. As she crossed the hall, Esther met her at the top of the stairs with a hug and they hurried into Judith's room.

"Just think," Esther said as she helped Judith settle a fresh *Kapp* over her hair. "It's September again. A year ago, we were helping Mary get ready for her wedding to Samuel."

Judith smoothed the white apron over her new rose-colored dress. "So much has changed in the last two years, hasn't it?"

The fragrance of chicken and noodles drifted up the stairs of Annie and Matthew's house. Pans of the simple meal were keeping warm in the oven and the scent made Judith's mouth water.

"You know who is getting married next, don't you?"

Judith nodded, rubbing her palms together. She wasn't nervous, so why were they damp?

"You think Ida Mae and Thomas are next?"

The corners of Esther's mouth twitched up in a little smile. "And soon only Sadie and I will be left. Two *maidles* living together."

Judith heard Guy's voice downstairs and her heart skipped a beat.

"You won't be a *maidle* for long. I thought you and Forest Miller were sweethearts."

Esther sighed. "He's been gone for the last several months, helping his *grossdatti* out in Iowa. Things have been bad there, with the drought."

"Has he written to you?"

"A couple letters. The last one came in June. It's been months since then, and I'm beginning to think he has found someone new."

"Or maybe he's just working hard."

Luke Kaufman came into the house, greeting Guy

and everyone else with a loud voice. If someone had told her that Luke would become Guy's best friend, she would never have believed it. But they had grown close during the baptism class over the summer, and even Luke's sweetheart, Susie Gingerich, had become good friends with Judith. They had spent many evenings together as the two couples courted.

Esther shook her head. "I think he has just forgotten me. But that's all right. Sadie can't live alone, and the Good Lord knows what He's doing." She smiled brightly. "I enjoy living with Sadie. Her house is pleasant, and the days are quiet."

More folks arrived and the buzz of the conversations downstairs grew louder. Judith chewed on her lower lip.

"You're doing all right, aren't you?" Esther peered into Judith's face. "You look a little pale."

"I'm fine." Judith swallowed. "Is my *Kapp* straight?"

"Of course it is."

"What about my apron? Are the ties even?" She stood up and turned around for Esther's inspection.

"You look wonderful. You're a beautiful bride."

"Then I guess it's time to go downstairs." Judith's mouth was as dry as if she had been eating chalk.

Esther paused with her hand on the doorknob. "You know *Mamm* would have loved to be here today."

Tears welled up. "Don't make me start crying. I may never stop."

Esther gave her a quick hug and started down the stairs. The furniture had been pushed back to open the lower floor enough to seat all the congregation from Eden Township as well as folks from the Shipshewana church. Faces blurred as Judith slipped into her seat on the front row.

Across the aisle, sitting next to Luke in the front row of the men's side, Guy glanced at her, his face as pale as death. She gave him a smile and he grinned back, his skin returning to its natural color.

Judith tucked cold fingers under her skirt and watched the toes of her shoes, waiting for the service to begin. By the time the service ended in a few hours, she and Guy would be husband and wife, their lives joined together forever.

Her heart pounded until she glanced at Guy again. He smiled and gave her an assuring nod. Everything would be all right. She belonged to him, and he belonged to her. Forever.

* * * * *

If you enjoyed this Amish romance, be sure to pick up the first book in Jan Drexler's
AMISH COUNTRY BRIDES *miniseries*

AN AMISH COURTSHIP

And don't miss these other Amish historical romances from Jan Drexler:

THE PRODIGAL SON RETURNS
A MOTHER FOR HIS CHILDREN

Available now from Love Inspired Historical!

Find more great reads at www.LoveInspired.com

Dear Reader,

This story is close to my heart. I loosely based the hero, Guy, on a real person—my grandfather. I never met the real Guy, who passed away several years before I was born, but his story is one I had to share.

Born in 1902, Guy's life changed dramatically when he was five years old. His mother gave birth to a daughter and died of complications soon after the delivery. Faced with raising three very young children on his own, their father placed Guy and his younger brother in an orphan asylum and put his newborn daughter up for adoption.

It was a hard life for a young boy. When he was old enough to do farm work, he was hired out to farmers in the area as an indentured worker. Abuse of various forms were part of his life, while the father who had left his sons in the orphanage traveled from job to job, never able to provide a home for them but never signing away his parental rights. From 1908 to 1926, Guy lived and worked in thirty-two different homes.

But, as in every story of redemption, God stepped in. Early in his young adulthood, Guy dedicated his life to serving the Lord. He met my grandmother, and they married and had five children, including two sons who became ministers.

The year after Guy's death, Grandma wrote, "He wanted love and respect, but most of all he wanted a home and security, something he hadn't had since his mother died."

Everything else that happened in this story, including

Guy's father being a criminal, is fiction. But the heart of the story, Guy's longing for a *home*, a place where he belonged, is true.

I'd love to hear your thoughts! Connect with me on Facebook or Goodreads, or on my website, www.JanDrexler.com.

Blessings,
Jan Drexler

We hope you enjoyed this story from
Love Inspired® Historical.

Love Inspired® Historical is coming to
an end but be sure to discover more
inspirational stories to warm your heart
from **Love Inspired®** and
Love Inspired® Suspense!

Love Inspired stories show that
faith, forgiveness and hope have the power
to lift spirits and change lives—always.

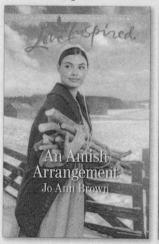
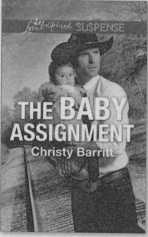

Look for six new romances every month
from **Love Inspired®** and
Love Inspired® Suspense!

COMING NEXT MONTH FROM
Love Inspired® Historical

Available April 3, 2018

THE RANCHER INHERITS A FAMILY
Return to Cowboy Creek • by Cheryl St. John

Rancher Seth Halloway is stunned when he inherits three sons from a recently deceased friend, but with the help of Marigold Brewster, the lovely new local schoolteacher, he settles into fatherhood. When the boys decide to become matchmakers, though, will he and Marigold find love?

MONTANA LAWMAN RESCUER
Big Sky Country • by Linda Ford

When Sheriff Jesse Hill rescues Emily Smith and a little boy after a stagecoach robbery, the woman can't remember anything but her name and that of the child. Now, while searching for the robbers and waiting for Emily's memory to return, he must resist falling for her.

MAIL-ORDER BRIDE SWITCH
Stand-In Brides • by Dorothy Clark

Fleeing a forced betrothal, socialite Virginia Winterman swaps places with Garret Stevenson's mail-order bride. But Garret needs a wife in name only to help in his new hotel... and Virginia hasn't worked a day in her life. Despite their differences, can she prove to him that she's his perfect match?

THE UNCONVENTIONAL GOVERNESS
by Jessica Nelson

If Henrietta Gordon wants to save enough money to reach her dream of becoming a doctor, she needs work—and Dominic, Lord St. Raven, needs a governess for his recently orphaned niece. It's a temporary arrangement, but the longer she stays, the more tempting it is to make it permanent.

LIHCNM0318

Get 2 Free Books,
Plus 2 Free Gifts —
just for trying the Reader Service!

Love Inspired®

LI17R3

SPECIAL EXCERPT FROM

Love Inspired HISTORICAL

When rancher Seth Halloway inherits a trio of
orphaned boys, he has nowhere to turn—except to lovely
schoolteacher Marigold Brewster. Together, they'll learn
to open their hearts to new family...and new love.

Read on for a sneak preview of
THE RANCHER INHERITS A FAMILY
by *Cheryl St.John*, *the touching beginning of the
series* RETURN TO COWBOY CREEK.

"Mr. Halloway." The soft voice near his side added to his
disorientation. "Are you in pain?"

Ivory-skinned and hazel-eyed, with a halo of red-gold
hair, the woman from the train came into view. She had
only a scrape on her chin as a result of the ordeal. "You
fared well," he managed.

"I'm perfectly fine, thank you."

"And the children?"

"They have a few bumps and bruises from the crash,
but they're safe."

He closed his eyes with grim satisfaction.

"I'm Marigold Brewster. Thank you for rescuing me."

"I'm glad you and your boys are all right."

"Well, that's the thing…"

His head throbbed and the light hurt. "What's the
thing?"

"They're not my boys."

"They're not?"

"I never saw them before I boarded the train headed for Kansas."

"Well, then—"

"They're yours."

With his uninjured hand, he touched his forehead gingerly. Had that blow to his head rattled his senses? No, he hadn't lost his memory. He remembered what he'd been doing before heading off to the wreckage. "I assure you I'd know if I had children."

"Well, as soon as you read this letter, along with a copy of a will, you'll know. It seems a friend of yours by the name of Tessa Radner wanted you to take her children upon her death."

Tessa Radner? "She's dead?"

"This letter says she is. I'm sorry. Did you know her?"

Remembering her well, he nodded. They'd been neighbors and classmates in Big Bend, Missouri. He'd joined the infantry alongside her husband, Jessie, who had been killed in Northern Virginia's final battle. Seth winced at the magnitude of senseless loss.

Seth's chest ached with sorrow and sympathy for his childhood friend. But sending her beloved babies to *him*? She must have been desperate to believe he was her best choice. What was he going to do with them?

Don't miss
THE RANCHER INHERITS A FAMILY
by Cheryl St.John, available April 2018 wherever
Love Inspired® Historical books and ebooks are sold.

www.LoveInspired.com